T0114763

The Legend of Cavenaugh Island

E. Thornton Goode, Jr.

THE LEGEND OF CAVENAUGH ISLAND

iUniverse books may be ordered through booksellers or by contacting:

iUniverse
1663 Liberty Drive
Bloomington, IN 47403
www.iuniverse.com
844-349-9409

ISBN: 978-1-6632-5422-1 (sc)
ISBN: 978-1-6632-5423-8 (e)

Library of Congress Control Number: 2023911944

Print information available on the last page.

iUniverse rev. date: 06/26/2023

In Appreciation

I want to thank my wonderful, kind and caring friend, Julian Green, for allowing me to use his pictures in several of my novels to represent certain characters. In this novel, he is the image of Andrew Cavenaugh. You left this life in 2017. I miss you so much and I will always love you.

I would like to thank my friend from Facebook, Terence Stokes, for letting me use his picture as the representation of Luke, the bartender.

Thank you again, Galen Berry, for letting me use your picture to represent the character, Tom, in this story, who is a TV reporter based in Boston.

Phillip McDonald is the perfect representation of the character of Alan in this story. My Phillip left this life in 1996. He was a kind and caring man. I miss him and I will always love him.

Dan Glass is perfect as the image of Mark. My Dan was such a funny guy. He passed away in 2014, six months before we were to come down here to our retirement house near the ocean. I miss him and will love him forever.

Thank you, Tris Coffin, for letting me use your picture. You are the perfect image of the character of Jack, in the story. You and I were best friends until you left this life in 1999. You are truly missed.

My friend, Galen, who is incredibly helpful with proofreading and editing of my novels prior to publication, suggested that I would make the perfect representation for the character, Brian Durnam. And so, I have used a photo that was taken back in 1985 to use. What can I say? This is the second time I have used one of my pictures to represent a character in one of my books.

Galen, I gratefully appreciate your help with this novel just as you have on several of the previous novels. In this one, you made many suggestions to improve and enhance the storyline. I loved them and incorporated the ideas.

For Saying Goodbye, Galen suggested an alternate ending to the one I had originally written. It was so good, I completely rewrote the ending of the last chapter to incorporate his suggestion.

Jeff Dillow, with KAHN MEDIA, was incredibly helpful and instrumental in directing me to Wikimedia Commons. Without his help, I would never have known of that website and been able to obtain the picture of the 1914 Ford Runabout I inserted in this book. It's like I told him, a picture is worth a thousand words. Thank you, Jeff. I gratefully appreciate your help.

Julian

Terence

Galen

Phillip

Dan

Tris

Me

Biographic Information

Well, folks, this is novel number eleven hitting the presses. That leaves two more to go of the novels completed so far. Then, I will consider the possible publication of the seventeen short stories that are presently written.

I love it down here on the southwest coast of Mexico. As I've said before, it is summer all year round here. A bit humid but the ocean breezes during the day and the breeze off the mountains at night seem to make it not so obvious.

It's so sad. Dan passed away of a heart attack in May of 2014, six months before we were to retire and come here.

Julian was planning to come here after he retired in June 2018 but unfortunately, he passed away in December of 2017. He told me that when he got here, we could paint together as he was an incredible artist. The world lost a great talent when he died. I will forever be in his debt for allowing me to use his pictures to represent so many characters in my writings.

PROLOGUE

Do you believe in ghosts? Do you believe in the supernatural? Do you believe love can transcend time and space? These are issues that will be dealt with in this story.

I have never experienced a ghost during my waking hours but I have had the dead come to me in dreams. It was George Anderson who said in his book, Lessons from the Light, that dreams are the easiest way for the dead to communicate with the living.

If you want to see an absolutely wonderful romance movie regarding a ghost, watch the 1947 movie, 'The Ghost and Mrs. Muir' with Gene Tierney and Rex Harrison. No matter how many times I watch it, the ending is so emotional, it always makes me cry.

CHAPTER I

It was 2018 and June had finally arrived. I'd been planning my vacation for months and was really looking forward to it. The place I'd chosen to go to in Maine was not the typical place someone would go, as it was not very touristy. I wanted chilled out and laid-back. Living in the city, there was enough hustle and bustle and I wanted to get away from all that.

The sound of the ocean and the cool breeze made this place just perfect. Renting a room in the lodging house located in the small town by the sea was a wonderful idea. There was a small restaurant and bar situated nearby where a lot of local people went to eat and drink. It was obvious that most of the people made their living from the sea.

After some twenty-four hours of driving, taking two days of almost twelve long hours each, it was Saturday, June 2nd, very late afternoon when I got in on the first day. I was completely exhausted, so I went to bed early.

Getting up the next morning, I walked down to the restaurant to get a little something to eat. My plan for the day was to take a stroll around town as well as some walking on the beach. Many of the locals looked me up and down, seeing I was an obvious 'out of towner'.

That evening I went to the restaurant again to have something to eat as well as a few drinks. After eating my meal at one of the tables, I moved to the bar to have a drink. This is where I introduced myself and also got the name of the bartender, Luke.

Luke was at least six feet tall and around a hundred and ninety pounds, very well-built, with dark hair, a full, trimmed beard and mustache. Around thirty-five and quite attractive.

He looked at me and smiled, "I see you're from out of town. How long are you staying?"

I clapped my hands. "Got here late yesterday. I've taken off a whole month from work to come here and paint. Not houses." I gave a big grin.

"You're an artist! Wow! So, you took off a whole month. What do you do for work?"

"Waiting tables is my main source of income. Love it. I work in a great restaurant with a bunch of terrific folks. But on the side, I paint. A major gallery in Atlanta where I live sells my work. I'm also a writer. Guess that about sums it up in a nutshell."

Luke's face was filled with surprise, "Wow! A writer, too. That's cool. There are some beautiful locations around here you might consider as subject matter for a painting or two. Every once in a while, I've seen someone painting down near the old lighthouse. There's another place, too, that you might want to consider. It's a bit out of the way but since you're going to be here for a whole month, you might want to check it out."

Luke had piqued my interest, "Really? Please, do tell."

"There's an island about two miles offshore." He actually pointed in a direction. "It's a little spooky. But there are some beautiful locations there I think would make great paintings. You should check it out. Check with Abel Johnson. He'll rent you a boat. He's down where all the boats come in. I think he'll have one suitable for you to use." He paused for a moment, shaking his head. "But."

"Yes? What?" I was curious.

"Well..... It's about the island. There's this old legend." He looked straight at me.

I tilted my head and raised my eyebrows. "Old legend?"

"Yeah." Luke continued, "There's the ruins of a big old mansion there. It sits high on a bluff, overlooking the ocean. It's now deserted and no one ever goes there. Many believe it's haunted and cursed."

"Oh. Wow. Really? Please, tell me more. Being a writer, I'm constantly looking for things like that for a story."

"Well, the legend goes that a man lived there over a hundred years ago. His name was Andrew Cavenaugh. He actually lived in New York City but was building the big house in anticipation of his marriage. This was to take place not long after the house was completed. Before the house was even finished and long before the wedding, he found out the woman he was to marry never loved him. The only reason she was going to marry him was to kill him, making it look like an accident, so she could get his wealth. It's a very sordid tale."

"It is said he moved into the unfinished house with several boxes of his belongings, a few pieces of furniture and a bed. Food was delivered on a daily basis from the restaurant in town and he became a recluse. Story goes, he went away and disappeared in June of nineteen nineteen just a few months after arriving. He'd written in a letter to Williams, the restaurant owner at the time, as well as Jake, the boat keeper, that the house was filled with pain and sadness. He had to leave. A friend with a boat would be coming to take him away along with his personal belongings. It indicated that if he had not returned after a while, his belongings in the house were to be given away. Yeah. No one ever knew where he went but the thinking was that he went back to New York."

"Everyone believes that when he died, his ghost came back to the house and now roams the island. Some say they have seen the ghost but nothing could ever be confirmed."

I was surprised, "Wow! That's a terrific story. And it's such a shame, too. Why didn't he seek another wife? Was he ugly? Did he treat people badly?"

"It's my understanding he was a very handsome man and very kind and generous. But he'd been so damaged emotionally, he became a recluse. After he left, the island and house were abandoned. Never finished. No one wanted to go there for fear some curse might come upon them. I know that sounds ridiculous but it's true."

"How old was he when he left?"

"I understand he was around thirty-nine or forty. Yep. He just disappeared and never returned. After about a year, he hadn't shown up and all his things were removed from the house and given away. This was done by a person from some law firm from Boston."

"Forty years old! That's two years older than I am right now. What a shame."

"Guys were afraid if they went there, something similar might happen to them. Even today, no one frequents the island. Younger men fear that if they do, they will never find a true and honest woman to be their wife. Older guys are afraid the curse may change the way their wives feel about them. So, it's definitely off-limits."

I was shocked, "You can't be serious."

Luke nodded his head. "Serious as a heart attack. So, if you go out there to paint, you will have the whole island to yourself. But be warned. Watch out for the ghost. And pray that you're not struck with the curse and an overwhelming feeling of sadness and grief." He bent his head down and began to snicker.

I shook my head. "Sure. Believe it. Struck by the curse." I raised my arms in the air and wiggled the fingers on both hands. "Woooooooo."

We both roared with laughter.

I finally collected myself enough to speak, "Okay. That definitely calls for a refill on my drink." I pushed my glass in Luke's direction.

Luke gave a big smile, "Coming right up."

CHAPTER II

Luke was correct. Abel Johnson was just the man I needed to see about renting a boat. He gave me a great rate when I rented it for a month. It was big enough to carry anything I needed with me going back and forth to the island. I told him I was familiar with handling a small sailboat without a keel and would be very careful with it. This made him very happy. He also told me that if I actually didn't need the boat for the full month, he would give me a small refund. That made me very pleased. It told me he was an honest and fair man.

On my first day out, I had a terrific wind. It took just over an hour to reach the island due to the tacking needed because of the wind direction.

Once there, I decided to sail completely around the island to check for possible locations to do paintings. Reaching the far eastern side, I could see what would have been a stately home if it had been completely finished, sitting on the bluff, overlooking the miles of open sea to the east. I could only imagine its beauty right after it had been built. It was strange. In my head, I could hear the opening lines of the movie, 'Rebecca', spoken by Joan Fontaine from the novel by Daphne du Maurier, 'Last night I dreamt I went to Manderley again.' Yes, the structure was not as large and imposing as Manderley, yet it did retain an air of the elegance of another time. Continuing to look at it, I began having a sense of foreboding and pain. After a few moments, those sensations slowly passed away.

By the time I got back to my starting point, it was going on four o'clock in the afternoon and I realized it was time to head back. I would sail over again in the morning and do some exploring on foot. A closer look at the house was in order as well.

A trip to the grocery store was necessary to stock the little refrigerator in my room with drinks and snacks to take with me on my excursions. If I planned to bring a lunch with me, I'd have the restaurant make me a little picnic basket.

After dinner at the restaurant, I moved to the bar to talk with Luke.

Luke came over when he saw me sit down. "Well, how was your day?"

"I went out to the island to check it out. You are correct. There are several locations there that would make terrific paintings. I'm going out again tomorrow. Seeing the house from the ocean has me very curious. I got a very strange feeling as I stared at it. The Alfred Hitchcock movie, 'Rebecca', popped into my head."

"Hey. I saw that movie some time ago. Interesting. Just be careful. If you don't show up by evening, I'll have someone come looking for you." He raised his eyebrows.

"Thank you very much for your concern. That's very considerate of you."

"You're very welcome." He gave a 'thumbs-up'.

"Yes, looking at the house gave me the strangest feelings. I can only imagine what I might feel when I actually check it out."

"Seriously. No one's lived there since Andrew flew the coop. That's been a long damn time. It could be kind of dangerous."

"Thanks but it won't be the first time I've been in an old dilapidated structure. I'm sure it must be locked up, so I doubt I'll be able to get inside."

"You're probably right as someone comes up this way from Boston like every six months to check on the place. He goes out there in the morning, comes back that afternoon and then heads back to Boston the next day."

"That's interesting. Very interesting."

I finished my drink, thanked Luke then headed back to my room at the lodging house. I'd planned to turn in early but got on the computer instead. Thought I would do a little research on this Andrew Cavenaugh.

It took a little while to find information about the man and what Luke referred to as the legend. But most of the information was exactly what Luke had told me. One thing that became quite clear is that Andrew was reported to be an extremely wealthy man. No wonder he could afford to buy the island and build on it. I also found it very interesting that he'd set up a trust with a major law firm, Brice and Walters in Boston, to prevent anything ever happening to the property. "If he lived in New York, why have a law firm in Boston? I'll bet the someone who comes to check on the house every six months is from that law firm." What was also curious to me is that all his investments and holdings were being held by this same law firm. From what I could find out in reading, there appeared to be no heirs to any of it. I couldn't imagine why none of the properties or investments had ever been sold. There had to be some reason.

Getting up early, I placed some drinks in the small cooler I'd be bringing with me. Then, it was to the boat.

Again, it took nearly an hour to reach the island. Maneuvering the boat into the small cove located on the west side of the island, I lowered the sail and used the paddle to reach the beach. I climbed out, placed the anchor to prevent the boat from drifting away and grabbed the cooler.

Looking around at the edge of the cove, I noticed a narrow roadway at the edge of the beach, heading up into the vegetation. I was sure it would lead directly to the house. Yes, it looked like a roadway. But being out here on the island, there were no vehicles. It definitely made it easier for walking.

Going slowly up the roadway, once again my mind recalled the opening scene of the movie, 'Rebecca', where the viewer is at the gated entrance. Then, slowly, the viewer moves forward and goes right through the iron gates without opening them. The viewer continues traveling up the driveway toward Manderley. Many don't realize that this visual effect was something that had never been done before in a film. Kudos to Alfred Hitchcock.

After about twenty minutes of an uphill walk, I was finally approaching the dwelling. Much unruly vegetation had grown up near the house. The only real clear areas were the paved roadway on which I was standing and the paved area across the front of the house and at the entrance.

I stood there, looking at the dwelling with the eye of someone with an architectural background. It was obvious to me, the house was extremely well-built. For it to have stood vacant for some one hundred years, it was in very good condition even if it hadn't been completed. I was surprised that more of the window panes had not been broken or knocked out. Looking closer, I realized all the window sections looked to be about three feet wide and at least six feet tall. Larger openings were made up of two or more of these same-sized sections. I smiled and nodded, "Smart move. Mass production. Cuts the cost and allows it to be completed quicker. A gold star to the architect."

I placed the cooler on the broad stone steps, leading up to the wide paved area in front of the house and the front entry portico. I looked closely at the front columned portico. It was about sixteen feet wide and eight feet deep. An ornamental stone balustrade went around the top of the frieze work, mimicking the stone balustrade that went around the complete roof of the house. Looking up, I saw a set of French doors from an upstairs room that would open out onto the flat roof of the portico.

In no time, I reached the front door. Looking closely, I noticed there was no rusting on the handle, it being made of brass but there was some patina from the atmosphere reacting with the surface. The handle was cold to the touch as I pressed down on the lever and slowly opened the door. It struck me very odd that it had not been locked. Was it possible the guy, who came up from Boston the last time to inspect the house, had forgotten to lock the door?

Walking into the large entryway, I noticed the hinges on the door were also brass, preventing them from rusting. There was a large archway on either side, leading into very large empty rooms. In front of me was a beautiful staircase, spiraling up to the second floor. Its carved wooden railing looked like mahogany. Curiosity drew me to one of the walls. As like all the rest, there was a stucco covering over brick masonry, evident in a few small places where the stucco had broken away. The masonry was within a reinforced concrete structure evident at the doorways. This being the case, it was obvious there was no wood in any of the major structural construction that would have deteriorated or rotted over time. All the floors were of stone pavers. Looking closely at the staircase, I could see it was made of stone. No wonder the house seemed to have little deterioration. It made me rather sad to see such an incredible house being vacant and abandoned. It would have been amazing if it had been completed.

Going further, I came to the high-ceilinged great room on the first floor located at the back of the house. It extended some sixty feet across the back of the house. There was a large fireplace at either end. The long exterior wall had many windows, allowing a view of the open ocean beyond. These windows were of the same design as the others of the house only taller. I would have said around ten feet tall. In the center of that wall was a set of French doors that would open out onto a paved patio area.

Looking around the huge space, I could only imagine the room filled with fine period furniture, crystal chandeliers hanging from the high ceiling, the fireplaces ablaze and a wonderful grand piano in the center of the long interior wall. Then, I shook my head, knowing none of this ever occurred.

The large rooms on either side of the entry hall led to many other large rooms beyond. At the far north end of the house was the kitchen area with an adjacent storage room and what looked like living quarters for several servants. There was also a large bathroom located in that same area. The rooms to the south could have served several purposes, I was sure. But there was no indication as to their possible use.

The second floor of the house was much like the first, solidly built. Unlike the first story, many of the walls had not yet been completely coated with stucco, allowing the brick fill work to be visible. Only two rooms were completely stuccoed. They were the hallway linen closet and the front room with bookcases on the north and south walls. It also made it clear that electric wiring had been installed. Even with the few broken window panes, storms would have done virtually no damage to the structure. Looking closely, I realized all the doors, cabinetry and such were made of mahogany. This would have deterred termites. It was obvious from the outside, the roof was flat. My walk through the second level of the house showed not a single crack or leak in any of the ceilings. The house was built extremely well and strong.

I spoke quietly, "Wow. Incredible. Three bathrooms upstairs for use by all the guest bedrooms. A master bedroom with its own bath. A nice big linen closet with lots of cabinets and shelves made of mahogany. And a large front room that was probably going to be a library of sorts with all the bookcases on the south and north walls. This is the room that has the set of French doors on the west exterior wall that open out onto the roof of the front portico. Very, very nice. What an amazing house."

Heading back downstairs, I commented to myself. "Andrew's architect had been a good one and knew exactly what he was doing when he designed this place."

Finally, finishing my tour of the interior, I walked back outside and looked up at the front façade. It would be an excellent subject for one of my paintings.

I grabbed my cooler and returned to the great room of the house. As I drank my diet cola, I was peering out the windows and noticed something ominous on the horizon. There appeared to be a storm approaching. This was my signal to hurry back to the mainland before it hit.

Leaving the house, I made sure the front door was secure then hurried down the drive. I stopped and turned to take another quick look at the house. Shock and surprise filled my body. I could have sworn there was someone briefly, standing on the roof of the portico at the balustrade, looking down at me. But there had been no one in the house when I made my tour through it. Who could it have been? Then, I remembered the story Luke told me. Could it have been the ghost of Andrew Cavenaugh? As much as I wanted to investigate, I knew there was no time. If I didn't leave now, the storm would hit and there is no telling how long it would last.

Quickly, I ran down the drive to the cove. Grabbing the anchor, I placed it and the cooler in the boat. Using the oars, the boat was finally far enough out to raise the sail. The wind was picking up and in the direction of the mainland, so there was no need for any tacking. It would be a straight shot.

It seemed I reached the mainland in record time. Down came the sail and I used the ropes to secure it to the pier. Taking hold of the cooler, I climbed onto the pier.

Abel was there to take over. "Glad you made it back in time. You better get to cover. I'm sure the storm's going to be here shortly the way the wind is picking up."

I gave Abel a 'thumbs-up'. "I'm sure you're right about that. You be careful and get in from the storm, too." I grabbed the cooler and quickly headed to the lodging house.

When I got to my room, I looked out the window and saw I had just enough time to run to the restaurant and bar. I was on my way. It was definitely time for a cocktail.

The minute I walked through the door of the restaurant, the rain began to pour. Immediately, I thought of the old movie, 'The Rains Came', with Tyrone Power and Myrna Loy. Yep! I really did need a cocktail.

Luke saw me walk in. "Well! Looks like you made it just in time!" He gave a big smile.

"You've got that right." I walked to the bar and sat down.

"And what can I get for you this afternoon?"

"With what happened earlier, I need a good stiff whiskey sour. You bet."

Luke had a questioning look on his face, "Oh? Something fluster you?"

I nodded. "Yes, it definitely did."

"Do tell. Do tell." Luke flexed his eyebrows.

I finally gathered my wits and realized what I had said, "Never mind. It would sound stupid."

"Hey! You opened the door. Now, 'Enquiring minds want to know.'" He pointed at the bar with his right index finger, tapped it a few times then went to make my drink.

I looked around the room to make sure no one was within earshot then spoke softly, "I know you're not going to believe me when I tell you."

Luke was busy making the whiskey sour. "Hey! I'm a bartender. Do you know how much crazy shit I hear? Even in this small town. Nothing surprises me anymore." After he finished shaking the drink, he began pouring it into a glass.

I looked at the glass. "Oh. No need for the orange slice and maraschino cherry. I'll take it just as it is and you can start another one if you don't mind. Thank you."

Luke gave me a strange look. "Wow. Something's really bugging you. Can't wait to hear what it is."

I began my story, "Last night when I left here, I got on my computer to do a little research on Andrew. The story you told me is basically what is out there. Also, there is a law firm in Boston, Brice and Walters, who take care of Andrew's holdings. I have a feeling the guy who comes to check on the house every six months is from that firm. I sailed over this morning to the island. Was curious about the house. Took a walk through the whole thing. I was very surprised the front door wasn't locked. Did you know the damn thing is built better than a fortress? Even though it was not completely finished, it's going to be around for another five hundred years or more. Easy. Whoever the architect was, he knew what the hell he was doing and so did the builders. It's a shame it's abandoned. Now, this is the business side of my mind speaking. With all the rooms and space, it could have made a terrific bed and breakfast. Seriously, a nice bed and breakfast."

"But, moving right along. While I was in the great room and looking out the windows, I could see the storm coming and knew I had to get my ass out of there and back here again before it hit. As I was leaving the house and heading down the driveway..." I paused for a moment, "I call it the driveway because it's as wide as one. But obviously, it would never be used by any vehicles. Anyway, as I was saying. I turned and looked back to see the house one more time." I stopped talking, turned to look around the room again, leaned in towards Luke and spoke quietly, "That's when I saw him."

Luke's face was filled with surprise, "Who? Who did you see?"

"I swear. I swear I saw someone. Only for a fleeting moment. Standing and looking down at me from the top of the front portico. With what you've told me about the place, I think it was Andrew."

Luke gave a quiet gasp, "You're shitting me. Really? But wait. Is it possible that maybe someone is staying there?"

"There was no other boat in the cove or any evidence someone else being on the island. I went through the whole house. Thoroughly. And I saw no one or anything indicating someone else was there. Not a single soul."

Luke bent his head down, shaking it. "Well, it could have been..... a single soul." He paused a moment. "You know. Soul. Spirit. Ghost."

I bent my head down and started snickering, "Okay. I sure as hell walked right into that one, didn't I?"

We both just laughed and gave a high-five using our right hands.

Luke nodded. "Yep. You sure did."

"What can I say?" I just shook my head.

Luke poured me another drink. "Okay, let's get serious here. So, you're pretty sure you saw the ghost. Are you sure it was a man?"

"It was a man. I only saw him for a very short time. But, yes. I know it was a man. A person with all that face fur had to be a man."

Luke flexed his eyebrows. "Question. Are you going to go back out there again?"

I looked directly at him. "Of course. It just gives me more reason to paint the place. If a painting can have a story behind it, it's more likely to sell. And..." I gave a big Cheshire Cat grin, "...I can charge a higher price for it."

Luke clapped his hands. "What can I say? What can I say?"

CHAPTER III

It was Wednesday and time to head out. It was clear and sunny as the rain had stopped during the night.

In my backpack, I put the bottles of turpentine and linseed oil, two empty jars and some paint rags to wipe my brushes. My easel when folded up had a strap I could put over my shoulders to carry it. I put on the backpack and easel. With my left hand, I got the case, containing all my tubes of paint, palette knives, wax paper palette and brushes. I placed a twenty-four by thirty-six canvas under my right arm as I grabbed my cooler, containing two soft drinks and headed to the boat. There were no edibles in the cooler as I wanted to spend all my time painting. I would eat when I got back that afternoon.

Reaching the island, I knew my first painting would be of the house. I contemplated for a while whether or not to paint it as it presently was or how it may have looked in its heyday if completed and all the overgrowth cut down. I set my easel up where I had the greatest vantage of capturing the structure. I must admit that while painting, I could not resist, continuing to look up at the top of the front portico where I had seen the figure the previous day.

As time progressed, the painting was coming along quite well. Before leaving, I decided to leave all my art supplies, the easel, as well as the painting inside the house. After all, there was no one on the island to bother it. If what I had seen the previous day was a ghost, I doubted that would be an issue. I set everything in the entry hall near the staircase. This would prevent any breeze that would possibly blow through from knocking over the easel with the painting clamped to it. With its three legs spread out, it would not have been an easy thing to do anyway.

I placed the jar containing my brushes and turpentine and the jar of linseed oil on the second step of the staircase along with my palette. I did have to giggle, thinking about some rodent walking into the paint on the palette and leaving footprints everywhere. Something told me, I had no worry as I had seen no evidence of creatures being in the house. If the house really was haunted, I seriously doubted any creatures would be hanging around.

Before grabbing my empty backpack and the cooler, I took one last look at the painting clamped securely to the easel. I was truly pleased with how much I'd accomplished that day. It was possible that I would finish the painting in just a few more days. And yes, I decided to paint it as it would have looked in its well-kept, finished state.

Closing the front door, down the front steps and heading for the beach, my curiosity got the best of me. I wondered. Stopping, I turned and looked back at the house. Surprise and shock filled me. There, in the same place as before, was the figure again, looking down at me.

I could not hold back. I placed everything on the driveway and ran to the house, opening the door and up the staircase to the front room of the house. Opening the door to that room, I looked into the room. Nothing.

Quickly walking over to the French doors, I opened them and looked out onto the roof of the portico. I went out onto the roof and walked to the balustrade then looked down at the things I'd left on the driveway. There was no evidence of anyone having been there. Returning, I slowly scanned the room. There was no place for anyone to hide. There were no closet doors or openings on the north wall. Just bookcases. The south wall was the mirror image of the north wall with bookcases. I closed the French doors and slowly headed out of the house again, closing the front door behind me.

I walked down the driveway, picked up my things but turned wanting to take one last look at the house. I spoke softly, "Holy shit! There he is again." Yep. Looking down at me from atop the portico was the smiling face of a man. I could see him much clearer this time. After a short moment, he slowly faded away.

I headed to the boat with his image still in my head. From what I could see, he was a very handsome man, looking to be maybe forty years old.

Reaching the mainland and putting everything in my room, I headed to the restaurant. I was looking forward to a good steak and salad for dinner. A drink was definitely in order.

Luke saw me as I walked in. "Well, how did your day go? I see you made it back. Any strange events happen?" A big grin filled his face.

I walked over to the bar and sat down. I looked directly at Luke. "Actually, you're not going to believe it. Yes, it was a very productive day. I should have the painting completed in a couple more days. I left everything over there in the house. But!" I took a long pause.

Luke looked at me with surprise, "No! No way! Not again!"

I nodded. "Yep. In the same place as yesterday. I even ran back in the house to the room upstairs. Nothing. No one. When I finished looking, I went back outside and got my stuff to leave. I turned around and looked again. To my surprise, there he was. I could see him much clearer, too. Have to say, he may be a ghost but he's a damn good-looking one. Very handsome."

Luke put my drink down in front of me. "I know you're ready for this one."

I looked at the cocktail. "You've got that right."

Luke continued, "Okay. You know I want to see this painting when it's done." He paused for a moment. "Do you do portraits?"

"Very few. They are very difficult to do. Why do you ask?"

"If you got a decent look at him, do his portrait. Maybe a sketch."

I clapped my hands together. "Luke! That's a great idea. I'll work on it when I get back to my room."

After having dinner, I headed back to my room, took a shower and pulled out my sketch pad and pencils. After some three hours, I had a fairly good likeness of the face of the man on the portico. I was really pleased with how well it had turned out. Looking at the drawing for a few minutes, suddenly, a crazy feeling came to me. There was a slight chill that accompanied it. I had no idea what it meant. But I needed to get to bed. I was looking forward to finishing the painting, it was turning out so well.

The next day, I got over to the island. There was no evidence of any rodents walking through the paint on the palette. That made me very happy. The whole day was spent painting. There was no sign of Andrew, either. That night I brought my sketch pad to the restaurant to show Luke but he was not at the bar. I was told he was in the back office doing some paperwork for business purposes. I told them not to disturb him. I'd see him tomorrow.

Morning came and I got up and headed to the restaurant for some breakfast. Luke was not there but that made sense as it was not the time of day people would be ordering cocktails.

When I got to the island, I went into the house to get all my things to continue painting. I did run and checked the upstairs room again. Still no evidence of anyone being there, so I went back downstairs.

I got my things and set everything up in the same place I had the day before. Continuing to paint, it was coming along so well, I only stopped to have a drink of soda.

It was late afternoon when I decided to stop for the day. Placing everything back in the entry hall again, I went outside and looked up at the portico. There was no sign of him. "Interesting." Being slightly disappointed, I ran down to the boat and headed for the mainland.

I put the cooler in my room before going over to the restaurant and bar. I was so pleased with myself and how well the painting was coming along, I decided to have a lobster dinner with a nice white wine. I grabbed my sketch pad in case Luke had returned.

Luke saw me as I walked in. "How's the painting coming along? You should have it done by now. And what's tucked up under your arm there?"

Walking to the bar, I gave a big grin, "You are correct. It will be finished tomorrow. I'm so pleased with myself, I'm having lobster and a nice white wine for dinner. Was here last night but they said you were busy. I told them not to disturb you."

"Yeah. It's the one thing I hate about being in business. All the damn paperwork. What can I say? So, what's with the sketch pad?"

I placed the sketch pad on the bar. "I took your advice. Now, let me show you what the..." I looked around the room to see who was close by then spoke softly, "...what the ghost looks like." I picked up the sketch pad, opened it and held it up with the drawing facing Luke.

Luke's mouth fell open. "Are you shitting me!? Holy fuck! You're damn right. He is one handsome dude. Wow!" He gave a 'thumbs-up'. "Excellent!"

I closed the sketch pad, placed it on the adjacent stool and sat down. "I know for the last few nights I've been eating here at the bar. If I'm taking up space and it would be better for me to eat at a table, let me know."

Luke placed his hands on the bar then slowly looked around the room and up and down the bar. There were several tables occupied in the room and two people seated at the far end of the bar. He looked at me and grinned, "Ah. Yes. We are so crowded. You definitely need to sit at a table."

Immediately, we both broke out laughing.

Luke went to the kitchen of the restaurant, placing my order and getting a bottle of wine. As he was opening it, pouring me a glass, he questioned, "Okay. 'Enquiring minds want to know.' Was everything still there where you left it?"

I took a sip of the wine. "Everything was right where I'd left it the other day."

"Glad to hear the painting is coming along so well. You say it might be finished by tomorrow? That's terrific. At that rate, you should be able to finish quite a few paintings while you're here. You're still staying for a month, aren't you?"

"Yes. And I brought four canvases with me, knowing I would be doing seascape-type paintings. Twenty-four by thirty-sixes. That might be wishful thinking but who knows? The owner of the gallery in Atlanta told me he's looking forward to displaying and selling the paintings I do while I was here. He's a great guy. He's been showing and selling my work for several years now. I just have to be careful bringing them home, so they don't get smeared. Oils don't dry overnight. I might even get a short story or novel out of the legend and history that's here."

"Yeah. That's right. You're a writer, too. I think that is so cool. You have anything in print?"

"Yep. Three novels. All available on Amazon." Humor filled my face.

Luke questioned, "What's so funny? I think that's terrific."

"I actually never had any aspirations of publishing. It's all due to the urging of my tenth and eleventh grade English teacher. Seriously. Believe it or not, I still keep in contact with her. I sent her the manuscript of my first novel. After reading it, she told me I needed to get it in print. To be honest, I was totally amazed, she thought it was that good. She also paid me a huge compliment. Knowing I'm an artist, she said, 'You paint with words.' And as the great Paul Harvey used to say at the end of his radio show, 'And now you know... the rest of the story. Good day.'"

Luke smiled, "That is such a terrific compliment. I think it's wonderful. I just may have to get one of your books and read it."

Just then, the bell rang, indicating my dinner was ready.

When he returned and placed the food in front of me, I looked right at him. "As much as I've seen you in here, do you ever get a day off?"

Luke bent his head down. "Well, when you own a place, you have to take a vested interest in it."

I was totally surprised, "You own this place!? Really!? Luke! That's fantastic!"

Luke nodded. "There are two others who are silent partners with me. They live down in Boston. They know I like living here and have no problem working and doing the bartending."

"I think that's incredible. I wish you continued success."

Luke bent his head down again and began to chuckle.

I looked at him. "What?"

With a smile on his face, he explained, "Well, this was a venture to be a tax write-off. You see, my two partners and I are really good friends, going back to high school. They just happened to do extremely well in their business ventures and investing and they needed something for a tax write-off. They pay me very well since I don't mind being up here. And it's kind of funny. This place doesn't do that bad even being out of the tourist realm. The local folks love the place and with their patronage, it stays in business. Also, gives a few locals a job doing the cooking, dishwashing and cleaning. I put some of my money into some investments, too."

I clapped my hands. "Luke! I think it's cool. Again. Congratulations to all three of you."

Finally finishing my meal, I paid the bill, said good night to Luke and headed to my room. After taking a nice warm shower, I got in bed and looked forward to a peaceful night's sleep. Little did I realize the kind of dream I was about to have that night.

I found myself walking up the driveway to the house on the island. It was as if I were a silent observer. Slowly up the steps to the front door. It seemed totally natural as I passed right through the closed door and into the entry hall. I could see my painting on the easel over near the staircase. The jars with turpentine and linseed oil along with my brushes were sitting on the second step next to my palette.

After a short time, I became aware of a figure coming down the staircase. For some reason, this all seemed normal and I was not shocked or surprised. I just continued to observe.

Immediately, it became obvious the figure was the man from atop the portico. I could see him much more clearly than before. He truly was an incredibly handsome man. He looked to be just over six feet tall, very well-built and wearing the clothes of a gentleman of the late 1800s or early 1900s. He had a head of dark wavy hair. A nicely trimmed beard and mustache accented his face.

I could not explain it but seeing him, for some reason, caused feelings of caring and emotion to well up inside me. There seemed to be some connection to the man.

Having completed descending the staircase, he walked to the middle of the entryway then turned and looked at the painting. His left hand moved up and began to stroke his beard. Several times I saw his head tip to one side, hold that position for a moment and then return to normal again. After a while, he turned back around and walked toward me, stopping about three feet from me. He looked directly at me.

He stared into my eyes. His were an intense crystal blue color. Once again, I was surprised this did not shock or fluster me. There actually was a feeling of closeness with him. A big smile slowly filled his face and to my amazement, he spoke with a voice, sounding much like that of Sam Elliott, "I must say your painting of our house is exceptional. I look forward to seeing it completed. I hope you plan on doing other scenes on the island."

Then, very slowly, he turned and headed back up the stairs, fading into the darkness.

I woke up, eyes wide open, recalling every second of the dream. "Wow! Holy shit! Wow!" I got out of bed and began fixing a cup of coffee. Looking at the clock, I saw that it was going on six in the morning and beginning to become day outside.

Not feeling hungry, I decided to just go to the island and continue painting. By mid-afternoon, it was completed. I set everything up in the entry hall. I didn't want to take it back to the room yet. It was possible that I might make some final touches on it the next day.

Starting out the front door, I stopped and snapped my fingers. "I wonder." Quickly, I turned around and ran upstairs to the empty room and opened the door. Nothing. No one there. I shook my head then went back down again and out the front door.

Reaching the spot just before where the house was no longer visible due to the vegetation on either side of the driveway, I turned around and looked again at the house. There, in the exact spot as before, he was looking down at me.

I yelled out, "Andrew! Hello!" I waved and smiled.

A big smile immediately filled the figure's face. A moment passed before he slowly disappeared.

Running down to the boat, I was ready for an early dinner and several cocktails, having not eaten all day.

When I got back to the mainland, Abel was there to greet me and secure the boat. Since I didn't have the cooler with me, I went directly to the restaurant and bar. I was hungry. With it being Saturday, I expected the place to be busy.

Luke was there and spoke when he saw me, "I thought you were going to finish your painting today. Where is it?"

I nodded as I headed to the bar. I was surprised the place was not really crowded like I thought it might be. "It is finished. Sort of. I like a work to sit for at least a day in case I want to make some final touches to it. It's still over there in the entry hall. Tomorrow. I'll bring it home tomorrow." As I sat down, I bent my head down.

Luke noticed this. "Okay. What is it? What happened? Did you see him again?"

I looked right at Luke with a big grin on my face, "Yes. Yes, I did. But! I need a drink to tell you about it."

Luke clapped his hands. "YeeeHaw! Coming right up!"

Shortly, Luke placed my cocktail down in front of me, got my order and took it to the cook. Returning, he leaned on the bar. "Okay. I'm ready. What?"

I looked right at him. "Last night Andrew was in my dream. And I know it was Andrew. He saw the painting and then actually spoke to me. He told me he liked the painting and thought it was good." Just then, my whole body shook with shock, "Oh, my God!"

Luke stood straight up with concern. "What? What's the matter? What happened?"

I looked right at Luke. "I just realized. It seemed so natural at the time. It didn't sink in till just now."

Luke was anxious. "What? What?"

"Luke. He said, 'Your painting of our house is exceptional.' Our house. Our house."

"No way! No fucking way! Really!? That's crazy as shit. Are you sure that's what he said?"

"As sure as I'm sitting here."

Luke shook his head. "I wonder what the hell that means? Damn. That just adds to the mystery. I can't imagine him referring to the damn bitch who wanted to kill him. I know this is going to sound crazy as shit. But it sounds like he knows you and somehow you have a connection to him and the house. Is it possible you look like and remind him of someone?"

"Now that you say that, I'm beginning to wonder the same thing. And I must tell you. For some strange reason, I did feel some connection with him. Wow." I took a drink of my cocktail. "Is it possible he did have a relationship with someone else and had planned to move into the house with that person? Maybe that's where he went when he left the house back then?" I tilted my head to the side. "But that would make no sense. If he had someone else, why would he be depressed and in pain?"

A questioning look came to Luke's face, "Yeah. You're right. If he had someone else, why would he be depressed and want to leave the house? Good point. It's something to think about."

After a moment, I gathered my wits, "Well, let me tell you. He has the most amazing blue eyes. And his voice sounds like Sam Elliott's."

Luke was shocked, "You do realize how incredible this is. Damn! And he has blue eyes? Holy shit! A ghost! In color, no less! And sounds like Sam Elliott." He was speechless for a moment, "You do know this is outrageously left field? I've only known you for a short time but for some reason, I do believe what you've been telling me is true. Otherwise, I'd think you were some lunatic wack job and totally out of your mind."

I nodded. "I know. I really am surprised you actually believe me. It sounds so off-the-fucking-wall. I'm also going to improve the drawing I did of him to make it more accurate, now that I saw him face-to-face."

Just then, the bell rang to let Luke know my food was ready. Getting it, he placed it in front of me. "Okay. Eat up. I've got to head out for the night but will see you tomorrow. Same bat place. Same bat time. With the painting!" He slapped his hand on the bar then we did a high-five.

I had to chuckle at his reference to the old Batman TV show. It's always fun when there are things one can share and enjoy if you catch the inference.

It was still early when I got back to the room. But I was tired and decided to hit the hay early. Shortly, I was asleep.

Once again, I found myself walking up to the house in my dream. Again, I passed through the front door without opening it.

This time, Andrew was standing on the first step of the staircase, looking right at me and smiling, "I'm so glad to see you again. I hope you don't mind but I have some very important information to tell you. I am going to show you where it is located and how to get it. What you find there will help you understand what I said to you before regarding 'our house'. Eventually, you will know the whole story and maybe it will help me find peace. Now, come with me." At that, Andrew led the way upstairs.

CHAPTER IV

When I awoke, I was totally taken aback by what I'd seen, heard and was shown by Andrew during my dream. From what he told me, the task at hand would answer many questions. I quickly got out of bed. Getting dressed, I headed down to the front desk.

I was so glad the landlady was there. "I was wondering if you might have a flashlight I could borrow for the day?"

She responded, "I think we do. Just a minute. Let me check." She went into a back room. Several minutes passed before she came back to the desk and handed one to me. "Yep! I thought there'd be one in the back."

I was happy and called out, "Yes! Thank you ever so much. I'll bring it back this afternoon." I was out the door and to the boat. I couldn't get to the island fast enough.

Walking into the entryway of the house, I looked at the painting. I was pleased with it. There would be no further changes or corrections.

Suddenly, I looked over to the wall behind the painting. It was obvious, one of my paintbrushes had been used to paint on the wall. EXCELLENT PAINTING. I was both shocked and surprised at the same time. A feeling of joy filled me. Somehow, I just knew it was Andrew who'd done it. I turned all around, looking in all directions and called out, "Andrew! Thank you!"

Still carrying the flashlight, I needed to see about working on the task given to me by Andrew in my dream the previous night. He had shown me and indicated everything I needed to do in the dream.

I headed upstairs to the hallway linen closet, the room intended to store linens, bed coverings and other such things for all the bedrooms in the house. This was located just south of the library and sitting room.

I opened the door and walked inside. I left the door open as there was no source of light in the room. Against the far wall was what I was seeking, a set of cabinets and shelves. Kneeling down, I opened the doors on the right side of the bottom cabinet. I turned on the flashlight, shining the beam into the cabinet interior. Just as I was instructed, with my left hand, I lifted the wooden shelf that was just over a foot from the bottom of the cabinet and removed it from the cabinet. I placed it on the floor. Then, I knocked on the bottom of the cabinet. I did find it interesting that the bottom of the entire set of cabinets on that wall were almost a foot from the floor of the room. It began to make sense what I had been told in the dream.

Going to the adjacent cabinet on the left, I opened the doors. Using the flashlight, I looked all around the bottom interior. I knocked on the bottom. The right and left parts were completely separate units with a wooden partition between them.

After examining further, it finally came to me. The bottom of the right side was a little lower than the bottom of the left side. Now, the instructions I was given by Andrew made sense.

I went back to the right side and began to check out the interior again. That's when I noticed a small hole about half an inch in diameter on the far right side of the wooden bottom. It was just big enough for anyone to stick a finger into it. Using my left hand index finger, I stuck it into the hole and slowly pulled to the left. The bottom panel began to move to the left, sliding under the bottom panel of the cabinet on the left.

I shined the light into the space below where the bottom panel had been. I saw something wrapped with cloth. It had a box shape. Putting down the flashlight, I leaned into the cabinet and with both hands grabbed hold of the item and pulled it out, setting it on the floor of the room. "This must be what Andrew was talking about in my dream."

Removing the cloth wrappings, I could see that indeed it was a wooden box about a foot wide, around eighteen inches long and some ten inches deep. There was no rusting on the hinges or the latch to open it as they were made of brass. There was no lock.

Since I was in a kneeling position, I grabbed the latch and carefully opened the lid. I took my time to make sure I would not do any possible damage to the box. I was pleased, it opened with ease. It looked like the box was filled with papers and a book. On the right side adjacent to the stacked papers and book was a cloth pouch. I carefully closed the lid. As much as I wanted to check things out, I did not want to do it with dirty and dusty hands.

Immediately, I knew what I was going to do. I slid the bottom panel back in its original position, placed the shelf back in, closed both cabinet doors, stuck the flashlight in my belt and placed the box under my right arm. When I got downstairs, I took hold of the painting with my left hand. It was time to go. The easel, palette and brushes would stay for now. Going far enough down the driveway, I turned to look.

There, up on the portico, was Andrew. A big smile was on his face as he nodded and gave me a 'thumbs-up'. I chuckled and called out, "Andrew! I have it!" He nodded then immediately vanished. I did have to laugh inside myself, wondering how Andrew knew about a 'thumbs-up'. Did they do that during his time period in history? I went quickly to the boat.

Arriving at the pier, Abel saw the painting. "Very nice! Very nice! I hold a candle to you artists who can put reality on canvas. Very nice."

I called back, "That's very kind of you. Thank you very much."

I quickly went to my room, putting the box on the desk and the painting on the floor, leaning it up against the wall. Then, I ran down to the front desk to return the flashlight. "Thank you so much. It did come in handy."

She nodded. "Any time."

Going back to my room, I went to the box on the desk. Again, very slowly I pulled on the latch to lift the lid and opened it.

With the lid fully open, I looked inside at a good-sized book on top of a pile of paper. I was really curious about the cloth pouch. I ran to the bathroom and washed my hands. I made sure they were completely dry using the bath towel.

My hands clean and dry, I reached to pull out the pouch first. Opening it, I saw there was a key and a gold ring inside.

I pulled out the ring to look at it closely. It was a signet ring with the initials 'A' and 'C' on the top. I also noticed there was an engraving on the inside. I read the words aloud, "I will always love you." Immediately, an old memory shifted me back to a time when I heard Dolly Parton singing that song for the first time. It was so emotional for me, it brought a flood of tears to my eyes back then.

After a few seconds, I was back to reality again. "I know his bitch fiancée would never have given this to him. There had to have been someone else. But if there was, why wasn't that person part of the legend? And why was Andrew depressed?" I placed the ring back in the pouch.

I had no idea what the key would open. I left it in the pouch and placed it on the desk next to the box.

Then, I pulled out the book and placed it on the desk. Next, the entire very large pile of paper, setting it next to the book. I could only imagine what would possibly be there. I knew it would take some time to go through everything and see what might be written in the book and on all those loose pages.

Thinking about what time it was, I stopped and placed everything back in the box. "Maybe tomorrow." I giggled, "Afta all, tamarra IS anotha day." I closed the box lid, went over and picked up the painting. I was hungry. Time to eat.

I was very careful with the painting, so as not to smear it. Entering the door of the restaurant, I saw Luke behind the bar. I raised the painting up in front of me, so he could see it.

Luke clapped his hands and cheered, "Wow! That's a really good painting. No wonder galleries want to show and sell your stuff. Yeah. Hey! I have an idea." He ran in the back and was soon out, carrying an easel. "Here. Put it on this, so folks can see it." He set the easel up in an out-of-the-way area but in the view of customers. "Just a second." He went to the back again and got a large piece of butcher paper. Using a magic marker, he wrote on it. 'WET PAINT..... DO NOT TOUCH'. Below the bold black letters, he wrote in small black letters. 'Or I'll break your fingers!' With some tape, he posted the sign on the easel between the front legs and just below where the painting would sit.

I walked over and placed the painting on the easel. "Wow. Thank you. You're very kind. And love the sign."

Everyone who saw the sign did snicker.

"No sweat. Now, I just know you have something to tell me and believe it or not, I have something to tell you."

I was curious, "Really? Do tell. You first."

"Well, have a seat, so we can talk. First, what can I get you to drink and eat?"

"Yes, I am hungry." I made my order and Luke took it to the back. Coming back out, he fixed my drink. I was very interested. "Okay. What's your news? I'm really curious."

"I told you I have two other partners in this venture here. One of them is Tom. He's a TV reporter down in Boston. I told him your story and he was so interested, he's taking the train up here tomorrow to talk and interview you. What do you think of that?"

"Wow! That's fantastic. I'm surprised he actually believes the story."

"As I said, I've known Tom since high school and he knows I would never feed him bull shit. He was totally ecstatic you're an artist and even did a portrait drawing of the ghost. I'll run down to the station and get him in the afternoon when the train gets here."

"Would it be okay if I went with you?"

"That would be terrific. I was hoping you would. Yeah. Now, tell me what's new with you."

"Are you ready for this? I had another dream last night. Andrew showed me a secret hiding place in the house. He led me to its location and wanted me to go to it and find what was there."

"You can't be serious! Did you go!?"

"Yep. I went over this morning, found the place and there was a wooden box. But!" I bent my head down.

"What!?" Luke was anxious, "What!?"

"You're not going to believe this but where I had the painting in the entry hall, written on the wall, using one of my paintbrushes, someone had written 'excellent painting' in all capital letters. I have a feeling it was Andrew who somehow did it."

"You are shitting me! You ARE shitting me!! No way!"

I nodded my head. "Yep. Seriously."

Just then, the bell rang. My food was ready. Luke turned. "Just a sec. I'll get that." In no time at all, he placed the meal in front of me. "This is unbelievable. I'll bet Tom will love it. You didn't smear the writing on the wall, did you? Or try to wipe it off? Please say you didn't."

"Nope. It's still there."

"Excellent!" Luke clapped his hands.

Finishing my meal, I paid my bill, took the painting off the easel and headed to the door.

Luke called out, "Wait! Would you mind if you left the painting? I'd like folks to see it. I'll make sure no one dicks with it." He gave a 'thumbs-up'. "They know I WILL break their fingers."

That made us both break out laughing.

"Thanks. Not a problem." I walked back and placed the painting on the easel. "Luke. Later. Later." I headed to the door.

Luke called out, "Come over for breakfast as I'll be here. Then, we can run down and get Tom from the train."

I gave a high-five in the air. "Sounds good. See you tomorrow morning."

I was tired when I got to my room. It surely had been an exciting day. I left the box shut. It was going to take some time to go through the things in it and see if they made any sense or had some relevance to this time period.

It was around nine-thirty the next morning when I got to the restaurant. I went directly to the bar and sat down. Looking around, I didn't see Luke anywhere. He was probably dealing with stuff in the back.

After a few minutes, he appeared and called out with a smile, "Good morning! How about a nice omelet?"

"Sounds good to me. And some coffee."

In the time before going to pick Tom up, we both began to share more of our history as well as general small talk. Some of the things Luke told me about his past made me ponder. "I hope you don't mind but I sure could use some of that stuff in a story or novel. You bet."

Luke raised his eyebrows with a smile, "Be my guest. But do me one favor."

I looked inquisitively at him. "Oh? What's that?"

"In the credits. Spell my name right."

We both did a high-five and roared with laughter.

The train was pulling in about thirty minutes after we arrived at the station. Shortly, Tom appeared but he was not alone. Both were carrying fairly large suitcases. It was obvious Tom saw Luke when they started walking towards us.

Luke and Tom shook hands and did a quick man-hug as Luke spoke, "Good to see you again. It's been a while. Geez. Three maybe four years? Damn! How time flies. So, this must be Alan." He looked right at the other man.

Tom turned toward the man. "Yes, this is Alan. He's my camera and soundman. I want to make sure I have some great video for any report I do." He looked over at me.

I smiled and extended my hand, "I'm the guy who saw the ghost."

We all began to laugh.

Luke took one of Tom's suitcases. "Hope everyone's ready for a late lunch. I had them fix something really special for our reunion. Let's go."

Tom and Alan were staying in the same lodging house I was. Dropping their things off in their rooms, Tom pulled out his tape recorder from his luggage. Then, we all headed to the restaurant and bar. It was almost two o'clock.

Since it was not the busiest time of day for bar customers, Luke had one of the waiters stand in for him just in case. He joined us at one of the tables. Another waiter brought our drinks. The food that Luke had specially made would arrive shortly.

Tom looked at me after peering at my painting. "I have to admit. It's obvious you're no slouch when it comes to slinging paint with a brush."

Tom continued, "Seriously. Very nice. But let's get to things at hand. I want you to start from the beginning and tell me what happened without interruption. Don't leave anything out, regardless of how trivial it may seem. That way, I'll know what kind of questions to ask when you are done. We can start now and when our food gets here, we can eat. Afterwards, we can continue while we have cocktails. How does that sound?"

I nodded my head. "That sounds fine with me. If I say something that brings up a question for anyone, please take note of it and we'll talk about it later."

Tom agreed, "Excellent idea. Four heads are better than one."

Tom turned on the recorder and I began. Tom's interest was piqued when he heard about the portrait drawing and the wooden box. I knew he would want to see them. Eventually, I had finished all I had to say. There was a moment of silence when Tom turned off the recorder.

Tom nodded. "Yep. I especially want to see the writing on the wall. It's true that many will say you did it but I don't care. I want to include everything I can regarding this story. Due to its strangeness, many will scoff at it all anyway. I definitely want to take a good look at the drawing and all the items that are in the box. It's very fascinating to me that Andrew came to you in a dream to show you where the box was located. I'm curious why he's having such a close connection with you. And his reference to 'our house' is very intriguing. Very interesting. I know of no one ever coming forward indicating he's had a dream regarding Andrew."

"We can head up to my room if you'd like and I can show you." I turned to Luke. "Luke, tally up my bill so far and I'll pay you later when we come back for dinner."

"Not to worry. You guys get over there and check things out. I'll stay here and take care of business. See you all when you're finished and ready to eat some dinner."

Arriving at the lodging house, Alan went to get his camera and Tom wanted to get another cassette for his recorder. Then, we headed to my room. Alan took several pictures of the sketch.

"I'll do an in-depth interview with you tomorrow and Alan will video it. It's going to be at the house in order to have the proper surroundings and atmosphere." Tom was pleased, "I'll want you to bring your painting and sketch pad with the portrait as well. The reason I wanted you to tell me the whole story earlier is so I know what to ask you tomorrow during the video interview."

Tom wanted to check out the contents of the wooden box. Making sure that everyone's hands were clean and dry, Tom removed the book and placed it on the desk. Picking up the cloth pouch, he opened it and peered inside. "There's a key and a gold ring in here. Looks like a signet ring." He closed the pouch and placed it next to the book.

Next, he removed the papers from the box and placed them on the desk. He looked at Alan and me. "Everyone take a page from the pile and read each page very carefully. If you find something that appears to be of major importance, make a comment and we'll place it in a special pile. The book we'll save for another time."

Each one of us began examining the pages closely, one by one.

Eventually, Tom came across a paper and commented, "This makes reference to the law firm of Brice and Walters. I wonder if it's still in business?" He set that specific page aside. It began the special pile.

I responded, "I did some research online. I'm pretty sure it is. I understand someone comes up from Boston around every six months to check on the house. I'd sure bet that person is from the firm."

Tom snapped his fingers. "That's right. Luke told me that ages ago. I just never equated it since I had no clue of the law firm."

After a while, Alan spoke up, "This page looks like a reference to several bank accounts. That could possibly be important." He set it in the pile Tom had begun.

Tom commented, "If you run across anything regarding any relatives, that would be important. There could be possible heirs who have no clue of a possible inheritance. The least of all is an island with a house on it. But since there's mention of bank accounts, there could also be some money involved."

Suddenly, Alan shouted out, "Okay! Here we go! This indicates that major information can be found at a law firm and there is a paper amongst these that will be a letter of introduction to that law firm. I'll bet it's Brice and Walters that Luke told us about. It will allow the gaining of access to important information pertaining to Andrew." He looked at Tom and me. "When one of us runs across that, we need to make sure nothing ever happens to it."

The next page for me was exactly what we had just been talking about. It was the introductory letter. "I found it! Here it is! It's the letter and it's got the name of the law firm on it and it is Brice and Walters."

"Let me see that if you don't mind." Tom took it and read it, "And there are signatures, too. That will absolutely prove it's not a fake. I'll check into this more closely when we get back to Boston. Alan, please take a picture of the letter. We'll leave the original with everything here."

It took the rest of the day and into the evening to finally go through all the papers and separate them appropriately. Alan took pictures of the pages we thought were vitally important before all were placed carefully back in the box.

Tom picked up the book and opened it. He flipped through several of the pages. "It's a kind of diary or journal." He turned back, looking at the first written page. "The first line here says he is twenty and starting to write. Now, if he was around forty when he disappeared, leaving the house and never returning, there could be information covering some twenty years of his life in here. It's definitely going to take some time to go through all of it. Obviously, there's quite an extensive amount of reading matter here. This can surely wait for another time. Wow. And I'm getting hungry." He placed the book in the box.

We decided it was way past time for dinner and headed to the restaurant and bar.

Tom commented, "Tomorrow we can head over early to the island, do some filming and I can do my report for the broadcast. Afterwards, Alan and I will have to head back to the city. Will get the story on the air as soon as possible after we do any necessary editing."

Conversation at dinner was basic conjecture, regarding all the information we'd read on the papers from the box. None of us could imagine what kind of information could be found at the law firm. We all knew it was most likely going to be one hell of a story when all was said and done. We wondered if there might be a clue to any heirs located in the information there.

I commented, "Being a writer, I can only imagine the story that exists in the book."

Tom looked at me. "After we leave tomorrow, why don't you start reading the book? You can let us know if it's an interesting tale worth telling."

Everyone expressed their agreement.

CHAPTER V

The next morning, we gathered early and went to the restaurant for a quick breakfast, just something to hold us over until dinner. Since Tom wanted me to bring the painting, I grabbed it off the easel.

Returning to the lodging house, Tom spoke up, "If you don't mind, get your sketch pad with the drawing, so it could be in the video of the interview. I know your painting is still wet. We'll be very careful with it."

I nodded. "Not a problem. It's not every day my artworks get into a televised news report. Yeah. Talk about free publicity and promotion. YeeeHaw!!!" I started cheering.

Alan responded, "I promise, I'll make them look really good, too. But I really don't have to because they are quite excellent."

"Why, thank you, Alan. I appreciate that."

We gathered up the things we wanted to bring. I carried the painting and the sketch pad. Tom had his recorder and some other sound equipment. Alan had all his camera stuff. It was time to head down to the boats and see Abel for a motorboat.

Abel had just what the doctor ordered and we were off. Alan handled the motor. I held the painting tight, so as not to have it get caught in the wind and smear. We were at the island in seemingly no time at all.

The easel was still exactly where I'd left it set up in the entryway. Placing the painting on it and standing back, the writing on the wall was visible right behind it.

Tom and Alan did a relatively quick tour of the house, filming the interiors and especially the upstairs library and sitting room where the ghost had appeared just outside the French doors near the balustrade. His interview with me was in the entry hall with the painting. There was a good close-up of the portrait in the sketchpad as I described the visions I'd had of Andrew in my dreams.

Alan walked over to where the writing was painted on the wall. "I know this may sound crazy but what if this place gets bought and finished? Wouldn't it be great if a clear plastic cover was placed over this writing and your painting framed and hung right above the writing?" He pointed to the wall space directly above the writing. "It's the perfect height for the painting. What a story could be told about it. And right next to it, mat and frame the portrait drawing you did of Andrew and place it right here next to the painting." He moved his hand to the right of where it had been. "Wouldn't that be terrific?"

Tom turned to Alan. "Alan, personally, I think it's a fantastic idea. If someone does end up buying this place, that needs to be suggested." He looked around and then continued, "Well, I think that's about it. We can get back to the city, start doing the editing and get the report ready to put on the air as soon as possible. It's going to take a little time but I think we can have a report ready in about two days. I want it to be an awesome piece. I'll call Luke to let him know when it'll air. Before you put your camera away, I want you to get a really nice shot of the outside of the house when we get a little way down the drive."

I grabbed the painting. "I'm leaving the easel and all my paint stuff here since I'll be back to do more work."

Collecting all the things we wanted to bring with us, we walked down the driveway and Tom stopped. "This should be good."

We all turned and Alan began filming the house. Suddenly, up on the portico, standing at the front balustrade, appeared Andrew with a big smile on his face.

Alan yelled, "Holy shit! It's him! It's Andrew!" He kept filming. He also slowly zoomed in on the figure. "This is fantastic!" He continued to film until the figure slowly faded away. "I have a terrific close-up of him! And he really does look just like your drawing." He looked at Tom. "You do know everyone's going to say it was a plant."

Tom laughed, "I don't give a fucking rat's ass what anyone thinks or says. We know the truth. And truth will out!"

Getting back to the mainland, I put the painting and the sketch pad in my room. Tom and Alan gathered their things and Luke drove us all to the train station. They would be catching the later one, coming through around nine that evening. Luke and I stayed until Tom and Alan left.

Returning, Luke dropped me off as he headed home. "Bring your painting back to the restaurant tomorrow and put it back on the easel. I want folks to see it."

"Thanks, Luke. Will do. See you tomorrow." Nothing was going to suit me more than a nice shower and a good night's sleep.

The next morning, I got up fairly late and fixed some coffee. I really wasn't hungry but I did run over to the restaurant to put the painting back on the easel there. I quickly came back to my room and fixed another cup of coffee.

Staring at the wooden box, I decided to get out the book and start reading what was written within its pages. Opening the lid, I took out the book and sat in a comfortable chair near the desk. After a sip of coffee, I opened the cover and began reading.

It is the year of our Lord, 1899 and I, Andrew Cavenaugh, now age twenty, have decided to record my current affairs as something to reflect upon in the times to come. And to what do I owe in doing this? It's all because of what happened when I recently went to a traveling carnival.

But first, I must explain. I am still in university. It is the fall of my Junior year. Just outside the town, located some miles from school, a traveling carnival had come and set up their facility. Classes were over, it was Saturday and I decided to go see the festivities.

It took me a little over two hours to walk the distance. It is a time in my life when doing so is not a major effort. Ah, youth. I wonder if I will be able to do such a feat when I am old. It being Saturday, many of the townsfolk were there, checking things out. Several of the sideshows looked quite interesting and intriguing.

One tent, with a sign hanging on it, caught my eye. Something I had heard and talked about but never experienced. I shook my head and snickered as I spoke the words on the sign, "Fortunes told by Madame Faruschka." It was the tent of a gypsy fortune teller. I pondered for a moment and wondered what I should do. Yes, I knew there were fakes and this could be another one but I thought it would be fun. I snapped my fingers. "Oh. Why not?" I walked toward the old gentleman, wearing gypsy-type clothes and sitting at a small table near the entrance. There was a little sign on the table, showing the admission fee.

He saw me approach and smiled, "Yes, young man. How may I help you? You desire to have Madame Faruschka tell your fortune?"

I nodded. "Yes, Sir. I think it could be very interesting and fun."

"Let me see if she is ready to see someone." He got up and entered the tent.

In the meantime, I opened my money pouch and pulled out a quarter more than the entry fee. Hey. I had been lucky at a card game several nights before. I believed you should share your good fortune.

Shortly, he returned and sat down. "Yes. She will see you now." He gestured with his left hand toward the entrance.

I handed him the money and started for the entrance.

"Young man! You have given me too much."

Turning, I looked right at him. "It's okay. I have been fortunate in my life. I recently won some money in a card game. It's my way of saying thank you and doing my part in paying forward a little bit."

I stopped reading for a moment. "A quarter back then would be almost nine dollars today. Yeah. That was generous of him." I started reading again.

The old gentleman bowed his head. "That's very gracious of you, young man. May the stars smile and shine brightly upon you." He bowed his head again.

"That is very kind. Thank you so very much." I headed into the tent.

The interior had been set up with a hallway created by sheets of canvas forming the walls. Walking along the passageway, I soon came to an open space. It was dimly lit with candles. In the middle of the space was a table covered with a plain tablecloth. In the middle of the table was a glass globe that appeared to be about ten inches in diameter supported by a strange-looking base. In front of the table was an empty wooden chair. Behind the table, sitting in a cushioned chair, was an elderly lady dressed in gypsy attire.

She looked at me and smiled, "Come in, young man. Have a seat. Let Madame Faruschka tell you your fortune."

I must admit, I loved it. It was so incredibly everything I had imagined it to be. Anticipation was building inside me, "Thank you so much." I sat down in the chair.

"First of all, let me see your hands. Place them, palms up, on either side of my crystal ball."

I did as she asked and said nothing.

She first went to my left hand, examining it carefully. Then, she did the same with my right. After a moment, she spoke quietly, "Thank you. You may take your hands back."

As I did, she slowly moved both her hands over the crystal ball. "You are a very smart and intelligent young man. Because of this and your logical abilities, you are going to be extremely successful in business dealings and finance." She paused a moment, "You are going to move to a large city. New York. And you will make a lot of money due to your smart business dealings. A lot of money. You are going to have many wealthy clients, too. Yes. Continue on the road you have chosen."

She paused for a moment as she seemed to peer deeper into the globe. "Interesting. I see an island in your future. But wait!" She looked directly at me. "You have a brother?"

I shook my head. "No. Not to my knowledge."

"I could have sworn I felt a brother link connection." Her head tilted as if there was some question not resolved. "This is something we may address later. Anyway, soon, you will seek an excellent law firm. It is one you want to be in business for a very long time. You will find this firm in Boston. 'B' and 'W'. Brice and Walters. There, you will keep all your important papers and information." Her head tilted to the side again. "I'm not quite sure what this means but when you have your wisdom teeth pulled, you are to put them in a small box and keep them in the same secure box at the law firm with your important information. I know it sounds quite unusual but I get a sensation there is significant importance for this to be done."

I nodded my head. "I will do that. Thank you."

"What I am about to tell you now is extremely personal. Extremely personal." She looked directly into my eyes. "You are going to meet someone in about twelve years and you are going to fall madly in love. I see the letters 'B' and 'D'. Your relationship will be what some would call unconventional but you both will love each other deeply and intensely. You both will know it immediately when it happens."

She paused for a moment and looked very hard at me. "The love you both will share will be one that few ever experience. To know such a love is very rare. Consider yourself extremely lucky that it happens for you. Go with your heart. I am glad for you."

"Now. The island. You are going to find an island and you will like it so much you are going to buy it and build a house there. Yes."

She continued, "You are going to start writing a book. No, not a novel. It will be things that will be happening to you that you want to remember. When you are done with it, you are going to put it in a special place in the house you are going to build on that island. Yes. I see this is necessary as someone is eventually going to find it. It will be significant in understanding a mystery that everyone has wondered about for a very long time."

After a moment's pause, she continued, "I see you now at thirty-nine. There is a thick fog I cannot see through. I do not know what it could mean. I am so sorry about that." She paused again. "I can't see any farther into the future because of this fog." She shook her head.

She looked at me. "Follow your intuition, your dreams, your senses. Be happy. Success will follow you wherever you go. Make sure you save something for a rainy day and the future." She looked deeply into the glass globe once more for a moment then back at me. "That is all I have for you today. Be careful. There is no need to say it because I already know you will be kind to others."

I gave her a big smile as I stood, "Madame Faruschka, thank you so very much for your wisdom. I gratefully appreciate it." I reached and got out my money pouch, found four quarters and placed them on the table next to the globe. "Thank you so very much. I will remember this always and I will do as you have instructed."

She looked lovingly at me and smiled, "Thank you, Andrew. That is very kind, considerate and generous of you. Be safe, my child."

I bowed my head, turned and walked through the passageways to the outside. I nodded kindly to the old gentleman as I left the tent and continued walking into the festivities of the carnival. It did not dawn on me until I was walking on my way home and thinking about all Madame Faruschka had told me. Suddenly, I stopped cold. "Oh, my God! She called me by name! How did she know my name?" Then, it dawned on me. "She said something about a brother and that we would address it later. But we never did. How stupid of me not to ask about that. What an idiot." I paused for a second. "I know. I'll go see her after my classes next Friday. Yes. Then, I can ask about that."

Little did I realize that when I went the next Friday, the carnival was gone. It had moved on to some other location unknown to me. This question is going to haunt me, I know.

One thing I did do since I was so moved by this event, I bought this large notebook and I have started this writing. What is here so far in my book is that experience. I shall continue to write in it as long as I feel it is necessary to record events, happenings and my feelings on them. I will have a record in case I need to remember something that has happened in the past.

And so it begins. It should be interesting to see if the things she told me will actually come to pass.

CHAPTER VI

I was so intrigued by the storyline in Andrew's book, I spent the next few days just reading. I know I should have been painting but I wanted to know more about Andrew.

I discovered much about Andrew over the next ten years of his life. He finally graduated with honors and got involved with a legal team and also into finance in New York. This made me start to rethink my own perception of gypsy fortune tellers. "Wow. Madame Faruschka was right about him moving to New York." There was indication that he wanted to try and get any information regarding the brother Madame Faruschka said he had. Unfortunately, he wasn't sure how to do it by himself. He did make a promise that when he could afford to hire a detective to look into it, he would do so.

As luck would have it due to his position, he got connected with many of the wealthy as well as men of big business and the railroad. Dealing with them, he became quite wealthy himself. Not only businesses and ventures in the States but gold mines and diamond mines in Africa. Andrew was having an incredible time, thoroughly enjoying what he did. It seemed he had the Midas touch when it came to making money. His clients benefited as well.

Finally having money, he did hire a very good detective to do research and try and find his brother. This venture did not have any good results. There was just no information to be found on that matter and so the search came to an end.

Due to his interest in business ventures and dealing with his clients, he'd not had time for personal affairs or any romance. This was of no consequence. He was enjoying life and being single was not a problem. Interestingly enough, some of his clients had occasionally intervened, introducing him to several eligible women. For Andrew, there just was no attraction or connection. It made him chuckle as none of them had the initials of 'B' and 'D', either.

I sat there contemplating the information I had found out, "I'll bet most of the women that were introduced to him were gold-diggers, knowing he had money." I just shook my head and giggled. It was time to get back reading again to see what Andrew was up to.

It was 1909 and my thirtieth birthday was coming up. I decided to take some time off from work and get away from the hurried atmosphere of the city. Yes, some quiet place by the ocean would be fantastic. Looking on a map of the upper east coast, I found a small town in Maine that was by the sea and accessible by train.

Packing my suitcases and trunk, I headed to the train station. It was the 1st of June and it was going to be a relaxing time near the ocean. I couldn't wait.

Finally arriving at my destination, I wasn't even sure if there would be a place to stay. After checking with one of the personnel at the station, I was told of a small lodging house in town where I could rent for the month. This pleased me greatly.

It was a couple of days after arriving, I was sitting in the local bar, having a drink, when I heard some of the patrons talking about a roaming carnival that had set up close to the next town over. Many were mentioning how much fun it was for family members.

Hearing this, immediately, my memories were taken back some ten years to the one I had visited when I was at university. I spoke to the bartender, "It might be fun to go check out the carnival tomorrow. Do you know of anyone heading in that direction? I'd like to see if I could catch a ride."

He responded, "Actually, I'm taking the wife and kids over there tomorrow. You can come along with us."

"Why, thank you. That's so very kind of you. What time are you leaving?"

"I thought around nine. That should get us there by ten or thereabouts. And we can decide on a time to meet to come home."

The next morning the bartender came by and picked me up in his wagon. His wife and kids stayed in the back. It was a relaxing ride. The decision would be to meet and return around four in the afternoon.

Walking around, seeing the sights and smelling the aromas brought me back to that time in my past. It was giving me a strange happiness I'd not felt in a long time.

As I walked down one of the avenues between sideshows and tents, I looked ahead and noticed something that brought a shock of surprise to me. It was a tent with a sign on it. I mumbled the words written on it, "Fortunes told." I began to wonder, "Wouldn't it be funny if..." I stopped in my tracks. Sitting outside behind a small table was an old gentleman dressed in gypsy attire. I couldn't help but stare at the old man. "No. It couldn't be. No way could it be." I continued to walk toward the tent.

The old gentleman saw me approach. "Hello, young man. Would you like to have your fortune told?"

I nodded. "Yes, Sir. That would be fun."

"Just a moment. Let me see if she is ready." He got up and went into the tent.

I went into my money purse and pulled out a two and a half dollar gold piece. Yes, it was significantly more than the fee written on the small sign on the table but it didn't matter.

Shortly, he came out and sat down. "Yes. Madame Faruschka will see you now."

"Madame Faruschka?" I was absolutely surprised.

"Why, yes. Is something wrong?"

"Oh! No! No! It's just that..." I felt I had stepped back ten years in time.

"Yes?" He looked at me with a questioning expression.

"It's just that about ten years ago I had my fortune told and it was by this same lady. I'm sure of it. And virtually everything she told me then has come to pass. I truly look forward to seeing her again." I placed the coin in his hand and turned to enter the tent.

The old man took the gold coin then called out, "Young man! You have given me much too much." He looked at me very hard then spoke quietly and calmly, "I remember you now. I see your kindness and generosity still continues. Bless you, young man." A warm smile came to his face.

"Thank you, kind Sir." I nodded, turned and went into the tent.

Walking slowly, it was the same as before. Soon, I came to the open room. I felt as if I had stepped back in time as it was set up just as it had been ten years earlier.

Madame Faruschka looked up and smiled, "Come in young man and sit down." She gestured with her right hand.

After I sat down, she looked very closely and hard at me. After a moment, a huge smile filled her face, "Andrew. You have come back to see me again."

I was so shocked, I could hardly speak. I know my face expressed my surprise but I nodded my head. Finally, I gathered my wits and spoke quietly, "Yes. Yes, I have. After seeing you last time, I had one question. But when I was able to return, you and the carnival had moved on." I looked at her with gladness, "It is nice to see you again."

She continued, "I hope you have been well and the Fates have been kind to you."

I was excited, "Madame Faruschka, everything you have said has come true. I have been extremely successful and I have become quite wealthy. Thank you. Just as you told me ten years ago."

She spoke quietly, "There are still some things that will come to fruition. Believe it or not, the island I told you about is right around the corner. And be patient. You will meet someone special in two more years. I still see the letters 'B' and 'D' associated with this person. And it is very strong." A sense of joy came to her face, "One day you both are going to recognize something quite humorous about your relationship. When it happens, you both will find it very funny. I will tell you. When you meet your special someone, you both will be happy and enjoy life. Just like I told you last time. You will come to know what real love is. I am so glad for you. There are so many who never do."

She paused for a moment. "This is very interesting. The fog is still there when you are thirty-nine and I cannot see into it. Maybe it is not for me to know what is there. I have no idea what it means."

She then wanted to talk about my childhood and how I had been given up as a baby to a family who had the means to take care of me, "I will tell you now. There is a twin brother who was adopted by another family yet neither family knew of the other baby. He is out there somewhere."

I looked at her. "That is the question I wanted to ask you about. Yes, I have tried."

"Unfortunately, I have no more information about this to give you. I am so sorry. I know you have tried very hard to find him but have been unsuccessful. If the Fates deem it so, you will find him."

Then, I told her I had found a wonderful law firm and it truly was Brice and Walters. I had my wisdom teeth taken out several years earlier and they were in a special security box at the firm along with other important things. No one had a key except me. "And yes, I am writing my book like you said. I started shortly after the first time I saw you."

She did explain to me the need to write a paper of security and have certain people sign it. Then, I should keep it in the same secret place as the book to be used in the future. I should make duplicates of other documents of importance and keep them with the book but keep the originals in the security box at the law firm. After a few more minor comments, she took my hand in both of hers, "Andrew. Enjoy every day. Be happy. Tell those that matter how much you love and appreciate them. It is so good to see you again. You have grown into such a handsome young man. Bless you and take care."

I stood up and walked around the table. She stood and I gave her a big hug. "Thank you, Madame Faruschka. Thank you." I backed off, went into my money purse and pulled out four twenty-dollar gold pieces and placed them on the table next to the globe. Walking over to her again, I gave her another big hug. "Thank you for your caring, kindness and wisdom."

She looked up into my eyes. “Andrew. Thank you for your kindness and your great generosity. Bless you. The next time I see you, we will be in the great beyond. Take care, my child.” She hugged me again.

Before leaving, I turned, looked right at her, smiled and bowed my head.

Looking back at me, her face was filled with warmth and joy.

When I left the tent, there was a sense of sadness, knowing what she had said was most likely the truth. It had been a wonderful reunion. I was so glad I came. Finally, I began to walk through the carnival area to see the other attractions. Soon, it was time to meet the bartender and his family and head back. When we arrived at the lodging house, I gave him a nice gratuity for taking me. He was very thankful.

I stopped reading and sat there thinking about all I had read. “I wonder if Andrew ever did get the chance to find his twin brother?” I stared off into space for a moment. I could feel the sense of the sadness he must have felt, knowing he was not going to see Madame Faruschka again in this life. Then, it was back to reading again.

I had been in the seaside town for a week when I ran into a local individual who told me much about the area and the people. This is also when I discovered there was an island about two miles offshore that was for sale. Madame Faruschka was right. Especially, when I discovered the seemingly low price, I was very interested in seeing it. A trip to the island was arranged.

I could not believe how beautiful it was. Standing on the top of the bluff, overlooking the ocean to the east, I just knew it would be the perfect place for a wonderful house. Now, all I'd have to do is find an architect to design one for me.

Before my vacation was over, all legal paperwork was done and the sale had been completed. I was ecstatic about the buy. When I returned to New York, I sent all the paperwork regarding the island to Brice and Walters to hold for me. I would place everything in the secure box there the next time I visited. Now, I would begin my search for an excellent architect. My birthday vacation had been a huge success. I couldn't have been happier.

It was the end of August and a little over two months after my thirty-second birthday, I got invited to a summer gathering of several of my major clients. Not long after arriving and expressing 'hello's, I was introduced to a young man. The minute my eyes saw him, I could not believe how attractive he was. Somewhat shorter than myself. Dare I say, I got pleasantly aroused. Not so much that it was visible. All those years of being single were finally having an effect on me.

I immediately stopped reading, shaking my head. "What!? What!? What the hell was that about? Okay. This could get very interesting if it's what I think it is." I continued reading to see what was going to happen at that party.

The host spoke, "Andrew, I would like you to meet Brian. Brian Durnam. He is an architect who is becoming the talk of the town with his new concepts and ideas."

I turned. "Brian. Nice to meet you. I'm not sure if this is providence or not but I'm actually looking for an architect to design and oversee the construction of a house I want built."

He looked up at me and smiled, "I would definitely be interested in working with you. Here is my card. Please, give me a call. I live here in the city." He reached into his vest pocket and pulled out one of his business cards, handing it to me.

I nodded. "Thank you. I will." Reaching into my vest, I pulled out one of my cards and handed it to him.

"Thank you. I await your call."

I smiled, turned and walked away as I was afraid if I kept looking at him, I would lose control and make a fool of myself right there. What was wrong with me? Never had I had such feelings or sensations come over me before like that. It was insane. One thing I did know is I had met someone quite unique and special. I already knew he was going to be the architect to design and oversee the construction of a wonderful house I wanted built on the island, overlooking the ocean.

That night I lay in bed and could not get Brian out of my head. I knew I couldn't wait to see him again. Suddenly, I recalled what Madame Faruschka had said years earlier. She had seen the letters 'B' and 'D' associated with the one I was to love. I sat up in bed and yelled out, "Brian Durnam! It is YOU! It is YOU I will fall in love with!" I started laughing.

Again, I stopped reading and called out, "No way! Holy shit! Andrew is GAY!? What!? If that's the case, how the hell did that story get started about him getting married to a woman? Did he suppress his homosexuality? Wow. I can't wait to see where this goes." I started reading again.

I kept laughing, "And it seems it has already begun." Then, I stopped. "But this cannot be. What if he doesn't feel the same? But Madame Faruschka said that person would have deep feelings for me." I shook my head. "But this is NOT acceptable behavior. This kind of relationship is sorely frowned upon and disdained. But she did say it was a relationship others would call unconventional. I must be careful and go slowly." I lay back down and was quiet until I finally was asleep.

It was two days later, I decided to call Brian about meeting. The reason I waited is because I didn't want to seem too anxious. I retrieved his business card to get his phone number. "Hello, Brian. Andrew here. Doing well, thank you. And you? Excellent. Listen. I was wondering if you might be free tonight for dinner here at my apartment around five. You are? Excellent. Yes. I would like to talk to you about the house I want to build. Perfect. I will see you then."

Immediately, I got on the phone and called my favorite restaurant, ordering dinner for two to be delivered. I also ordered two bottles of excellent wine to go with the dinner. It would arrive around four o'clock, so I might have everything ready by the time Brian got here.

Promptly at four, dinner arrived. After we had placed all the boxes in the kitchen, I turned to the young man before he left, handing him a gratuity. "Thank you very much. I appreciate you getting everything here on time."

The young man looked at what I had given him then back at me with a big smile, "Mister Cavenaugh! Sir! Thank you for being so gracious and generous. If you ever need anything in the future, let us know. Have a good evening, Sir." He bowed politely as he went out the door.

I immediately started taking the food out of the boxes and placing the items in serving dishes to go on the buffet in the dining area. I had already placed the flatware, china and crystal in their appropriate places on the somewhat small table. I finished opening one of the bottles of wine and getting everything in place just as there came a knock at the door.

I must admit, knowing he had arrived, my heart began to beat a little faster. I took a deep breath and shook my head. "Settle down." I walked to the door and opened it. A big grin was on my face, "Brian. Welcome. Please, come in. Let me take your hat."

Brian looked up at me and smiled as he was holding two bottles of wine, one in each hand. "I wasn't sure if white or red would be appropriate, so I brought one of each." He handed them to me. "Thank you. I've been looking forward to this. I'll give you my hat in a minute when you put down the wine."

I looked down and noticed he was carrying a very large sketchpad pressed against his right side with his right elbow. "And what do we have here?"

"I thought I'd bring my sketchpad, so I could write things down. That way I'd have that information for future use. If there's time, we might even get an idea as to a possible floor plan. One never knows."

"Excellent. Have a seat there in the living room while I get us a glass of wine. I'll get your hat in a minute." I placed the two bottles of wine that Brian brought next to the ones I had on the buffet.

Brian looked around the openly connected rooms. "You have a lovely apartment."

I returned from the buffet and handed Brian a glass of wine then took his hat and placed it on the hat rack in the corner before I sat down. "Thank you very much. As you can see, I am rather unconventional. I use this whole area for a workspace as well as for relaxing and eating. I don't do much entertaining. One reason it seems somewhat cluttered. But I do have seating for clients should the occasion arise."

I continued, "I'm sure you've noticed I have no servants like many of my clients do. It's that I like doing a lot of things myself. I do have a wonderful couple who come in once a week on Wednesdays to do the housecleaning. They do excellent work and are very trustworthy. I would recommend them highly to anyone requiring such a service."

"But let's talk more at the table. Everything is on the buffet, so it's self-service. Oh! And by the way. No! I did not do the cooking. I had it delivered from my favorite restaurant."

Brian grinned, "Hey! Why not? Especially, if it's excellent food. And I'm sure it is. Being single, I fully understand."

We both grabbed our plates and went to the buffet. Shortly, we were sitting at the table.

I got up from the table, went to the buffet and picked up the bottle of wine. Returning, I filled both of our glasses, returned the bottle to the buffet and took my seat again. I held my glass in the air. "I do hope this is the beginning of a lasting friendship." I looked at Brian and smiled.

Brian smiled back and raised his glass in the air, "Hear! Hear! I absolutely agree."

During dinner, we began to share bits and pieces of information regarding our pasts. Brian went first. It was gratifying to find out more about him even though I knew he had only scratched the surface.

Brian looked at me and flexed his eyebrows. "Okay. Now, it's your turn."

I began explaining several events in my life that had some importance. But then, I said something without thinking, "It's kind of funny. Much of my success was foretold by a gypsy fortune teller." Suddenly, I almost choked, realizing what I had said. There was no way I could retrieve the words and put them back in my mouth. I looked at Brian.

Brian looked directly at me with an inquisitive expression on his face. He spoke quietly, "Really? A gypsy fortune teller?"

I bent my head down shaking it. "I'm sorry. I didn't mean to say that. It just came out. You must think I'm a lunatic."

"Au contraire. I find that extremely interesting."

"You can't be serious?"

"But I do. And there's a very good reason why."

I tilted my head to the side and peered at Brian with a questioning look on my face.

Brian looked at me very intently then spoke in a quiet manner, "Are you ready for this? My future as well was foretold by a gypsy fortune teller. Many years ago. I didn't mention it before as I didn't want YOU to think me strange."

I was surprised, "No way. You are kidding me?"

Brian shook his head. "Nope. Not kidding."

"Okay. Let's finish eating and retire to more comfortable seats. I want to hear more about this."

"Sounds good to me. And you can share as well." We both were nearly finished anyway.

Shortly, we were done and I started to remove the plates when Brian spoke up, "Let me help move the dishes to the kitchen."

"Thank you. Yes. You're so helpful. I just might have to keep you around." Suddenly, I realized what I had said. What was wrong with me? Why was I making an ass of myself?

Brian looked at me. "Who knows? We just might have to work on that." A big grin filled his face.

We both broke out in laughter as we went to the buffet to fill our glasses and retired to more comfortable chairs in the living room area.

Finally getting settled, Brian turned to me and asked, "Please, do tell about your experience with the gypsy fortune teller. I find things like that very unconventional but extremely interesting."

"If you insist." It took a little time to tell of both experiences. One thing I did leave out was the information regarding the letters of the someone special who was supposed to come into my life. Another thing I forgot to mention was the name of the gypsy lady.

I didn't realize that till later. "And that's really about it. So many of the things she told me have come to pass."

"I find it quite interesting that you have a twin brother somewhere out in the world. Have you had any success in finding him?"

"No. With nothing to go on to point in a direction, the detective I hired indicated it was virtually fruitless."

I went to the buffet, opened the new bottle of wine, came back to the living room area, refilled our glasses and placed the bottle on the coffee table adjacent to where we were sitting.

"Thank you very much." Brian bowed his head. "Guess it's my turn. To do so, we must go back to when I was about to get out of university. It was the spring of my Senior year. I'd be graduating in just another month." He began his story.

CHAPTER VII

Three friends and I found out a traveling carnival had set up not far from campus and thought we'd check it out. We decided to go after morning classes that Saturday. Since it was so close, it was not a problem to walk.

Brian paused and chuckled, "I hope you don't mind if I tell you a little side story that happened when we arrived. Every time I remember going to the carnival, it comes to mind. It has to do with Richard. He was a really nice friend of mine."

I looked at Brian and gestured with my right hand. "Hey. The floor is yours. Go for it."

Brian was happy I didn't mind and he continued his story.

When we got to the carnival, one of the first things we saw was the place where you take a big sledgehammer and hit a pad to see if you can ring the bell. My friend, Richard, was up for it. "Okay, guys. How many of you think I can do it?"

We all expressed our approval with cheers and whistles.

Brian paused again and looked over at me. "You need to know that Richard was built like a brick shithouse and around six-two. Yes. Tall like you and your stature but without a beard and mustache like you have. But let me continue."

Richard chuckled, walked over, paid the fee and picked up the hammer.

Interestingly enough, many of the folks in the vicinity stopped to watch, calling out, "You can do it! Ring the bell! Ring the bell!"

Richard raised the hammer up in the air and down it came. And what do you know? The sound of the bell resounded through the air and everyone cheered and clapped.

The man who ran the concession called out, "Excellent, young man! And here is your prize." He handed Richard a small stuffed bear. "A bear for a bear!"

Everyone clapped and cheered some more.

Richard responded, "Thank you. Thank you so very much." He looked around at all those who had stopped to watch him. That's when he saw a young mother and father with their young son, standing there watching. He walked over to them, knelt down in front of the young boy, handed the bear to the youngster and smiled, "Maybe one day you will grow up to be a big bear like me. Then, you can come and ring the bell."

Again, everyone loudly expressed their satisfaction at what he had done. The boy's parents were very happy at how thoughtful a gesture it was, thanking him.

As we turned to walk away, I commented, "Richard. You truly are a kind and considerate guy. I hope the Fates are kind to you in the future."

I interrupted Brian, "Sorry to break in but I have to say, Richard sounds like a really great guy. Do you still keep in contact with him?"

"No. Not long after we graduated, he married his girlfriend and they moved to Australia. I lost track of him after that."

"That's too bad but you still have memories of him and the one you just told me is a very good one. Now, please continue."

Brian smiled and continued where he had left off.

From there, we continued to walk around through the different concessions and tents. That's when we came upon one with an older man sitting at a small table near the entrance dressed in gypsy-type attire.

I called out, "Oh! Look! It's a fortune teller!" I could see her name on the sign.

John turned and looked at me. "Don't tell me you want to go see a gypsy fortune teller? Really?"

I responded, "I think it could be fun."

Matt patted me on the back. "Okay. If you want to waste your money on crazy shit, go right ahead. The rest of us will go check out more stuff here. We'll come back in about half an hour and get you."

I answered, "Okay. See you guys in about half an hour." I started walking to the table as the others walked down another avenue between the tents.

Seeing the charge written on the small poster hanging on the front of the table, I went into my money pouch and obtained the correct amount. Walking to the table, I handed the man the money.

He looked up at me. "One moment, young man and I will see if she is ready to see someone." He got up and entered the tent. Shortly, he was back and gestured with his left arm, he spoke, "Please. Go right in."

I headed to the entrance and walked in. Laughing to myself, I shook my head, speaking quietly, "Well, this should be VERY interesting. Am I actually doing this?"

Canvas panels had been used to create walkways, finally ending at a dimly lit open space. In the middle, sitting behind a small table with a glass globe in the center, was an older lady, wearing gypsy clothes.

She looked up at me with a warm expression on her face. "Come in, young man. Please sit down." She gestured with her right hand to the chair in front of the table. "You are young and have your whole life in front of you. Maybe I can help you choose the correct roads to take."

"Thank you." I sat down at the table.

She spoke quietly, "First, let me see your hands."

I stretched my arms out in front of me. "Sorry. Stupid me." I turned my hands over, realizing it was very likely she wanted to read my palms.

She took both and placed them flat on the table, palms up and went to the left hand first. After examining it closely, she went to the right, looking at it very closely. Soon, she leaned back. "Thank you. You may take your hands back now." As I did, she used both of her hands to sweep over the surface of the glass globe in front of her. "I see you are going to become a very well-known and respected architect. You are going to live in New York City. You are going to do very well and people will be extremely pleased with your designs and ideas."

After a slight pause, she continued, "This is very interesting. This is very private and I hope you do not mind me telling you this. You are going to meet someone special when you are thirty. You are going to fall very much in love. Your love will be considered as unconventional but that should not concern you." She paused again. "Ah, yes. This makes sense now. I see the letters 'A' and 'C' regarding this person." She had a very happy expression on her face, "I'm so glad to see I've not lost my touch." Looking right at me, she smiled, "There's a little funny puzzle you will figure out in time, showing that the connection you have with this special person is meant to be. You both will share happiness and love."

The words Brian had just said shocked and surprised me but I did not interrupt him. I let him continue.

She spoke quietly, "Do you know how many people never know real and true love? It is such a shame. You are going to be one of the lucky ones. I hope you realize this. Be happy together and express your love as often as you can."

Suddenly, she shook her head. "Something unusual has happened. I can see everything up until you are thirty-seven. But then, there is a door. I have turned the handle but the door will not open. I cannot see what is on the other side. It could mean you are to embark on a new adventure. Only time will tell." Pausing only for a moment, she continued, "Do you have any questions? If you do, I may be able to answer them."

I looked right at her. "Not really. It's good to know I will be a success in my profession." I giggled, "It's really nice to know I will fall in love, too. And it's only eight years away. By then, I hope I am very successful. Thank you so very much for what you have told me. I will remember it. I can only imagine what is beyond the door. I hope it's a great adventure."

"That is all I have for you. Take care and enjoy your life. Be happy."

As I got up, I reached into my money pouch and got the last of my money. It was a quarter and I placed it on the table. "I wish it was more. It's the only way to express my thanks to you. I appreciate your time and wisdom."

She stood, walked around the table and gave me a big hug. "Thank you for your generosity and kindness."

I returned the hug and then turned to leave. When I got to the opening to the room, I turned and smiled, "Thank you so much again."

A big smile was on her face, "You are so welcome, Brian. Take care, my child, and be happy."

I bowed slightly and walked to the entrance of the tent and out into the open air. "Wow. That was exhilarating." I looked down at the old man at the table. "Thank you very much." Then,

I started walking away. At that moment, I saw the guys coming in my direction.

Matt called out, "I hope she told you some good stuff and not some gloom and doom. Or about some damn marriage that ends in divorce."

"She told me I was going to become the emperor of the world."

They looked at me really hard with questioning expressions on their faces. Then, realized I was joking.

At that, we all laughed out loud and walked away. The guys mentioned there wasn't much more to see, so we headed back to campus.

Halfway there, I stopped. "Holy shit!"

John questioned, "What? What's wrong?"

The guys all looked at me as I answered, "She called me by name. She called me Brian."

Richard shook his head. "Are you sure? You didn't imagine it?"

"I have no idea how she knew my name."

John joked, "Well! Excuse me! She IS a fortune teller after all."

We all looked at John and just broke up laughing again as we continued going back to campus.

Brian looked at me. "And that's the story of my encounter with the gypsy fortune teller."

I shook my head. "There are things you mentioned that brought up several questions for me. I must be honest. I did not tell you everything the gypsy lady told me. I didn't want you to think me crazy and outlandish. But hearing your story, I find it necessary to share it with you. She told me I was going to meet someone very special who would become significant in my life with the letters 'B' and 'D'. Believe it or not, she knew my name as well without me telling her. Yes. She also said I would realize something humorous about the connection with that person." I started to laugh, "And it really is funny. I have figured it out." I kept laughing, "Are you ready? Put your initials with mine and what do you get?"

Brian stared at me for a moment and then began to laugh, "Holy shit! WOW! And it's so simple."

We both looked at one another and cried out in unison, "'A'! 'B'! 'C'! 'D'!" We both roared with laughter.

I picked up the bottle from the coffee table and began refilling our glasses. "I have to admit. Madame Faruschka was a very nice lady."

Brian yelled out, "No way!"

"What?"

"The gypsy lady you saw was named Madame Faruschka? Well. Guess what? So was mine."

I almost knocked over my glass as I set the bottle down. "You are joking? What are the chances?"

Brian giggled, "I guess I forgot to mention it when I was telling you about my encounter. You're right. She was a caring and kind lady. It really did make me wonder how she knew my name. I swear I never told her."

"I felt the same way. I thought about it for some time, trying to figure out how she knew my name, too. But your friend, John, said it. She was a gypsy fortune teller."

Just then, I heard the hall clock chiming. "Geez. What time is it? We've been chatting for some time now. I had no idea it was getting that late."

"Yes, I really should get going. I'm sorry we didn't get to talk about your house."

I thought for a moment. "I don't know what you have planned for tomorrow but I have two bedrooms here. If you would like to stay, it would be fine with me. That way you won't be on the streets at night alone."

"How kind of you. That would be wonderful. I have nothing planned for tomorrow."

"Fantastic." I grabbed the bottle of wine and poured the last of it into our glasses, setting the empty bottle back on the coffee table. I stood, looked at Brian and raised my glass.

Brian stood up and raised his glass. "To a newfound friend."

I responded, "To a newfound friend." I looked Brian directly in his eyes. "And to so much more." A huge grin filled my face.

We both called out as the glasses clinked together, "Hear! Hear!"

I looked up from reading and started to snicker, "With as much as they both had to drink, I wonder if they ended up in the same bed? I have a feeling Andrew would not expose such in his writings. But we shall see." I closed the book and got up. "I wonder what time it is? I'm getting hungry. I need a drink, too." I placed the book in the wooden box and headed to the restaurant and bar. It was Saturday evening and time to eat something other than from the fridge.

Luke was there and saw me walk in. "Well, what have you been doing the last couple of days? Did you go over to the island and start another painting? Glad you brought the painting back. Lots of folks have said how much they liked it." He pointed to the painting on the easel.

"No. Didn't go to the island and start a new painting. Actually, I started reading the book that was in the box. I just couldn't put it down, not even to come over here and eat. I had some things in the fridge in my room. It's been explaining Andrew's story. It began when he was at university and the time he went to see a gypsy fortune teller for the first time." I walked over and sat down at the bar. "From what I've read so far, I need a drink and something to eat. Yeah. Some real food."

Luke commented, "That's interesting. How about a burger?"

"Sounds good to me."

"If you don't mind sharing, I'd love to hear what you've discovered so far." He went in back and came out shortly. "Burger will be on the way shortly with some fries. Now. Let me get you a nice cocktail."

While I drank and ate, I hit the highlights of what I had read so far.

Luke was rather surprised, "Wow. This is incredible. From what you've said so far, it seems to me that Andrew was gay. But it sure doesn't jive with the story everyone knows that goes with the legend. I mean, how did the story come out about him getting married? And he has a twin brother? Wow!"

I took a sip of my drink. "Well, I'm not finished reading the whole book yet. Maybe there's some explanation yet to come. Now, don't forget. We're talking turn of the century here. Being gay was not something someone would just announce to the damn world back then. Do you know how many older guys I know who got married back in the fifties and sixties and even the seventies to hide their sexuality? Hey. It took the Stonewall event in New York in June of nineteen sixty-nine for gays to finally ban together and form the gay community and organize the gay rights movement."

Luke agreed, "Yep. You've got that right. And look how long it took from Stonewall to have the damn Supreme Court get off its ass and legalize gay marriage in June twenty fifteen." Luke paused a moment. "By the way, come over tomorrow, so you can watch the six o'clock news. Tom called me today and said he's going to give his cover story about all this in hopes it will lead to a possible hour-long special."

"That's terrific. I'll be right here. Drink in hand. I can't wait for him to hear the story in the book. That information will definitely add to his report."

Luke responded, "You've got that right."

I looked directly at Luke. "I'm rather surprised that you would know stuff regarding the gay community."

He looked at me with a big grin, "Well, there's a good reason I would and should know such information."

A shocked expression filled my face, "No way! No way!"

Luke raised his eyebrows. "Yep!" He paused for a moment. "I guess since you seem to be quite informed, you're a member of the club as well."

We both could not hold back and just broke up laughing and high-fived.

"I'm going to read the rest of Andrew's book tomorrow and see how things go with him and Brian. It's obvious, there's a budding relationship beginning. I'll see you tomorrow. I may come in early if I have anything interesting to tell from what I've read." I paid Luke for my drinks and food and started for the door. "See you tomorrow.

Maybe there will be some clue as to how the story of the legend got started."

Luke called out, "Tomorrow. Have a good evening. And don't get distracted and forget to get here in time."

I called back, "Yeah, I know what you mean. If I'm not here in time, give me a buzz over at the lodging house. I don't want to miss that report."

"Will do. Tomorrow!"

Getting back to my room, I was so tempted to start reading again but decided I would get a fresh start in the morning. That would be soon enough.

CHAPTER VIII

Getting up around eight-thirty, I went over to the restaurant for a quick breakfast. I didn't expect to see Luke there since it was too early for him. Returning to the room, I fixed a cup of coffee, retrieved the book from the box and sat down to continue reading from where I'd left off the day before. I could hardly wait to see where Andrew and Brian's story was going.

Brian did spend the night and slept in the second bedroom. The next morning when we woke up and got dressed, I thought we would walk down to my favorite restaurant and have breakfast.

While there, we had the chance to talk some more. Since Brian had nothing scheduled for that day, he indicated it would not be a problem to spend the day talking about the house I wanted to build.

Brian completely understood that I wanted the house designed in the same fashion as the major country houses in England. Large rooms, fairly high ceilings and a large great room on the back of the house, overlooking the ocean were of main importance. The second story would be for bedrooms and bathrooms. There would also be one room to be used to store linens, bathroom accessories and the like. Brian suggested there be a room as a sitting room and library where guests could go and just relax and maybe read. I thought it was a great idea.

Brian commented, "You do know that to do this properly, I really should see where the house is supposed to be constructed.

That way, I could get a sense of the land and how to position major rooms in the house."

I snapped my fingers. "Well, I'll tell you what. Let me know when you have about a week's time and we can go check out the island. How does that sound?"

Brian nodded. "That sounds excellent. How does next week sound?"

"That would be perfect for me. I have no major engagements. It also means we can get it done before any of fall's bad weather comes into play. We can go up this coming Saturday."

We spent the rest of the morning discussing how many major rooms I wanted on the first floor of the house. It was also essential to have a nice sized kitchen, storage pantry, at least one major bath for the first floor, maybe two, and two bedrooms and a small bath for live-in assistance.

By early afternoon, Brian was ready to head back to his apartment. "Before you go, why don't we run down and have a late lunch, early dinner?"

This was very agreeable to Brian, "That would be terrific. I would like that."

Finishing eating, Brian headed to his apartment and I went back to mine. It was after four o'clock in the afternoon and I decided to take a nap. The next day would be rather hectic as I had to meet with two of my clients. Doing that was going to take up the better part of the day.

Before taking my nap, I wanted to take some time to catch up with things here in my book. And having done so, I must be honest with myself. I truly enjoyed every moment I had spent with Brian. Just being near him gave me a sense of warmth. I so look forward to the trip we will take to visit the island. It will give me a whole week to be near him.

Closing the book, all I could do was chuckle, "All I can say is Andrew has it bad." I placed the book back in the box and decided to check my emails on the computer. I knew this would take some time.

I was correct. After going through all my emails, responding and checking out what was happening in the world on the Yahoo news clips, it was going on four o'clock. Time to head over to the restaurant and bar and have a cocktail. I'll definitely be there in time to see the report and chat with Luke a little bit beforehand. "After all, as Jimmy Buffett and Alan Jackson sing it, 'It's five o'clock somewhere.'" I left the room and closed the door.

Luke saw me walk in. "Hey, I didn't expect you this early. Glad you didn't forget. So, what else have you found out about Andrew?"

I sat down at the bar and shook my head. "He's got it bad. You remember the old song that goes, 'I've got you..... under my skin.'? Well. He's got Brian under his."

Luke placed my drink in front of me. "I know it's early but I'm sure you could use it."

"'It's five o'clock somewhere.'" I raised my glass in the air.

Luke gave a 'thumbs-up'. "You've got that right."

I took a sip of the cocktail and began catching Luke up on the story, "They're about to take a trip to come up and see the island, so Brian can get a feel for the place. They're planning to stay a week. I'll let you know how that turns out when I read more."

Luke giggled as he nodded his head, "I think that's so cool about the 'A' 'B' 'C' 'D'. And what are the chances of them both going to the same gypsy fortune teller? Wow. I spoke with Tom earlier and told him what you've told me so far. He's on cloud nine with all that new information. He's really excited about the fact that Andrew has a twin brother." After a moment, he asked, "How about something to eat?"

"Sounds good. If you have the fixings for a chef salad, that would be great."

Luke slapped his hand on the bar. "Coming right up!" He headed to the back to place the order.

Soon, it was time for the news report. Luke fixed me a fresh cocktail then went to adjust the TV, so we could see it clearly. He also made sure the sound was loud enough for us to hear it well. He called out, "How's that?"

I gave him a 'thumbs-up'. "That's terrific."

Within five minutes, the news report started. Before all the major news reports began, there was a quick comment, regarding Tom's report that would be at the end and for everyone to stay tuned. It took a while to get through the local and national news, the sports and the weather but finally, Tom's smiling face appeared on the screen.

"Good evening, ladies and gentlemen. Tonight I'm going to tell you of an incident that happened to me just recently. Many of you will laugh and scoff at the story. And that's okay. But I am a reporter who believes in telling the truth and the facts regarding any story. What I'm going to tell you is something I personally experienced. There's an old expression that the proof is in the pudding but in this case, proof is in the video. Think and believe what you may. For me, this is the truth."

"Before I show you any video, I must explain the legend of Cavenaugh Island which is located off the coast of Maine. It is a sad story that has been going around in that area for virtually a hundred years."

As I watched the report, Tom told of the legend, using video footage of Luke telling the story. Then, it went into the interview with me. I was very much impressed with the edited video Tom had made with me and showing the painting and the portrait drawing I had done. Alan's camera work was excellent. I was truly surprised at the mental effect it had when he slowly zoomed in on the painting I did of the house, sitting on the easel in the entryway of the house. And after a few moments, the view slowly moved up over the top of it, allowing the viewer to see the painted words on the wall. All the while, Tom was making commentary.

The clincher was the video Alan had taken of the ghostly image, standing on the roof of the portico and slowly zooming in on his face. The video then paused to a still picture. With excellent camera work, the portrait drawing I had done was slowly superimposed over the face in the video, holding for several seconds to allow the TV viewers to see that they were the same man. The portrait drawing was then removed and the video continued right to the point of the ghost slowly fading away and vanishing. Seeing that even disturbed me.

Luke called out, "Holy shit! Wow!"

Tom's smiling face came back to the screen again. "Ladies and gentlemen. What you have just seen was not faked. No actors were used in any of the video. I was there and witnessed everything you've seen in this report. Whether you believe in ghosts or not is strictly up to you. But I must admit, my mind has been broadly expanded on the subject due to this experience."

"My producers have seen this report and were so impressed, they want me to do more research into this story and see if I can come up with a worthwhile, in-depth report as a special. Needless to say, I was extremely pleased they considered the subject worthy of a possible special report."

"Sometime down the road, I may be reporting again on this very subject. Until then, ponder what you've seen tonight. It could change your fundamental thinking on things such as this. Ladies and gentlemen, thank you for watching. And good night." The screen faded.

I turned to Luke. "Damn! No one can say that Tom is not a consummate reporter. It totally amazed me how he took all that video interview with me and edited it down to a most compelling report. And Luke. You looked terrific. Yeah. Alan's camera work was beyond expectation. The way he did that shot from the painting, transitioning to the writing on the wall, was almost creepy and eerie."

Luke agreed, "Yep! Tom's a great reporter and Alan's a great cameraman. Wherever Tom goes, there goes Alan. They're like Mutt and Jeff."

I shook my head and giggled, "Geez. With that kind of relationship, you'd think they were partners."

Luke bent his head down. "Well."

I looked directly at Luke. "No. No way. I got no indication. You ARE kidding?"

Luke responded, "They like to keep it very quiet. I've known about Tom for years but Tom told me some time ago about his relationship with Alan. When they were here is the first time I had met Alan."

"Well, my hat's off to both of them."

Luke and I did a high-five.

I raised my glass up. "That definitely calls for another cocktail. Why don't you have one on me?"

"Why thanks, buddy. I appreciate that."

Luke went and fixed two cocktails. Placing one in front of me, he raised his in the air. "To a totally cool guy. Thank you."

I raised my cocktail and a 'ding' sounded as our two glasses touched. "Thank you. Back at you. And to Tom and Alan."

After a moment, we raised our glasses together. "To Tom and Alan."

I continued, "You know this report could possibly increase the number of folks coming up here. There's a ton of people who are into this kind of stuff, ghosts and all. Someone might even have to start selling souvenirs for folks to take home with them. What do you think?"

Luke slapped his hand on the bar. "Hey! That's not a bad idea if that should happen."

We both did another high-five.

Luke nodded. "I consider myself really lucky to have Tom as a longtime friend. As I've said, he and Bob have been friends since high school. They've been quite good to me. Both have been very, very successful. And they're not poor either." He expressed his pleasure, "They could've hired anybody to run this place here and paid them a lot less, too. They're the ones who actually put up the money for this place. And yet. They wanted me to have equal share. Not only that, as I've said, they pay me very, very well. I love it here. I consider myself incredibly lucky when I think about those who have jobs they dislike or don't get paid enough. What can I say?"

I responded, "I am so happy for you. And you're so right. There are so many who have jobs they're not fond of. I, too, am lucky. Some, I think, were disappointed I didn't take a job based on my education as an architect. Now, trust me. I'm not sorry for going to school as it was a great broadening of the mind. But I just love waiting tables. The pay's not fantastic but it covers the bills with a little leftover for a rainy day. Plus, I love my customers. I could almost write a book with some of the stories I've been told and been privy to." I bent my head down and chuckled, "Actually, I do use some of the information in my writings. I just switch it around and change the names to protect the innocent."

My comment had us both chuckling.

I drank the last of my cocktail and placed the glass on the bar. "Since it's still early, I think I'm going to go back over and read some more in Andrew's book. It should be interesting to see how his trip to the island with Brian turns out."

Luke added, "I'm going to give Tom a buzz and catch him up on all the new stuff you have told me about Andrew."

As I got up to leave, Luke spoke out again, "Can't wait to hear what happens with Andrew and Brian. It should be quite interesting how they handle their relationship in that time period. See you tomorrow! I also hope there is some explanation as to how the story of the legend got started. I can think of nothing that would bring a woman into the story."

I called out, "We shall see! We shall see! Tomorrow!" I headed out the door.

Reaching my room, I retrieved the book and got comfortable in a chair. I, too, was interested in how things were going to move forward between Andrew and Brian. I began to read.

I could not stop thinking about Brian. It was as if I was possessed. I not only saw his attractive physical qualities but I could see he was smart, intelligent, had a sense of humor and more. I was really looking forward to our trip to the island. As planned, we would meet at the train station that Saturday morning.

I arrived early and bought the tickets. Knowing there was no need to take a lot of clothes, I was carrying one large suitcase. I set it down beside me and sat down to wait for Brian.

It was getting close to time for the train to leave Penn Station and Brian had not shown up yet. Maybe he had changed his mind. Maybe he really didn't want to go. I caught myself. "Stop thinking so negatively. He's probably running a bit late."

At that, Brian came running into the station with a large suitcase in his right hand and his sketch pad under his left arm. Seeing me as I stood, he came running to me and my heart began to pound. A big smile filled my face.

He cried out, "I'm sorry! I'm so sorry! There was a commotion, holding up traffic. I was so afraid I might not get here in time. Let me get my ticket."

I held the two tickets in the air. "Not to worry. I have your ticket already and you are here. That's all that matters. Let's head to the train and get our seats."

The trip north took several hours with a major stop in Boston before continuing north. We spent a great amount of time in the dining car, having something to eat as well as a few drinks. Conversation was basically about some of our business ventures and some gossip about several of our clients.

It was early evening by the time we arrived. We gathered our things, got off the train and headed to the same lodging house where I'd stayed two years earlier. We were fortunate that a local man with his wagon picked us up and took us to the lodging house.

When we walked in, the owner looked hard at me. "I remember you. You stayed here two years ago. You bought the island. Yes. Welcome back, Mister Cavenaugh."

"Yes, ma'am. You are correct. We are here for a week and I was hoping you had lodging for us."

A big smile filled her face, "Certainly, Mister Cavenaugh." She looked at Brian. "Two rooms?"

"Yes. This is Mister Brian Durnam. He is my architect and is going to design the house I want to build on the island. He wants to see the island and get a feel for the location. It will help him in the placement of the house and certain rooms within its walls."

She turned to Brian. "Welcome, Mister Durnam. And thank you so much for staying here." She reached up on a board behind the desk and grabbed two keys. "Let me show you your rooms. Don't worry about signing in. You can do that later. I'm sure you want to get settled from your trip."

I questioned, "Is the restaurant in town still open? I thought we could get something to eat before going to bed."

She nodded. "Yes. Yes, it is and the food is still pretty good."

We all headed upstairs to our rooms. Brian's room was right next to mine. We both understood that we would be using the common bathroom on that floor.

After the owner handed our keys to us, she commented, "Welcome, again, gentlemen. And if you need anything, just let me know." Then, she headed back downstairs.

I turned to Brian. "It's a bit rustic but it's really quite nice."

Brian shook his head. "Hey! If you only knew where I came from, you'd possibly reconsider me as your architect." He unlocked his door, picked up his suitcase and walked in.

I did the same and placed my suitcase on the desk in my room. I could get my clothes hung up later. It was time to get something to eat. I went next door. "Are you ready to go get something? I'm getting hungry."

Brian responded, "Yep! Let's go!"

Once seated at the restaurant, we ordered our food and drink. The food was simple and good just as I remembered it from my last visit two years earlier.

As the waiter left the table, Williams, the owner, came over. A big smile on his face, "Good evening, Mister Cavenaugh. Nice to see you again."

I responded, "Why, thank you very much. It's good to be back. I brought my architect to see the island since he is going to design and oversee the building of my house there. This is Brian Durnam." I gestured in Brian's direction.

"Good evening to you, Mister Durnam. I am Williams. This is my establishment. Welcome. I hope you have a nice stay here in our town. If you both should need anything special, let me know. I'll try to accommodate. Thank you for coming in again." He bowed slightly and returned to the kitchen.

While we ate, Brian told me of his past and how he was from a family of rather meager means, "The reason I got to go to university is due to my very good grades in high school. I was given a scholarship. I had wanted to be an architect ever since I can remember. I think it had to do with the books I got to read in the small library at school. I've been quite lucky at the work that's come my way and the wealthy clients requesting it."

I looked at Brian. "Well, to sound really snobbish and pompous, if the host of the party where I met you wasn't impressed with things you've done for him and or his friends, you would never have been there." I grinned, "Sorry. But it's true."

Brian took a sip of his drink. "Yes, I'm sure you are right. I know several of his friends and they all seem to be a bit much. But I don't mind as long as it is putting money in my pockets." He bent his head down to hide his giggle.

I chuckled and responded, "What can I say?"

Then, I changed the subject. "I can't wait to see the finished product on the island. I know it will be incredible."

"I have to tell you. I've been doing the drawings for your house in my spare time and they are coming along really well. I hope you will like what I've come up with, especially knowing you like the country homes in England. After seeing the island, I can refine them where needed."

I was pleased, "If you have time tomorrow, I'd love to look at them and see what you've come up with."

Brian smiled, "Excellent."

I was ecstatic, "With the drawing happening so quickly, we could get construction starting next spring. That would be fantastic."

Brian nodded. "You've got that right."

I looked over at Brian. "This is really off the subject, but I was planning a trip overseas next spring. Especially, if the house construction is started. Thought about hitting Rome, Paris and London. Didn't know what you might be doing at that time but would love for you to come along."

Brian raised his eyebrows. "That gives me time to wrap up two jobs I have recently accepted. They should be done by then. If construction can start in late February on your house, I would love to go."

I raised my glass in the air. "To our trip to Europe next year."

Brian raised his and they clinked together. "Hear! Hear!"

Finishing our meal, we returned to our rooms. It had been a tiring day. We would go to the island the next day.

As I closed the book for the night, I rejoiced in the happiness I could feel in the writing. But there was a nagging sensation in the back of my brain, knowing what was to eventually happen down the road. I spoke softly, "What could have taken place, causing the story of the legend? And whatever happened to Brian? There's nothing about him in the legend." I shook my head.

CHAPTER IX

Stretching and yawning, I got out of bed and looked at the clock. It was going on eight-thirty. I really wasn't hungry but I thought I might run over and have a light breakfast. Realizing Luke was not there, I quickly finished and returned to my room.

Looking over at the three blank canvases, I had to laugh to myself, "I came all this way to do possibly four paintings and I've only completed one. Took me two days to get here and it's June eighteenth. My month of vacation is more than half over. This ghost mystery is taking up so much of my time." I shook my head. "Well, who knows? I might get another novel out of it. What can I say?"

I opened the wooden box and retrieved the book. "Okay. Let's see how things continue with Andrew and Brian." I began to read where I had left off the day before.

The next day before heading to the island, Brian and I had a quick breakfast at the restaurant. Brian already had his notebook and pencil with him, so after eating, we went directly down and rented a boat from Jack.

Jack spoke with a smile, "Good morning, Mr. Cavenaugh. Good to see you again."

"Hello, Jack, and good morning to you. This is my architect, Brian Durnam. He wants to see the island and the location I want to build the house."

Jack bowed his head. "Welcome, Mr. Durnam." He then turned to me. "I think this is just what you will need to get there." He pointed at one of the boats.

I responded, "Excellent. We will be back by this afternoon."

Arriving in the cove, we took our time walking through the vegetation and up to the location where I wanted the house constructed.

I watched Brian walk within some ten feet of the edge of the bluff as he looked out over the ocean. He didn't get any closer. I called out, "If you get closer to the edge you can see how high up we are."

He turned and looked at me. "I can't! I am terribly afraid of heights!" He gave a nervous chuckle.

"Oh! Sorry! I didn't know!"

Brian turned back around again. "The view up here is spectacular. It makes perfect sense to have a large great room on this side of the house with many windows on the outside wall." He turned and looked at me again with a saddened expression, "You do realize that with so many windows, heating the room is going to be a real bitch."

I nodded in agreement, "I thought if there were two large fireplaces it might help. One at either end of the room."

Brian stomped his foot on the ground. "With all this stone, the foundations will have an excellent footing." He slowly turned his head from left to right. "And this looks to be one of the highest points on the island. Will definitely have to take into consideration any howling windstorms." He opened his notebook, pulled out his pencil and started writing entries.

As I watched Brian, a happiness and warmth grew inside me. I felt comfortable with him. I knew I was falling more and more in love. I walked over next to him and looked down into his face. "Brian. I can't hold back any longer. I'm not sure how you feel about me but I know how I feel about you. I'm falling in love with you every day. And it all began when I first saw you at the party."

Brian looked up and smiled, "From the moment I first saw you, I knew you were the one and immediately started falling in love with you. I had a sense you were having feelings for me but I wasn't sure how significant they were until now. Andrew, I want to spend the rest of my life with you. But." He paused for a moment.

I became concerned, "What? What's the problem?"

"You do realize the love we have and share will not be recognized by others. It is unconventional and would be ridiculed and disdained. We would have to be so very careful. No one could know. If your clients or mine ever found out, our reputations would be destroyed. We would be ostracized. We'd have to be extremely careful."

What Brian was saying made perfect sense to me. I completely understood. "Yes, I know. You're correct. We'd have to show extreme discretion in public. Only in private could we share and show the love we have for one another." I pulled him close to me and we passionately kissed.

After a moment, I made a suggestion I'd been pondering for some time, "What would you think about moving into the same building where I am? I know there's an opening on the floor above mine. You would have your space and I'd have mine but we'd be close enough that we'd be able to often share time together."

A huge grin filled Brian's face, "That's an incredible idea. I'd be the Watson to your Holmes. And no one would be the wiser."

Happiness raced through my body, "Now, that's funny. Yes, they did both have their own apartment on different floors but they spent a major portion of their time in Holmes'. You could set up all your architectural drawing needs in your living space since I have all my business things set up in mine."

Brian cheered, "Excellent idea! We can take action on it when we get back to the city."

I turned and looked out to sea. "You're correct. We will have to be careful. I so hope that one day love like ours will finally be accepted."

Brian added, "Well, as my mother would say, 'Don't hold your breath on that one. You'd look like hell blue.'"

We both laughed together.

Just then, my cell phone rang, interrupting my reading. It was Luke, telling me I needed to go online and see the news clips. Information regarding Tom's report was all over the internet. "Luke, thank you. I'll check it out right now. See you later on this afternoon."

I closed the book, put it away in the box and went to my laptop on the desk. The main Yahoo page had several articles and commentaries about Tom's television report the previous night. YouTube had video clips from the report.

It took quite some time to read the articles and view the comment postings made by several individuals pertaining to the video and the report. I found it rather interesting the opinions being shared on both sides of the fence, regarding the issue of ghosts. Needless to say, I had to post my own comments in the response forums below several of the articles and videos, "It should be very interesting to see what people have to say when they discover that I'm one of the people in the television interview."

Getting up to run to the bathroom, I looked at the clock. "Damn! I can't believe it's this late already. I think it's time for a cocktail." After letting the coffee I drank that morning escape my body, I came back to my room, turned off the computer and headed out the door to the restaurant.

Luke saw me enter and called out, "What did you think of some of those comments online?"

I shook my head as I walked over and sat down at the bar. "It truly amazes me at the diversity of thinking out there. To be honest, I did have to contemplate the ignorance and stupidity of some of the responses."

Luke just grinned, "I know what you mean. Some people just have no imagination."

He finished making my drink and placed it in front of me. "Okay. 'Enquiring minds want to know.' What else have you discovered in the book?"

I took a sip of my drink. "Wow. That tastes very, very good. Thanks, Luke."

"You're so welcome. How about a hamburger to go with that?"

"That sounds great. And some fries, too, if you don't mind."

Luke went to the back to place my order and returned shortly. "I'm ready. Let's hear it."

"Okay. Andrew and Brian have gone to check out the island. Their relationship is beginning to heat up. But they both know they have to be very careful. They're well aware of how things are in those times, regarding such relationships. Brian's actually going to move into Andrew's building. It'll appear, as Brian described it, they'll have a relationship similar to Watson and Holmes. Remember the story? Dr. Watson lived above the apartment where Sherlock Holmes did. They shared most of their time together in the living area of Holmes' apartment. There was never any indication that their relationship was anything but typical of two friends at the time."

Luke was surprised, "Wow. That's very interesting. You never really did get any impression there was anything more than a great friendship between the two. Another question. How much more of the book is there to go?"

"So far, Andrew is thirty-two and Brian is thirty. Since Andrew vanished at around forty years old, there should be about eight more years of information. I still find it so interesting that there's nothing about Brian in the legend. It seems they kept their relationship an excellent secret. Maybe they ran away together to a distant island, so no one would ever know of their relationship. I'm still trying to figure out how in the hell the story about Andrew getting married got started. I can't wait to find out how that took place."

Luke had a questioning expression on his face, "Do you really think that's going to be in the book?"

I looked right at him. "Oh, hell yeah. I'm sure of it. Believe me. It's going to be something so wonderfully conniving. I just know it is. It's something I can't imagine Andrew leaving out." I took a sip of my drink. "Not to change the subject. BUT. I wonder how all this publicity on the web today might change things here. As I mentioned to you before, this place could get inundated with ghost hunters and the like."

"I know! You're right! That island could possibly turn into a tourist attraction."

Just then, the bell rang, indicating my food was ready. Luke went back, retrieved it and placed it on the bar.

I looked at the hamburger and fries. "You all make a great hamburger here and terrific fries. This looks really good." After putting some mustard and ketchup on the burger, I took a bite and swallowed. "Yummy."

I picked up one of the French fries and stuck it in some ketchup. I held it up and turned to Luke. "Here's a touch of history for you. There was a restaurant in Atlanta over on Cheshire Bridge Road that started serving French fries with a thick beef gravy on top. Yeah. Back in the day, there used to be a number of gay clubs on that road and in that area. When they all closed at night, it was around two o'clock in the morning and a lot of the guys would go to that restaurant for something to eat. Especially, on Friday and Saturday nights."

"From what I remember hearing, a whole bunch of guys came in one night and one of them ordered French fries and asked the cook if they would put a thick beef gravy on them. When the order came out, several folks tasted them and were truly impressed. A whole bunch more orders were made and the word spread. Since it was a gay guy that ordered them, everybody referred to them as 'Gay Fries' and it stuck. It was the only place you could get them in the city. They definitely were different but very good."

Luke looked surprised, "Wow! That's different! And you say they were good?"

"Every time I went there I'd order them. They were that good. I haven't been to that restaurant in a thousand years, so I have no idea if the tradition is still going on."

Luke questioned, "You say it was a thick gravy?"

"Yep. A thick beef gravy. One that would stick really good to the fries."

Luke flexed his eyebrows. "You know what? I'm going to give it a try. And if they're as good as you say they are, I'm going to put them on the menu."

I bent my head down and started snickering.

Luke spoke, "What?"

"Are you going to call them……. 'Gay Fries'?"

We both just roared with laughter.

Finishing my food, I asked Luke for another drink.

Luke called out, "Coming right up!"

I spoke up, "Getting back on subject again, I'll bet Tom is going to be ecstatic with all the information and stuff in the book Andrew wrote. It definitely will be information to incorporate into his TV special. I can only imagine what else I'm going to find out the more I read. As much as I want to find out more, I really do need to get back to painting again. Geez. I had great expectations of completing at least four canvases on this vacation but I've only completed one. And my vacation is more than half over. I think tomorrow I will go back out to the island again and start another one. If I possibly can get the right angle, I'd like to do one of the columned pavilion with the house off to the side and in the background. If not, I'll sail around to the east side and do a seascape if I can find a good spot where there aren't so many rocks. I didn't really look that closely when I did it on my first day over there."

Luke tipped his head to the side. "Well, if you do go to the island tomorrow, just be careful and I'll see you here tomorrow night."

I drank the last of my cocktail. "Thank you. I will. See you tomorrow night." I left the bar and headed to my room.

CHAPTER X

The next morning, I got up and headed down to the boat, carrying a new canvas. I didn't eat any breakfast as I wasn't really hungry.

Finally arriving at the island, I carried the canvas up to the house. Opening the front door and entering, I walked over and placed the empty canvas on the easel. I looked over at the staircase. Everything was exactly where I had left it. I walked into the great room and peered out the windows. The edge of the bluff was some twenty-five to thirty feet from the wall of the house. Remembering what I had read in the book, I imagined Andrew and Brian standing together near the edge. I could feel a sense of the love they shared that day.

Walking to the set of French doors opening onto the terrace space between the house and the bluff, I left the house through those doors and walked close to the edge and peered over. It became quite obvious to me that to do a seascape down there, I would have to take a photograph from the boat as there was no sandy beach below the bluff where I could set up an easel. A painting at sea level with the ocean to the right and the bluff on the left would make a terrific painting the way the waves crashed upon the rocks. I would take that picture another day.

Since I was outside, I decided to walk to the domed and columned pavilion that was north and west of the house. It took some time but I finally found the right place I would eventually set up and do a painting. I wanted to make sure that the light and shadowing were the best. I would have to do this painting at another time because it would require a different size canvas than the ones I'd brought with me.

Down to the beach where I had anchored the boat, I decided to walk along the beach for a place to set up my easel and do the next painting. This little venture took some time but it was well worth it. I found two locations that would make excellent paintings.

I returned to the entry hall then ran upstairs to the room where Andrew left through the doors to the top of the front portico. I walked to the middle of the room and closed my eyes. I spoke quietly, "Andrew. I'm reading your journal. It's so wonderful you and Brian have found one another. I have reached the part where you have both come here for the first time, so Brian can see where you want this house built. I'm so happy for you that you both have figured out a way to share time together by living in the same building. I look forward to reading more." I stood there for a moment in silence.

Suddenly, I felt a slight breeze blow over my face and then was gone. I opened my eyes and smiled. I just knew it was Andrew letting me know he heard me.

I left the room, headed downstairs, out the front door and down to the boat. It was going on four o'clock and time to head back to the mainland. I was getting hungry.

When I got back, I headed directly to the restaurant and bar. It was time for a nice Delmonico steak and salad.

I had hardly walked through the front door when Luke saw me and yelled out, "Have I got news for you! You're not going to believe this. Have a seat while I fix your drink. I'm sure you're hungry. What can we fix for you this late afternoon?"

"And a good afternoon to you, too!" I called back and headed to the bar. Sitting down, I looked directly at Luke. "Yes. A drink would be perfect. Along with a Delmonico steak and a salad. Medium rare, please. Yes. Now, what seems to have your knickers twisted? And I have a little something for you, too."

Luke responded, "Let me get your order in and I'll be right back." Running to the back, he returned shortly making my drink. Pouring it into a glass and placing it in front of me, a big smile filled his face, "I'm glad you're sitting down. Tom called me less than an hour ago. He said it's essential for you and me to take the train down to Boston tomorrow morning. He indicated it's extremely important."

I was stunned. I knew it had something to do with all this craziness but I was totally surprised, "Did he give you any details? Anything?"

Luke shook his head in the negative. "Nope. But if he said it's important, trust me. It's important. I did tell him you've been reading more of the book. He was pleased. He wants you to bring the wooden box and everything in it with you. He definitely wants you to tell him everything you've found out so far. I almost forgot. He wants you to bring your sketchpad as well."

A questioning expression filled my face, "But he already has video of the drawing. I can't imagine why he'd need it again. This is very interesting. I know this is going to sound crazy but it's kind of spooky, too."

Luke clapped his hands. "Okay. What's your news?"

"While I was out there today checking on possible locations for a painting, I went up to the room where I had seen Andrew out on the portico. I stood in the middle of the room and closed my eyes and told him I was reading his book. That's when a small breeze blew over my face and vanished. I just know it was Andrew."

Luke was shocked, "Oh, wow. This thing just gets better and better." He paused for a moment then changed the subject. "Guess you didn't get a chance to start another painting today?"

I looked at Luke. "You do know if you were any closer, I'd smack you upside the head."

All we could do is snicker.

I looked right at him. "To answer your question. NO! I did not start another painting yet. But the empty canvas is sitting on the easel, waiting for me. I guess it's just going to have to wait for another day." I paused for a moment, leaned back and placed the back of my left hand on my forehead. "I'll think about it tamarra. Afta all, tamarra IS anotha day."

Luke let out a loud sigh, "What can I say? What can I say?" He chuckled, "I have seen that movie several times. I also love the line spoken by Clark Gable, 'Frankly my dear, I don't give a damn.'" He started laughing.

I raised my hand in the air and we did a high-five as I joined in the laughter.

The bell rang in the kitchen, indicating my food was ready. Luke ran in and brought it back, setting it on the bar in front of me. "Enjoy! I'll fix you another cocktail, too."

While I ate, Luke and I pondered what was of such significance in Boston. Yes, the law firm was there. Brice and Walters. Tom's suggestion to bring the wooden box with all its contents was an excellent idea. And if we did go to the law firm, we would have all the paperwork as well as the key that most likely went to a safe deposit box. We also had a feeling that there was something else besides the law firm that was of significance. Yes, the next day was going to be very interesting.

Luke commented, "Tom said he'd pick us up at the station and bring us to his office."

"Not to sound like a stingy asshole, but that will save us a taxi fare."

We both chuckled.

The phone ringing in my room woke me up. It was Luke, telling me to put a few things in a bag since it was possible we would be there for a few days. He said Tom had already booked rooms for us just in case.

Knowing I only had my large suitcase and backpack, he loaned me a small satchel for me to carry items in. Since he was only using his small suitcase, he also carried the wooden box. That left me with the small satchel and the sketchpad. Luke drove us to the station and we were there a little early. We decided to eat a little something on the train. It was mid-afternoon by the time we arrived in Boston.

Tom greeted us with a big smile on his face, "Hey, guys! Let me help you with your things." Everything went into the trunk of his car and we were off to his office. "I'll take you to your hotel rooms later on. It's more important right now for us to talk and let you in on something I have discovered."

When we got to the television station, I had to chuckle to myself. Tom didn't have to worry about a parking space as he had one assigned to him.

As we got out of the car, Tom commented, "I'm so glad to see you brought the wooden box. It's going to come in very handy, trust me. I've also put together a theory as to why the old gypsy lady told Andrew to put his wisdom teeth in a secure location." We all walked around to the trunk of Tom's car. "I think you both will be on the clue bus very shortly." He opened the trunk and pulled out the wooden box. "I'm going to make copies of all the paperwork in here, so we have backup in case we have to leave the originals at the law firm." He turned to me. "Bring your sketchpad along, too." He handed it to me.

Entering the building and taking the elevator, we were finally in Tom's office. "Gentlemen, before we get started on any of this, you need to see this." The expression on his face was incredible. Like he had a major trick up his sleeve. He walked over to the door of an adjacent room, placed his hand on the handle and opened it. He then turned toward Luke and me. "Let me introduce you to..... Ethan Groves."

Right then, a man appeared in the doorway and walked into the room. He had a big smile on his face, "Hello, gentlemen. I'm Ethan Groves."

I was so shocked and astounded, I actually let out a scream. Totally shaken and virtually losing my balance, Luke and Alan grabbed hold of me to keep me from collapsing on the floor.

There, in front of me, stood a man whose voice sounded much like that of Sam Elliott. He was just over six feet tall, dark hair, beard and mustache and with the most piercing blue eyes, staring directly into mine. I cried out, "Oh, my God! It's ANDREW!!" I tried to regain my balance.

Tom looked right at me. "No. His name is Ethan Groves and he lives in New York City. Now, do you understand what I said earlier? Luke had told me the things he said you had read in Andrew's book.

The gypsy lady had indicated Andrew had a twin brother. Well, it's very possible and very probable that Ethan is a descendant of that twin brother. Otherwise, how could the resemblance be so striking and astounding? I have a sneaking suspicion a DNA test on Andrew's wisdom teeth will prove the connection."

Shortly, I collected myself. I walked forward and extended my right hand in Ethan's direction. "Ethan. Please, forgive me. But you look so much like the man who appeared in my dreams. Seriously, you are the spitting image of Andrew."

Ethan shook my hand and gave a big smile, "Not a problem. I can only imagine and I do understand."

I quickly got the sketch pad and opened it to the portrait drawing, holding it up for all to see.

Ethan stared right at it and nodded his head. "This just gets scarier and scaier."

Luke responded, "The resemblance is truly uncanny. Geez."

Tom spoke up, "If everyone would please have a seat, I would like Ethan to explain why and how he got here." He turned to Ethan. "The floor is all yours."

After we all sat down, Ethan looked at Luke and me. "Living in New York City, we obviously don't get news reports from Boston TV stations. But! Tom's story that was on TV Sunday night went viral on the internet by Monday. It was just after lunch on Monday that one of my colleagues at work came into my office with his laptop. I had no idea why he was laughing."

"Ethan! You've got to see this online video report if you haven't seen it already. You're not going to believe it. It's a report that was on

TV last night in Boston. From comments I've seen about it, it has literally gone viral online."

Roger placed his laptop down on my desk in front of me and started playing the video. I sat there and watched the report and listened to the interview. But I could not understand how it was pertinent to me. Not until the camera focused in on a pencil sketch portrait. I was shocked, "Holy shit! That looks exactly like me! But how the hell is that possible?" I continued watching the video right to the end when the camera slowly zoomed in on the face of a man, standing on the front portico of the house. "Oh, my God! How the hell is this possible? I know it's not me." What was really shocking was to see the man slowly fade away and vanish.

Roger looked at me with a very serious expression. "Now, do you see why I wanted you to see this? It's incredible. And what if it's true? A hundred-year-old ghost that looks exactly like you. And a portrait sketch that looks like you sat for it. What are the chances?"

"Roger! I definitely need to get in contact with that TV reporter."

Roger grinned, "I had a feeling you might say that." He handed me a piece of paper. "All the information's right there. Also, his phone number. Personally, when I first saw the report, it almost blew me out of the chair. I couldn't wait for you to see it if you hadn't already. And from your reaction, it's obvious you hadn't." He pointed at his laptop. "You want me to leave my laptop in here, so you can see it again?"

"No. But thanks. I'm going to call right now and get to the bottom of this."

Ethan looked at all of us sitting there. "That's when I got on the phone and talked with Tom here. He gave me some details of the story that he was aware of and realizing I was not pulling his leg, he indicated it was imperative I come up here to Boston to see if we could sort some of this out. Interestingly enough, Roger had shown the story all over the office and even my boss wanted me to come check it out."

"And so. Here I am. I arrived on the train last night. Tom told me you both were coming up today but he didn't want you to immediately see me. So, he told me to wait in the adjacent room until he opened the door. Yeah. Knowing everything he told me Monday on the phone and last night, I could only imagine the impact it was going to have on both of you. Well, it was significantly greater than I actually imagined." He looked at me and smiled, "I'm so really glad it didn't give you a heart attack."

That made all of us laugh.

Tom spoke up, "I've already set up an appointment to go talk to the folks over at Brice and Walters. They will see us on Friday afternoon and sounded extremely interested in meeting and speaking to all of us. They indicated there had been no communication with them regarding Andrew since his disappearance a hundred years ago. I told them I hoped they didn't mind that some of us would be in casual wear due to the circumstances. They indicated this would not be a problem."

Ethan commented, "I'm so glad everyone is so open-minded about this. Because I now understand something I was told back when I was in college." He bent his head down shaking it. Shortly, he looked up and deliberately looked at each one of us in the room. He spoke quietly, "Yes. When I was a Senior in college, several friends and I went to a carnival that had set up not far from campus and the local town."

I heard Ethan's words and my whole body was filled with a feeling of shock, anticipation and surprise. A chill raced through me letting me instantly know what he was going to say next.

Ethan continued, "And at the carnival, there happened to be the tent of an old gypsy fortune teller." He paused for a moment. "Yes, I went in to see her. She told me many things regarding my future. One of them was that she saw an 'island' in my future but she never really elaborated on that. There was also mention of 'teeth'. I never really asked any questions. As time progressed, I wondered if the 'island', to which she was referring, might be Manhattan as that's where I ended up working and living. As for 'teeth', I took that to mean I should see my dentist on a regular basis to prevent any problems in the future."

He continued, "Now, I have to say. Having heard what Tom told me, throws a whole new light on the subject." He paused again. Then, he looked directly at me. "Oh. And by the way, the old gypsy lady's name was..."

At that, we all became anxious. I could see the suspense on everyone's face.

Then, Ethan looked at all of us and spoke quietly, "Madame Faruschka."

We all yelled out, "WHAT!" "NO WAY!" "HELL NO! OH, HELL NO!!"

At that, Ethan slapped his leg, rocking back and forth, roaring with laughter, "JUST KIDDING! Just kidding! Just kidding!"

We all realized we'd been HAD and roared with laughter, clapping our hands.

Luke just howled, “Yeah! I was going to say. That bitch would have to have been at least a hundred and fifty years old when you saw her!”

That made us all laugh even more.

Ethan finally gathered his wits. “Sorry, guys. But I couldn’t help it. The door was open and I just couldn’t resist walking through it. Actually, her name was Madame Zelda in case you were interested.

I was still snickering, “Okay. THAT was a good one. Kudos to you for the impromptu humor. But I do find it interesting that you actually did go to a fortune teller. To me, it shows you are not narrow-minded regarding things that are out there in left field and unconventional. I like that. But, I swear! This whole thing gets more strange and weirder than ever. But how did you know Madame Faruschka’s name?”

“Tom told me as he was telling me about what he knew. He had talked with Luke and Luke had mentioned her name when telling of what he’d been told by you.” He pointed right at me.

I shook my head. “Very interesting.”

Tom responded, “Okay, guys. Tomorrow, I’d like us all to meet here around ten, so we may find out the rest of the story in the book.” He looked directly at me. “I know we all basically know most of what is in the book so far but I’d still like you to tell it all again tomorrow.”

I quickly spoke up, “What I’ve read so far covers the time period from when Andrew was twenty years old until he was thirty-two when he met Brian. And then...” I paused for a moment and looked over at Ethan. “And then, I think Ethan should read the rest of the story. The reason I say this is because Ethan looks and sounds exactly like Andrew. Having him read the rest of the book would almost be like hearing Andrew, speaking from the grave."

Luke was anxious, "That's spooky as shit! But I also think it's totally cool!" He looked at Ethan. "Ethan. Please say you'll do it. I think it would be so awesome."

Tom clapped his hands together. "Wow! What an incredible idea. I can't imagine why I didn't come up with it. Alan can film the whole reading and use segments of it in my special." He turned to Ethan. "If necessary, would it be possible for you to read the entire book while Alan films it? I mean after tomorrow, you'll only have to read the first half."

Ethan gave a 'thumbs-up'. "Not a problem."

Tom raised his right arm in the air, formed a fist and pulled it down quickly as he called out, "YES!! I can have Alan get everything ready in the morning."

Everyone clapped and cheered, showing their approval.

Ethan spoke, "I have to be honest. I'm really curious how they handle their relationship in that time period. With the way society regarded this kind of behavior, knowing what they did should be very interesting since there is no mention of it in the legend. They must have done a really good job at hiding it." A questioning squint came to his face, "I still don't understand how the story of him getting married got started. That's a real puzzle to me."

I looked at Ethan. "Interesting you should say that. I said exactly the same thing."

Tom looked at everyone. "Okay, guys. I'm taking all of you to dinner, so everyone can sort of share your histories with the rest of us. I mean, who'd have ever thought?"

We all clapped our hands and cheered again.

CHAPTER XI

I usually don't sleep well on an unusual bed but the one in the hotel room was very comfortable. Waking up early, I pondered all the things I had heard at dinner the night before. From Ethan's occupation as a financier and stockbroker, it seemed he was doing very well. He never really indicated how much money he made but I was sure it was significantly more than I did. I did find it interesting that it was very similar to Andrew's occupation.

It's incredible how good-looking he is. I'll bet he could've been a high-paid fashion model. Possible movie star. I let out a sigh, "I just can't get over how much he looks like Andrew. It's kind of freaky and creepy at the same time." Then, I began to ponder his eligibility. I hadn't noticed any ring on his left hand. Still, I find it so difficult to imagine a man who looks like him not having someone of significance.

I got out of bed, did a quick shower and shave of my neck under my beard, got dressed and headed into the hallway. Interestingly enough, Ethan was coming out of his room at the same time. I called out, "Ethan. Good morning. Thought I'd run down for a little breakfast at the restaurant."

Ethan agreed, "That's where I was headed. Had planned to see if you were up yet but I see you are. Let's see if Luke wants to go down with us."

Before we could reach the door to Luke's room, he came out and saw us. "Good morning, guys. Guess you all are headed down to get a little something to eat. I was going to do the same thing."

We headed to the elevator and went directly to the restaurant.

We'd just finished eating when a gentleman came in and walked to our table. "I'm the van driver. Tom sent me over to pick you all up and take you to the TV station. Take your time. There's no rush."

Arriving at the TV station, we went directly to Tom's office. Shortly after entering and sitting down, someone arrived with a tray containing cups of coffee, sugar and cream.

Tom took a sip of his coffee. "Alan has set up one of the studios for Ethan. It will allow excellent sound and a green screen behind. That way, we can put any kind of background there. I was thinking of putting a rotating set of the pictures and videos Alan took when we were on the island."

I commented, "I think that's a terrific idea. It would give so much character to the reading."

Everyone finally finishing their coffee, Tom spoke up, "Okay, gentlemen. Let's get this show on the road. Everyone get comfortable." He gestured in my direction. "The floor is now yours."

For the next two hours, I told Andrew's story up to the point of them being on the island for the first time together as well as their plans of living in the same building when they got back to the city.

Ethan tilted his head to the side. "I have to say, Tom gave me the highlights of the story but hearing it in more detail from the very beginning has given me a greater appreciation for Andrew and the love he is going to share with Brian. I still can't imagine what brought all of it to such a strange ending as described in the legend. This may sound crazy but I feel a strangeness inside me, knowing that the answer is probably going to be found within the pages of Andrew's book. I'm hoping they both ran away together to some deserted island and lived happily ever after."

I responded, "Funny you should say that. I said the same thing. Unfortunately, I believe the thinking is that he returned to New York on the boat of his friend. If he went anywhere else is unknown."

Tom opened the wooden box on his desk and pulled out Andrew's book, holding it in the air. "Well, we shall see. Shall we all head to the studio? Follow me."

When we got to the studio, I was truly impressed with the setup. Alan's camera was directed straight at a comfortable-looking chair with a green screen behind it. Several more comfortable chairs were situated out of view of the camera.

Tom told Ethan to get comfortable in the chair and handed him Andrew's book.

After Ethan got situated, I walked over to him. "Let me show you where I stopped reading." I took the book and opened it to the correct page. Handing him the open book, I pointed to where I had left off.

Alan clipped on a small microphone on Ethan's shirt. "I want to get a sound setting, so just speak in your normal reading voice. That way I can make sure it's loud enough and clear enough."

Soon, it was time to begin. Alan turned on the camera and pointed at Ethan. Andrew's story continued again.

Brian and I spent a relaxing week in the local town, making frequent trips to the island to explore it to see the potential of developing it. The townspeople were ecstatic, knowing I was eventually going to build and that Brian was my architect. At every turn, the people were friendly and helpful.

Brian already had a contractor in mind who could either do the job or knew of someone closer to the area who could. Seeing some of the work several of the local men had done, Brian told them he would be recommending them to be part of the construction crew. Everyone was ecstatic that building would most likely begin the next spring. They were very pleased that the project was going to take several years to complete.

When we returned to New York, Brian notified his landlord he was moving but paid him through the end of the year. This pleased him greatly. The owner of my building was extremely happy to hear that Brian wanted the rooms above mine. By the end of the month, he had basically settled in.

It was amazing. I cannot describe in words the joy, happiness, closeness, pleasure and fun it was to share time with Brian. Every day with him was a gift to my heart.

We were together for virtually all our meals. During the day, it was necessary for him to work on his drawings upstairs in his rooms. It was the same for me, doing my work in my space. But the before, after and in-between times, we were together. The Watson and Holmes idea was working very well.

It was the beginning of November when Brian came down from his rooms with several large sheets of paper. "Wanted to show you what I've come up with so far. I've also got a site sketch of a nice round, columned and domed pavilion out on the grounds." He placed the drawing on the table in the dining area. "Now, this is the first and second floors."

I went over and looked what he had done. "These are wonderful. This will be a grand house. Please, get with the contractor and see if they can start in February."

Brian was very happy at my satisfaction, "Sounds good. Now, I've got to get back up and work on the plans of a country house for one of my clients. I told them I'd have it done by the end of the month."

It was early the next February. One evening while we were out to dinner, Brian looked at me with a big smile, "You know there have been several times I've wished I was able to tell Madame Faruschka how happy I am."

I looked right back at him. "Funny you should say that. I've done the same thing."

Brian picked up his wine glass and raised it in the air. "To Madame Faruschka. Thank you."

I raised mine as well, touching it against Brian's. "To Madame Faruschka. Thank you."

"I wanted to tell you. I met with the contractor back in January and he's reviewed the complete set of drawings that I gave him." Brian gave a snicker, "Actually, he and I took the train up there the end of last month, spent the night and then the next day showed him the location you want the house. He thought it would be a terrific site and he loved the view. We were back by that night."

I was shocked, "REALLY!? I didn't know. I guess I really was busy."

Brian continued, "I knew we could do it quickly. He is going to be working with another contractor up in that area. He's already lined that up. He's also contacted a company to work on making the windows and doors. Many of the craftsmen in town are going to help with the work. He's actually got men digging, so the foundations can go in. Rebar for the reinforced concrete structural construction has been ordered and is being sent to the site. There should be no problem with them starting the foundations by the end of the month."

He added, "One thing I stressed to him was regarding the flat roof. The roof would not actually be flat. It was to pitch slightly from the centers to the exterior walls where drain spouts would be located to prevent any water from standing on the surface. There would be no ponding or damage from roof leaks that way. As construction progresses, I will bring this up again to make absolutely sure this is done. Ponding can cause significant damage to a reinforced concrete roof."

I was very much surprised, "Wow! That's terrific. It's obvious you have this whole thing in hand. No wonder your clients love you. Maybe we can make a quick trip up there near the end of March to see how things are going. We need to run by the bank, so I can transfer funds to your account, so you can pay the guys. Just let me know what you need."

Brian winked his right eye. "Sounds good. Everything's covered right now."

After a few moments, I looked at Brian. "You mentioned the other day you were working on a project for one of your clients and it would be completed by the end of this March. I hope so." I flexed my eyebrows several times. "Because I've arranged our trip abroad. We're taking a ship to Europe a little over a week after the beginning of April."

Brian gave a big grin, "That's so wonderful. You do know I wish I could come over there and hug and kiss you." He quickly looked around the room of the restaurant. "But I don't think I better. I'd hate for us to cause a scene in here."

We both bent our heads down, trying to hide our snickering.

I explained, "Let me tell you first. We leave from here on April eleventh. Our destination is Fiume. It's a port at the northeast end of the Adriatic Sea. I thought that would give us a starting place, go to Venice, Italy, then Rome, maybe Florence, up to Paris and then to England. I hope that sounds satisfactory."

Brian was pleasantly surprised, "That's terrific."

I looked right at him. "Now, as to where we go in those different places, I'll leave that up to you since you're familiar with the art and architectural wonders of Europe. We can take our time to see what we want to see with no rushing."

Brian's face was filled with joy, "Why, thank you very much. I'll immediately start plotting our course to show you the places that you should see." He paused for a moment. "Such as the Eiffel Tower." He had a nervous expression on his face. "With my acrophobia, you might have to help me get to the top."

We both broke out laughing so loud that other patrons in the restaurant turned to look our way. We bowed our heads several times in their direction in apology.

Brian was ecstatic, "So. We leave on April eleventh?"

"Yes. It's not a grand ship but it should be nice. It's the *Carpathia*."

A big smile came to Brian's face, "The *Carpathia*. Excellent. I know we're going to have a wonderful time."

We did make a quick trip up to the island and things were coming right along with the construction. Brian was pleased that everything was moving along very well and even a little ahead of schedule. The contractor indicated that the entire reinforced concrete structure should be completed by the end of the year, including the poured roof and the floor of the second level. And since the structure would have reinforced concrete around where there were to be windows and doors, this would make them very secure. The brick masonry fill that would go within all the exterior walls would start in the spring of the next year. This work would be completed before starting with the masonry fill for all the interior walls.

We got back from the island a week before leaving on the trip overseas.

Little did we realize we were going to be caught up in a historic event on an unprecedented scale. What I'm about to write now was done after the fact as there was no time and it was impossible to get it down on paper while it was happening.

Brian and I both had a trunk and a suitcase to take on the trip. Arriving, checking in and getting on board on April 11th was not a major ordeal. We had separate but adjacent rooms. It was going to be a slow but relaxing trip since the ship only had a maximum speed of around fifteen to seventeen miles an hour.

It was the night of April 14th, I heard a commotion and disturbance in the hallway outside my room. Later, I realized it was actually early morning on the 15th. Getting up, I went and opened the door.

The door to Brian's room opened and he stuck his head out. "Something's not right. Crew members running up and down the hall is not normal, especially at this hour."

I nodded. "I think you're right. I'm going to get dressed and see what's going on."

Brian responded, "Wait for me."

I quickly dressed in warm clothing as the temperature was quite cold outside. I stepped into the hall virtually at the same time Brian did. I saw he also was dressed warmly. Together, we went up on deck.

Shortly thereafter, we ran into one of the crew who seemed in a hurry. I called to him, "Young man! What seems to be the problem?"

He turned and quickly answered, "We've all been told to prepare to take on passengers."

Brian questioned, "Take on passengers?"

"Yes. We're responding to a distress call."

I shook my head. "A distress call? There's a ship in trouble?"

He nodded. "Yes. It's the *Titanic*. It's struck an iceberg and it's sinking." He bowed. "Sirs, I must get to my duties." He was quickly off.

I looked at Brian. "The *Titanic*? How can that be? Everyone has haled it as unsinkable. There has to be some mistake. Let's see if we can find one of the officers and find out what really is happening."

It didn't take long for us to see the quick preparations being made to accommodate more people. Brian and I stopped one of the officers to verify what we'd heard.

He responded, "Yes. It's true. It's the *Titanic* and it's sinking. We're going as fast as we can to the location. Hopefully, we'll be there around four o'clock."

Brian spoke out, "Andrew and I would like to give up our accommodations to those in need."

He smiled and nodded, "Gentlemen, thank you so much for your consideration and kindness. I shall relay this to Captain Rostron." He was off again.

I looked at Brian. "I'm much too agitated to go back to sleep. I think I'm going to the dining room and see if I can get a cup of coffee."

Brian agreed, "I know what you mean. I could use a cup as well."

It was around four in the morning when the *Carpathia* arrived at the designated location of the sinking. For virtually five hours, lifeboats arrived with distressed passengers. The crew and many of the passengers of the *Carpathia* did as much as they could to keep the survivors warm and comfortable.

Brian and I helped several ladies down to our rooms and told them they could stay there until we reached port. He and I were going to sleep in the dining room or any other place we could hunker down. As Brian put it, "We do what we have to do."

The *Carpathia* headed back to New York around nine o'clock in the morning as there was no sign of any other survivors. The ship would arrive there after nine o'clock at night on the 18th.

Brian and I both agreed that this beginning of our first major trip together was too traumatic to continue. We disembarked and decided we'd plan to go later in the summer. Hopefully, things would go much more smoothly the next time.

It was the next day after we got back to our apartments that Brian came down from his rooms, so we could have a cup of coffee together.

Brian shook his head. "I cannot believe what we have just been through. It's unnerving to me. The most luxurious, well-promoted and famous ship in the world, sinking on its maiden voyage. Who'd have ever thought?"

I looked directly at Brian, sitting across the table from me. "Actually, someone did."

Brian took a sip of his coffee then looked at me with a questioning expression on his face, "What? Someone did? You have to be kidding me."

"Nope. If I remember correctly, it was about twelve years ago. No. It was fourteen. Morgan Robertson wrote a book called Futility. It was quite popular at the time."

"It's about a ship going from New York to England. Strangely enough, the ship in the story had virtually all the same features and descriptions as the *Titanic*. It was even labeled 'unsinkable'. On a mid-April night, it hits an iceberg and sinks, killing almost everyone aboard. Now, here's the clincher. The name of the ship in his book was... the *Titan*."

Brian's face was filled with surprise, "No way! You can't be serious?"

"Yep. That's the God's honest truth. And I'll bet you're going to see his book back in bookstores again. People will start saying he was psychic."

Brian drank some more of his coffee. "How about we plan going again towards the end of June? I should have the plans finished for the country house for one of my clients by then. I'd already contacted them to let them know my plans had changed. I'll meet with them later in June. We also need to run up and check on the progress of your house before we go."

I took a sip of coffee. "That sounds like a great idea. Now. You said... 'your house'. What would you think if I said... 'our house'?" I flexed my eyebrows several times.

Brian looked at me with joy and happiness on his face and he spoke quietly, "You know I love you so much."

I looked at him with a big grin on my face, "I love you, too. That's why I said it."

After a moment, I continued, "You know it's too bad it takes so long to get over there to Europe. Wouldn't it be great if one day there was a way to do it faster? Think about what happened at Kitty Hawk a couple of years ago. They actually got a flying machine off the ground and it flew through the air. Now, just imagine a BIG flying machine that could hold a lot of people and fly really fast. We'd be in Europe in no time at all."

Brian slapped his leg and started laughing, "Well, I wouldn't hold my breath on that one. I think hell will probably freeze over before that happens."

We both broke out in loud laughter as I got up to pour ourselves another cup of coffee.

CHAPTER XII

Ethan stopped reading and looked at all of us with a strange expression on his face, "That's so incredible. Wow." He shook his head and looked at Alan. "Oh! Alan! I'm so sorry for messing up the video you're doing. It's just that all of this is so incredible and I had to pause for a few."

Alan stopped his camera. "Not to worry. That's why there's such a thing as editing."

Alan's comment made everyone snicker.

After a few minutes for a break for everyone, Tom gestured with his hand. "Ethan. Please continue."

Ethan got comfortable in his chair, opened the book and started reading.

Eventually, discussing going on the Europe trip, we both settled on going to Europe around the middle of July. I'd make all the arrangements to get there. We decided to go to Paris and London. Brian could work out the details of the places we'd see in both cities. We would go on an extended tour another time.

As we were boarding the ship going to Europe, Brian turned to me and gave a nervous giggle, "Can I be honest? I do feel a little queasy about this after what happened in April."

I patted him on the back. "One thing we don't have to worry about on this trip is an iceberg."

We both broke out in stifled snickering as we continued up the gangplank.

Our first major destination was Paris. This was accomplished by the ship docking at Cherbourg and then taking the train down to Paris. Using that as our jumping-off place, we would take trips out to see Chartres Cathedral as well as Versailles.

While in Paris, we frequented several of the cafés. There was one we discovered that was often frequented by several artists. We were very fortunate to meet a couple of them and eventually got introduced to another. They told us of a gallery where we could purchase their paintings along with works by others. Needless to say after seeing several of their works, I decided to purchase a number of them, have them packed, crated and shipped back to New York. Once framed, they would look terrific in the new house on the island. It was a great honor to meet them.

While we were there, Brian insisted we go see the Eiffel Tower. He said it was one way to help him fight his demon, fear of heights. And yes, he was a sight to see with our trip to the top.

While going to the first and second levels as well as to the top, Brian sat in the middle of the floor of the elevators while calling out, "I can't look out! I can't look out!" He bent his head down shaking it.

Many of the passengers understood but we all did chuckle.

Once at the top, I had to help him to the outside deck. He stayed very close to the wall and would not venture toward the outside railing.

I walked toward the railing. "Are you sure you don't want to come over here and look?"

Brian called out in a very nervous voice, "How do you do that!? It makes me nervous just watching you walk over that way!" He looked out across the city. "I do have to admit. The view from up here is absolutely spectacular. I'm really glad you dragged my ass out here onto the deck to see it." He gave a nervous giggle, "You do know that when we get down to the restaurant on the second level, I'm going to have to have a drink."

While we were in Notre Dame Cathedral, Brian pointed out many things of interest. I did know the building was constructed close to an east-west axis with the altar being in the east end of the church and the entry on the west front.

Then, he pointed out the stained glass windows. "Notice that the windows on the north side of the church are of much lighter colored glass than those on the south side. It's because there is more sunlight on the south side of the building and would show off the darker colors much better." This is something I had not known before.

Our next destination was London. We would use that as a jumping-off place to go see a couple of the English country estates and Shakespeare's house.

Brian was absolutely correct about the architecture of these homes. It was exactly what I had in mind for the exterior finish of the island house.

While we were in London, we happened to meet a wonderful artist. Interestingly enough, he had recently returned from Spain.

After much conversation, we discovered he was actually an American who had moved to England. Realizing he did portrait painting, we asked if he would consider doing our portrait. I wanted Brian and me to be in the same painting. He said he would be very happy to do that for us.

He spoke out with a big grin on his face, "That will be no problem. But!" He raised his right arm in the air, his index finger pointing upward. "It will require a much larger canvas."

We all chuckled at his humor.

For several days, we went to his location and posed for the painting. It was going to be life-size. The first thing he wanted to do was rough in the bodies. Then, he worked meticulously on the faces and the hands. All the rest could be done later.

On the last day of our sitting with him, we were truly impressed at the quality and accuracy of our faces. Brian and I were both extremely pleased. We knew it was going to take time for him to finish the bodies and the background as well as for the paint to dry. I was so pleased with what I was seeing, I paid a significant amount more than what he was asking to do it. I also gave him additional funds in order to have the painting shipped back to New York when it was dry.

It was the end of August by the time we got back to New York. It had been a fun and successful trip. When all the paintings arrived, I took them to the Metropolitan Museum of Art. I was sure they would know someone competent to make the frames for all the paintings that would be appropriate for each one. They were extremely impressed with the works and indicated that they did know several good framers. They also made it clear that if I ever wanted to donate the paintings, they would gladly accept them.

Getting back to work again, we were both very busy into the spring of the next year. One unexpected and quite surprising thing that happened was that we both heard from a few of the survivors from the previous April as well as a couple of the passengers who'd been aboard the *Carpathia* at that time. They were requiring our assistance in areas of both our professions. Both of us were extremely pleased to be of service to them.

In June of 1913, we planned to take a quick trip to see how things were coming along with the house on the island. In the meantime, Brian had concocted a sneaky and conniving plan that would eventually allow him to live with me in the island house. This all came about one evening at dinner.

Brian set his wine glass down and looked directly at me. "I have an idea I want to throw out and get your opinion as to what you think of it."

After taking a sip from my wine glass, I looked in his direction. "Oh? And what could that possibly be?"

He gave a sly snicker, "It's an idea I've been thinking about for a while now. It would eventually give me a very logical reason for us to be living together in the island house."

I was surprised, "Oh really? And from that snicker and knowing you as I do, I'm sure it just has to be the cat's meow."

Brian began, "When we head up to the island to look at the progress, I will leave right after that giving some excuse of returning for business purposes. But in actuality, I will take the train down to the next station, change my clothes and return later that day on the next train north."

A questioning expression filled my face, "Change your clothes?" I squinted and tilted my head to the side. "But what would be wrong with your original clothes?"

Brian giggled, "Let me explain. I don't have the clothes right now but I can run down to Macy's and get them rather quickly."

I shook my head. "I didn't know you needed more clothes."

"I don't. These would be special clothes. Clothes to put on a performance." He couldn't contain himself and started laughing.

I grinned, "Okay. This should be good. I'm all ears."

Brian looked around the restaurant to see if anyone was listening. Then, he spoke more quietly, "I'll go down to Macy's to the women's department and will tell the person there that I want to get my sister several outfits, some shoes and a couple of hats with nice veils. They are for her birthday. I'll tell that person that she and I are virtually the same size and wear the same size shoe. I'll also run by one of the wig shops and get a really good wig to wear. After I get that completed, I can bring everything back and I'll be ready for the performance."

I looked right at Brian. "And?"

"I will dress in one of the outfits, put on a pair of shoes, put on the wig and a hat with a very thick veil. These are the clothes I'll be wearing when I return."

I shook my head. "Okay. I'm still not with you. What does all this have to do with us?"

Brian took a sip of his wine. "Here is the story we will spread around. You are going to flagrantly tell everyone that you are building the house for you and your future bride to live in."

I interrupted, "BRIDE!?" I quickly looked around to see if I had disturbed any of the other patrons in the restaurant. All seemed well.

Brian looked around, giving a 'shush' sound with his finger up to his lips, "I'm not finished. The story is going to be that you are engaged and going to be married not long after the house is finished. I'll get all dressed up in those women's clothes, so no one will actually be able to see my face. I will appear on the scene, so people will think I'm your fiancée. During the rest of the construction, I will make several trips up with you, with me dressed as your fiancée to reinforce the story."

"Then, just as the house is nearing completion, you will spread the story that you hired a private detective and he found out that she was going to have you killed, not long after you were married, so she could collect everything you own because she was in love with another man."

"You will then put on an act, convincing people that you are so extremely distraught and overwhelmed with grief. That's when I'll step in as your best friend and tell everyone that I'll stay with you and take care of you to make sure you are all right." Brian stared at me with a big grin on his face, "Okay. What do you think of that?"

I bent my head down and started laughing. I raised my left hand up, shaking my head. "No. No. I'm not laughing at you. It's just that I can see this whole thing in my mind and it's really quite ingenious. I like the idea. We'll need to do some practicing and hone it well. And you're right. It would give a truly legitimate reason for us to be living together."

For a couple of days, we did several role-plays and Brian was excellent at it. Because of his physical stature, he fit the part perfectly. He even used a falsetto to make his voice more effeminate. The bottoms of the veils were just thick enough to hide his beard and mustache.

On the first trip to the island, Brian and I met with the contractor. After conversing with him, Brian excused himself, making it clear he had to return to the city for business purposes. He was to catch the next train heading south.

He turned to me. "Don't forget! Your fiancée is arriving on the next train coming north." He said it loud enough so all within earshot would hear it.

I almost had to pinch myself to keep from snickering, "Yes! Yes. I know. I'll go to the station to meet her."

Needless to say, after Brian left, everyone came up, congratulating me and patting me on the back with smiles and good wishes.

While waiting for the train to arrive, I noticed several of the townsfolk had come to the station. Something told me it was their curiosity. It was absolutely perfect.

On the next train coming north, only one person got off. It was a well-dressed woman with white gloves and a brimmed hat and veil that came down completely covering her face. It was fixed in such a way that there was no way anyone would be able to see her face.

Watching Brian get off the train, with a suitcase and starting to walk my way in his new attire, almost had me in stitches. I had to contain myself to refrain from laughing out loud. I called out, "Hello, my dear! I'm so glad you could make it! I can't wait for you to see the island and how well the construction is coming along."

The falsetto voice came from under the veil, "Hello, my darling! I can't wait!"

I gave a big smile, "I'm so sorry but we'll have to wait till tomorrow. There's really not enough time to do it today."

"Maybe that's a good thing. I wanted to freshen up anyway." Brian walked right up to me.

"Let's head to the lodging house. The lady there has your room ready for you." I grabbed the suitcase with my right hand, took Brian's arm with my left and we walked together to take the ride to the lodging house. I was very much aware of everyone watching and listening. Brian's plan was working beautifully.

The landlady saw us walk into the front door. She gave a big smile, "Mister Cavenaugh, this is your lovely fiancée? Let me take you up to see her room."

As we headed up the stairs the falsetto voice came from under the veil, "I'm getting hungry but I have such a headache from my trip. Is there any way I can eat in my room tonight?"

I responded, "My dear. Certainly. I'll go to the restaurant and get us something to eat and bring it back here."

The landlady opened the door and gave the key to Brian. "I hope it's to your satisfaction, madam."

The voice came from beneath the veil, "Why, it's lovely. Thank you so very much." He walked over and sat on the bed as I placed the suitcase next to the desk.

I looked at Brian and smiled, "I'll run to the restaurant and get us something to eat. Be back very soon." I escorted the landlady down as I went to the restaurant to get some food and drink. It was nothing special, just something to hold us over. Within thirty minutes, I was back at the lodging house again. I acknowledged the landlady as I went upstairs to the room. I knocked on the door.

I heard the effeminate voice within, "Who is it?"

I snickered to myself, "It's me, my love." I opened the door, walked in then shut and locked the door behind me. I whispered, "In the future, keep the door locked. You definitely don't want someone walking in on you."

Brian had already removed the hat, veil and wig, placing them on the bed. He spoke in his normal voice but very quietly, "That's a good idea. You're right."

I bent my head down and started to quietly laugh, "I don't believe it. So far, this plan seems to be working like a charm. You should have seen all the people watching and listening to us. I'll bet the fact that you are here is already all over town."

Brian had a big grin on his face, "Yes, but we're going to have to be very careful. This charade is going to take some time to complete. And we don't need to have anyone questioning the reality of it."

"I definitely agree. Now, let's eat something and we can plot our strategy for tomorrow."

"Excellent. I really am hungry."

I responded, "It's nothing special but it will fill the void."

CHAPTER XIII

Ethan paused in his reading and turned to everyone. "Wow. Who'd have thought?" He looked at Alan. "Sorry, Alan but I just had to comment."

Alan just grinned and turned off the camera, "Not to worry. I totally get it."

We all gave a loud sigh along with comments of understanding. Everyone apologized for the interruption but we all needed to express our pleasure at finding out how the legend got started. Yep, the story of the legend was now perfectly clear. It explained the concept of a future wife. But there still was a question as to what happened with Andrew disappearing. Did the boat actually come for him and did he go back to New York? After we all finally calmed down again, Alan turned on his camera and Ethan continued reading.

During the entire construction phase of the house, Brian plans to periodically do his dress-up routine to keep the locals wondering. Most of the time, he will show up as himself to make sure everything is on schedule and being completed in a satisfactory manner. When we are here in New York City, it won't be necessary to perform the fake scenario as everyone here sees our relationship as very good friends. Brian's comparison of us to Watson and Holmes is right on the mark.

I was very pleased with the progress. In February and March of 1912, the foundations were down and set on the bedrock. That definitely assured the house would never be going anywhere. There'd be no settling or movement that way. There would be a big room built adjacent to the kitchen to hold the electric water pump and the tanks of natural gas for the kitchen stoves. Under its floor would be a large cistern for water.

A workman in town constructed a large icebox for me and was to bring it out to the island and place it in one of the rooms near the kitchen after the floor above and roof were completed. This could be used by the workman to store anything they needed to keep cold. Since the store in town had ice being delivered on a weekly basis, I asked him to make sure a few blocks were delivered to the island and placed in the icebox, during times when work was in progress. He indicated this would be no problem.

All the reinforced concrete structural framework of the building as well as the reinforced floor of the second story and the roof were completed by the end of 1912 just as planned. All the plumbing for the kitchen and bathrooms along with wiring for future electric lights would be put in as the brick masonry fill for the walls was completed inside the reinforced concrete structure. These would not be able to be used until electricity was brought to the island sometime in the future. My thinking was that if they could run a transatlantic cable from the United States to England for communication, there should be no problem running an electric cable two miles to the island.

Starting at the beginning of 1913, the brick fill work would begin on the exterior walls. This would carry over into 1914. The outer coat of concrete that would cover the entire exterior of the house would begin in late spring of 1914. So would the brick fill work for the interior walls of the house. The stucco work covering the interior walls would begin as soon as the brick fill was completed with each of the interior walls. Their first priority was to stucco all walls in the house wherever there were to be cabinets or shelving regardless of where those walls were located as well as around window and door openings. Also, since the brick fill work in the interior walls was being completed on the first level before the second level, the rooms on the first level would be completely stuccoed before heading to the second level.

Stucco was being used instead of plaster on the interior walls due to the humid and salty atmosphere at this location. Stucco would hold up much better than plaster in such an atmosphere.

Many of the local townspeople were extremely happy they were being included in the construction process. This was bringing extra money to the town over and above what they normally made doing their fishing. The workers coming in from elsewhere were staying at the local lodging house as well as several other homes where the residents rented them rooms. The local restaurant and bar started making a lot more money than they normally would have. When the men would come in for breakfast, the restaurant would take their lunch order at that time then deliver it out to the island at lunchtime. This eliminated the need for the workers to come back to the mainland until they were finished for the day. Yes, everyone was extremely pleased with the building of the house on the island.

In the meantime, Brian's and my relationship was growing closer and closer. I considered myself so lucky to have found someone to intensely love who in turn fully loved me. Our private times together were incredible and filled with emotion. Almost every night he would stay with me unless he was working on a project requiring his attention. Many early mornings he'd go quietly back up to his rooms just so other tenants wouldn't get suspicious. Since his rooms were upstairs, his being in my apartment was a routine occurrence, especially during the day.

My business and financial ventures have been continually making me more and more wealthy. I was not sorry for investing in the gold mines and the diamond mines in Africa. I was told I could expect to receive an excellent return on both of them.

It's 1914 and virtually a year now since I've last written. I'm now thirty-five. At the end of last month, a major conflict occurred in Europe. It's quite severe. Actually, I've been expecting it due to the information I've been getting and situations happening over there since the first of the year. The real trigger occurred in June with the assassination of the Archduke of Austria-Hungary. Major war broke out a month later.

Early that summer, a security service delivered a wooden box from Africa. Not long afterward, a small cloth pouch arrived from Africa. The box was so heavy, they had to use a dolly to move it into my apartment. The contents of both will end up in a very special place. I do not yet know where that will be. But obviously, it is going to be somewhere on the island. Brian told me that my special place was already in the design of the house and he would eventually show it to me.

I decided to refer to this little treasure as my 'stash for a rainy day'. In the meantime, it will be kept here in my rooms where I live in New York City until it is time to move it to the house on the island.

It's October and it's getting colder here in the city. Major construction on the house is to stop in about a week and not start up again until next spring.

My work and Brian's have not yet been affected by what's going on in Europe. I must say I'm happy about that. So far, the United States has not gotten involved in the conflict. Personally, I believe it's only a matter of time. We shall see.

It was morning time and Brian came down to have coffee with me. As I handed him his cup I began to giggle.

Brian looked at me and asked, "What's so funny?"

We both sat down at the table. "Christmas is just about a week away. I wanted you to know I got you something. I had to order it quite a while ago to make sure it would get here in time."

Happiness filled Brian's face, "Andrew! I thought we agreed on no presents for Christmas. We've had that agreement from the start."

"I know. I know. But I couldn't help myself. They said it would be delivered by tomorrow. I just know you're going to love it."

Brian responded, "Okay. To be honest, I got you something, too. And I'm going to give it to you on Christmas day."

The next day, I got a phone call, indicating Brian's gift would be arriving around noon at the front door. I could hardly wait to see it. I ran up to Brian's rooms to let him know.

Brian was so very excited, "This should be interesting. I can't imagine what it could be."

Just before noon, we both dressed warmly and stood outside the building to wait. It was a little after noon when I looked up the street and saw it coming.

I pointed. "And here it comes!"

Brian looked in the direction I was pointing. "Oh, my God! This is incredible. You do know I have no idea how to operate it."

I shook my head. "Not to worry. I understand they'll give you some instructions on how it works and things you need to know about it. Until then, we'll have to keep it under the roofed area in back of the building."

Honking and pulling up to the curb, was a gentleman driving a brand-new 1914 Ford Runabout with white wheels. The top was up to keep out possible weather. The gentleman who'd been driving gave us instructions how to raise and lower the top. He also gave some general instructions, regarding its operation and things to know about it. After doing so, I asked him to drive it around to the back of the building and park it under the roof where I had arranged with the building owner to use as a parking space.

When we returned upstairs, I explained about the car, "I got that car and not a Packard or a more expensive car because the Runabout is more sporty looking than those other ones and I thought it just said 'you'."

Brian gave me a big hug. "Thank you so much. I love it. And you're right. It is a lot more sporty looking than most cars. I promise I won't drive it till I get some lessons. I'll do that right after the first of the year."

"That's a good idea. It shouldn't be that difficult. You just have to be alert and watch where you're going." I paused for a moment. "And not run over anybody."

That had us laughing.

On Christmas morning, Brian came down to have coffee before we went to the restaurant to have breakfast. Brian called out as he opened the door, "Andrew! Merry Christmas!" He entered and shut the door.

I responded, "Have a seat at the table. I'll have the coffee in a second." Shortly, I brought a tray with everything on it to the table. I placed Brian's cup in front of him. Then, I went to place my cup down in my place.

Sitting next to my place was a small box wrapped in decorative paper. I placed the tray off to the side, sat down and picked up the box. "And what do we have here?"

Brian smiled, "I think it's just a little something from Father Christmas."

I looked across the table at him. "But I don't have anything for you."

Brian shook his head. "Excuse me!? There's an automobile parked in the back. I love it! Now, check and see what Father Christmas brought for you." He pointed at the box.

I carefully removed the paper and looked at the box. 'Tiffany & Co.' was written on the top. I looked over at Brian who was grinning. I slowly opened it. There inside was a beautiful golden ring with my initials in large letters in an oval. I took it out of the box and set the box on the table.

That's when I noticed something was on the interior of the ring. I tilted it so I could read it. I spoke softly, "I will always love you." I was silent and became overwhelmed with emotion. Tears started streaming down my face. I looked at Brian.

Brian saw I was incredibly moved with emotion and in an attempt to bring some levity, called out, "Geez! You hate it!" He began to chuckle.

I couldn't help myself. Through my tears, I began to laugh. I stood up and walked over to Brian who also stood. I wrapped my arms around him and pulled him close. I whispered, "I love you so much." I bent my head down and kissed him passionately.

Soon, Brian pulled away and looked into my eyes. "Andrew, I will always love you." He pulled my head down so we could kiss again.

We held each other for a while slowly rocking back and forth.

I looked into Brian's face and smiled, "I will love you forever. Thank you for being in my life. I promise I will always try to make you happy and feel loved."

We hugged again.

Brian pulled back. "Okay. Let's see if it fits."

I slid it onto the ring finger of my right hand. It fit perfectly. "I love it." I smiled.

Brian nodded. "Good. I'm glad it does. Now, I say we go get something to eat!"

I just shook my head. "Geez! You sure know how to wreck a moment! Okay! Let's go eat!"

We both began laughing as we headed off to the restaurant.

Ethan paused in his reading and just stared into space. He then spoke quietly, "I remember the first time I heard the song, *I Will Always Love You*. Dolly Parton was singing it and by the time it was over, I was a mess."

I nodded my head. "Same thing happened to me. There's another song that gets to me. It's the Roy Orbison song, *A Love So Beautiful.* Wow. If you've ever heard it, you know what I mean."

Tom spoke up and gestured to Alan, "Okay, folks. Let's take a little break. Personally, I need to go pee."

We all chuckled as Alan turned off the camera.

Shortly, a few of the crew brought in a couple of trays with drinks and finger snacks as a hold-me-over. After everyone had their snack, Tom called out. "Okay. Let's continue here."

After a few minutes, everyone got settled. Ethan got comfortable and picked up the open book. Alan turned the camera on and Ethan began reading again.

It was New Year's Eve, heading into 1915. Brian and I had decided to stay in for the evening and avoid all the craziness. Little did he know that I had a surprise.

Earlier in the year, I'd gone to Tiffany's and had them make two matching rings that were set with small diamonds. They'd been ready since the end of November. I was going to spring them on Brian right after the stroke of midnight on New Year's Eve.

We'd gone out to dinner that evening and saw all the insanity beginning. Brian was glad we were spending the rest of the night in my apartment.

Everything was set up. The bottle of champagne was in the ice bucket and I got each of us a crazy hat to wear that had 1915 in large numbers on them. We put them on about five minutes to midnight and started laughing. I uncorked the champagne and started pouring it into the two glasses on the coffee table. I had just finished pouring when we started hearing fireworks and the honking of horns. We even heard the clock across the room starting to chime. I took the two glasses and handed one to Brian.

Brian looked at me and smiled, "Happy New Year, my love."

I smiled back, "Happy New Year, to you. I love you so much."

We clinked the glasses together.

I looked at Brian. "I have something a little special." I reached in my pocket and pulled out the Tiffany box, opening it, taking out the two rings.

I walked over to Brian, took his left hand and slid one of the rings on his ring finger. "As long as gold and diamonds are forever, they will be a testament of the love I have for you." I smiled and took the other ring and began to put it on my left hand.

Brian immediately stopped me and took the ring. As he slipped it on the ring finger of my left hand, he looked into my eyes. "The Fates have been kind to me to let our paths cross and join together. I will love you forever. I will always love you."

I pulled Brian close and we hugged tightly as we passionately kissed.

Work began on the house again in February of 1915. Carpenters began installing the windows and doors. The interior trim would not be installed until all the stucco work was done where needed at each location. Shelving in closets would be done much later.

The world was shocked when the headlines appeared in the newspapers, regarding the sinking of the *Lusitania* on May the 7th by a German submarine. I had a feeling this act was going to be a tipping point as to whether or not the United States got into the conflict. It was obvious to Brian and me that there would be no traveling abroad until all of it was over.

It's now August. I turned thirty-six this past June. Brian and I have gone to see the progress on the island several times with him dressed up with wig, hat and veil. I had to laugh that the act was working so well. We've been told that all the doors and windows should be completed by the time the work was to stop for the winter. All the cabinets and bookcases and shelves had been premade to order, brought to the house and were waiting in the kitchen and pantry to eventually be installed where they belonged. Also, stone pavers were laid for the terrace area outside the great room, on the driveway leading up to the house from the cove as well as all in front and on the entry area directly in front of the main entry door to the house. We knew a vehicle would never drive on it but it gave a nice lead up to the house. Six broad stone front steps were put in place from the driveway level to the paved area across the front of the house.

Every day I share with Brian is a gift. I never could believe I could love with such intensity. He brings me more joy and happiness than I can explain in words. I feel so sorry for those who never experience it.

Life was and had been good. Both of us were still getting work and there was money in the banks. We were both looking forward to the new year coming up in less than four months.

Construction commenced with the coming of spring. Thinner stone pavers were starting to be installed throughout the house on top of the poured concrete floors. The men doing the stucco continued their work. So did the carpenters, finishing up places where the stucco had been completed.

The first room on the second level to be completely stuccoed was the front room that would eventually be used as a library sitting room. Brian wanted this room done first along with the linen closet off the hall and the closet to the library sitting room before any of the rest on the second level of the house.

Two things Brian got completely involved with were the instillations of the cabinets and shelves in the upstairs linen closet and the bookcases and door to the closet in the library sitting room on the second floor. He actually got in there with the carpenters to make sure everything was done exactly like on the drawings.

All the bookcases had been installed on the north wall in the upstairs room that led out to the roof of the front portico, the library and sitting room. I was in the room with him, where the carpenters and he were installing the wooden door and premade bookcases on the south wall. The closet opening was about two feet from the right corner of the room and the outside west wall of the house. This closet was a room that butted against the linen closet that was accessible from the hall. The hinges were on the right side of the opening to the closet and made of brass. Noticing there were eight hinges instead of the normal three, I did wonder why but said nothing. The bookcases all were four feet wide and had flat wooden backs. The first three were anchored to the south wall, one next to the other. They started two feet from the east interior wall of the room on the left. This left a six-foot space to the corner at the exterior west wall.

I noticed the door to the closet had no hole on the left-hand side to install a handle.

Before I could ask, Brian walked by me and whispered, "Don't ask. I'll explain later." He kept walking as if nothing had happened.

When we returned to the lodging house that afternoon, Brian began to explain, "What you saw happening in the upstairs front room is this. That room is to be an upstairs sitting room and partial library. The bookshelves were all placed together on the south wall for a reason just like on the north wall. It and the north wall will be the only ones with bookshelves. They will look like mirror images of one another. On another one of our trips here when no one else is on the island, I will go in that room and finish the project that was started today." A big grin filled his face.

I tilted my head and raised my eyebrows. "Okay. I'm totally confused. I'm not quite sure what you are talking about. How can the bookcases on the north wall be a mirror image of the south wall as there is no door on the north wall?"

Brian continued, "The door to the closet you saw being installed today on the south wall will actually be the support for another bookcase. That's why it has eight hinges. It has to support not only the bookcase but any books in it as well. That bookcase is down in the kitchen pantry. The closet in the upstairs front room, in actuality, will be your secret storage room. We will bring the unit that's in the pantry, upstairs and securely bolt it to the door completely covering it and butting it right up to the three bookcases already installed on the wall. It will be slightly off the floor, so it will open freely. It will blend in with the other three bookcases to the left because they are all the same size. The hinges on the right-hand side are two feet from the corner of the room and will not be that obvious. I will install two hidden latches to open it in a less conspicuous place than a normal door handle."

I was truly surprised because it was now quite evident. That would be the perfect place to keep my 'stash for a rainy day'. "What a terrific idea. When I was reviewing the floor plan I just assumed that was a regular closet for that room."

Brian grinned, "That is exactly what everyone was supposed to think. The special cabinet for the linen closet is also in the kitchen pantry. When we come back, I'll bring the proper tools and finish things up with it as well."

I clapped my hands. "Well, Mister Genius. Thanks for being so clever. I think that deserves a cocktail. Let's head down to the restaurant and get something to eat."

Brian gave a 'thumbs-up'. "I'll second that!"

I looked at Brian with a questioning expression, "What was that gesture?"

Brian started to giggle, "In ancient Rome, it was used when gladiators would fight. If the thumb pointed down, it meant to kill. If it pointed up, it meant live. So I am using it as a good sign. A let live sign. A YES sign. An I agree sign."

I gave a big smile, "I love it." I gave a 'thumbs-up' with my right hand.

We headed out the door.

CHAPTER XIV

I immediately interrupted Ethan, "Hearing what you just read, I remembered the time I saw Andrew on the portico and he did a 'thumbs-up'. I wondered how he knew about it. Now, I have my answer. Yeah. He got it from Brian. And the linen closet cabinet. That's where I found the book and the other things in the wooden box. It's incredible how Brian got it all installed in such a way it was not obvious at all that the secret compartment was there. I have to hand it to the cabinet builders, too. They did a terrific job. Excellent craftsmanship." I looked around. "Sorry for interrupting."

Tom spoke up, "Ethan. If you would continue."

It's June 1916. Yes, I just recently turned thirty-seven. What can I say? Recently another heavy wooden box arrived by secret security service along with a pouch from Africa. I told both services to give messages to management, indicating not to deliver any more until the conflict of war is over. After the war is over, they were to deliver them to my law firm in Boston.

All the stucco work in the first story has been finished but is still being done on the second floor. The kitchen stove has been installed and several gas tanks have been hooked up located in the pump room. The stone paving on all the floors has been completed. All the woodwork of window trim, cabinets and bookcases on the first floor has been done. Trim work has started on the second floor where the stucco work is finished. Brian has done what he wanted in the linen closet but has yet to complete his project in the upstairs library and sitting room. He said we could do that soon.

It's finally happened. Almost all the workers and construction crew have been called into service due to the conflict in Europe. They are going for training. Major issues of the war are finally having a significant effect here. Because of this, virtually all work has stopped on the house. It's too bad since it's so very close to being finished. I had the delivery of ice for the icebox discontinued since no one would be using it.

Since he started, Brian has continuously pulled his charade and it seems everyone so far believes it. I jokingly brought this up one time, "You know you do this so well, you should have been on stage."

Brian called out, "Believe it. Sure. Sorry. Not to sound callous or smug or a greedy bitch but there just isn't enough money in acting."

His comment made us both laugh.

It's August and Brian wanted to take a trip to the island to complete his project in the library and sitting room upstairs. He brought the necessary tools to do the job. I helped him carry the bookcase from the kitchen pantry to the room, hold it in place while he attached it to the already installed door, making sure it would open properly without scraping the floor.

I stood back and looked at the bookcase. "Damn. You did a great job. No one would ever know it's actually a secret door to the space behind. I'm really impressed. Now, I understand why you said the north and south walls would be mirror images of one another."

Brian commented, "Glad you approve. On our next trip up here, let's see about bringing some of the things you want to keep in there."

I nodded. "That's a great idea. Now, let's head back to the mainland and get something to eat."

Not long afterward, we did make another trip, bringing all the crated paintings I'd gotten back from the museum after they had them properly framed. We had to hire a truck to get them from the apartment in New York and directly down to the boat to the island. It was necessary to rent a bigger boat due to the amount of crates. After getting them up to the house, we removed all the crating from around the framed paintings and placed them in the secret storage room. Here they would remain until it was time to hang them throughout the house. We took the crates out into a clear area and burned them. That completed, we drove back to New York and returned the truck to the place from where we rented it.

It required two additional trips from New York to bring up my 'stash for a rainy day'. We actually went in Brian's Runabout. On each trip, we brought one of the wooden boxes since they were so heavy. I was afraid to bring them both at the same time due to their weight. With great effort, Brian and I were able to grab a handle on either side of the box and carry it. For that reason, Brian drove the Runabout right down to the boats and each time we carried the box to the boat. Each time we placed the box in the center of the boat, we were amazed at how much the boat lowered in the water. It made us chuckle.

I was really pleased with Brian's driving ability. His significant practicing had paid off. Both trips were great fun and we got to see the countryside that we couldn't see from the train.

Due to the size of the storage room behind the bookcase, everything fit quite well. Since there still was so much more space left, there would be no problem putting more items in it if I so desired.

Once all the construction was finished and the interior walls painted, Brian and I could find appropriate places for all the paintings. We already knew that the portrait painting would go in the center of the interior wall of the large great room of the house. It would take some time to furnish the house since none of the furniture in the apartment where I lived in New York belonged to me. Brian indicated that he had no furniture as well.

Mid-November arrived and we decided it was finally time to get the tragic last part of the ruse story rolling. It would be the part about my fiancée wanting to kill me. The minute the train arrived in town, we both grabbed our suitcases and started to leave the train.

I looked at Brian and snickered, "Okay. Curtain going up. The play now begins."

Brian whispered in a scolding manner, "Don't you dare laugh. You'll blow the whole thing out of the water."

I shook my head. "I know. I know." I stepped from the train to the platform with my head bent down and my shoulders shrugged.

Brian was walking to the right of me with his left hand patting my back. Periodically, he would speak quietly but just loud enough for those standing nearby to hear, "Don't worry, my friend.

Everything will be all right. Everything will be all right." He was quiet for a moment as we continued to walk to catch a ride to the lodging house. He whispered, "It's incredible. Everyone's looking. It's obvious they're all wondering what is wrong." He then began speaking in a louder voice, "Not to worry. Not to worry. Everything will be all right."

When we arrived at the lodging house, Brian went into the house in front of me and saw the landlady.

The landlady called out with a big smile on her face, "Mister Durnam! Mister Cavenaugh! So good to see you again and an early Happy Thanksgiving!"

Brian spoke up with a sad inflection in his voice, "Nice to see you again, too. Mister Cavenaugh needed to get away after what's happened to him."

I was still standing somewhat behind Brian with my head still bent down.

The landlady looked concerned. "Oh! What's the matter? What happened?"

Brian began to speak in a sad and forlorn tone, "It's sad. So sad. Mister Cavenaugh is in pain. It's unbelievable what's happened. Just sad."

An expression of pain filled the landlady's face. She spoke quietly, "I'm so sorry. What happened? He's not sick, is he?"

Brian shook his head and spoke quietly, "Oh. No. No. It's Mister Cavenaugh's fiancée. She planned to do some terrible things. He found out when a private detective came to him. She actually loved someone else and was marrying Mister Cavenaugh only for his money. She never loved him. He also heard she planned to have him killed right after they married, so she could inherit everything he had."

The landlady's left hand moved up near her mouth and pain was still on her face, "Mister Durnam. That's so sad. How terrible. No wonder he looks so sad and broken. Let me get the keys and we'll go up to your rooms immediately." She stepped behind the front desk, grabbed the keys then led us upstairs to the rooms. She opened the door, handed Brian the keys and spoke quietly, "I'm so sorry what's happened." She looked directly at me. "Mister Cavenaugh. I'm so sorry. I hope things will get better for you in time. I'm sure Mister Durnam will stand by you in this time of pain and help you get through it." She turned and headed back downstairs again.

Brian closed the door. He turned to me with a huge grin on his face, reached up in the air with his right fist and then pulled it down, quietly saying, "Yes!" After hugging each other, I went and sat on the bed. He looked right at me and in a quiet voice, he spoke, "Perfect! Exactly what I hoped! I have a feeling that within the next two hours, this will be all over town." He bent his head down and started to giggle, he was so ecstatic.

I couldn't help it. I began to giggle, too, "You're right. It's perfect. From now on, if ever I need a terrific idea, I'm definitely consulting you first."

We both grabbed pillows off the bed to stifle our chuckles.

Brian commented, "I'll run down to the restaurant and get us something to eat and drink. I'll also ask them if they can fix a picnic basket for us to carry over to the island tomorrow. The more we're away from everybody, the less chance of any slipups. We definitely want this story to sink in with everyone. That way there'll be no problem with me being there with you on the island when the house is finished."

I looked at Brian. "How can I be so lucky? I love you so much. I'm so glad you're in my life." I stood, walked over to Brian and hugged him tightly.

Brian looked up at me. "Remember. It's not a one-way street. I never thought I would come to know such love as you have given me." He hugged me tightly.

Brian went to the restaurant to buy us breakfast as well as pick up the picnic basket to take with us to the island. By late morning, we were at the island and up in the house.

I commented as we walked into the large front room, "I'm really pleased. Your plan has worked from the very beginning. One question. What are you going to do with those women's clothes now?"

Brian answered, "I'm sure I can donate them to some good cause." After a pause, he began looking around the room and completely changed the subject. "You're absolutely correct. The portrait will look terrific on that wall." He pointed to the center of the main interior west wall. "In my mind, I can see this room fully furnished and the fires burning brightly in the fireplaces."

I smiled, "One day down the road we'll be able to have electricity brought out to the island with an underwater cable. When that happens, we can have the electricians come in and install electric lights since the wiring is already completed. And since the plumbing is also installed, I can have a water pump put in, so we'll have running water, too."

Brian clapped his hands. "That's true. Then, we could eliminate the use of candles and actually flush a commode."

"Yes!" We both yelled out.

Even though it was rather cool outside we took a walk around the island. We did come back into the house to eat a late lunch then did some more walking around outside.

It was late afternoon when we returned to the mainland and the lodging house. Brian told the landlady we would be leaving in the morning.

When he returned from the restaurant that evening with our food, he looked very happy, "You'll be glad to know that several people asked me how you were doing and to send you their condolences. They were very sorry for what has happened to you. I told them I would relay the message."

We both just began to chuckle, trying not to laugh too loud. We didn't want it to be heard anywhere in the building.

I just turned thirty-eight two months ago. In April, the country got involved in the war in Europe. Brian and I decided to take another trip up to the house on the island. Again, we pulled our old sorrowful charade. It was to reinforce the appearance that deep pain and anguish were still being felt by me. Of course, it worked beautifully. The main reason we were going to the island is because I wanted to check the secret room.

Not that I didn't trust people but after all, it was a big empty house with no one living there yet. I was also curious if we would see any signs of someone being there. Each time we had arrived with the crated paintings as well as the very heavy wooden boxes, many saw them being moved down to the boat. It was obvious everything was being taken to the house on the island.

After arriving, we checked around. I was pleased that we saw nothing to indicate that anyone had been in the house. Going into the upstairs room, I went over to the bookcase on the south wall. "Seems like everything's okay. Looks like it's not been opened since the last time we were here."

Brian walked over to the right-hand side of the bookcase. He looked down at the floor and began to giggle, "No one's opened the door. It's still there and not been moved."

I asked, "What?"

Brian looked over at me. "I put a very small rock, actually a pebble, right up against the side of the bookcase. If it'd been opened, the pebble would've been pushed away, making it obvious the door had been operated."

I could not believe his cleverness. "You sneaky, sneaky guy. Very clever. Bravo."

Brian walked out into the middle of the room and took several bows.

I couldn't resist. "And you say you never wanted to be an actor. What a ham."

Laughter filled the room.

We were there for only two days. Then, it was back to New York again.

The 1917 Christmas and New Year's holidays in the city were rather low-key due to the war. As the spring of 1918 arrived, Brian and I were quite lucky. Both of us still had work to keep us busy. Unfortunately, in the world, a flu had begun to infect people. Since there was no vaccine, it was beginning to spread rapidly around the world.

All through the summer, we were very careful due to the flu going around. Because it was so contagious, we noticed a reduction in our work. We attributed it to the reluctance of people wanting to gather or be out in public.

It was early October when Brian decided to head to the store. "I'm going to run down and get a couple of things. Did you need anything?"

I called out, "No, I can't think of anything right now. Just be careful out there. Make sure you wear your face mask."

Brian responded, "No problem. I'm putting it on the minute I step outside."

It was about two hours later when Brian returned. He walked in the door a little flustered.

I looked at him. "What's wrong?"

Brian shook his head. "I don't believe it. I was getting ready to go in the store and an elderly lady in front of me fell down and was coughing. She was coughing really bad. I went over and tried to help her up when my face mask accidentally fell off. She was coughing so badly, I helped her inside where she could sit down. The store called the local hospital for assistance. I ran back outside and got my mask that had fallen on the ground and put it back on again. Finally, medical assistance arrived. I then went and bought the few things I needed, came home, put the stuff away then came down here." He looked at me with a concerned expression, "Don't come near me. It's possible I could've been infected. The medical folks were sure the lady had the flu. If that's true, I could now have it and I don't want you to be infected."

I was shocked, "Brian! Come sit down! Let me fix you some hot tea. I'll also call my doctor and see if there's anything we should do."

Less than a week later Brian was coughing badly and having difficulty breathing, I took him down to the hospital to see if they could do anything for him. We both wore masks when we went. It was mid-morning when we arrived. Seeing his condition, they immediately admitted him, saying he did have all the symptoms of the flu.

Before they took him to be admitted, I gave him a big hug. My face mask was still on. "You hang in there. I'm sure they'll be able to help you get well soon. I'll check with the admissions desk and see when I can come back and see you." I hugged him again and whispered in his ear, "I love you so much. I love you more than life itself. Get well and come back to me."

Brian pulled back and looked up at me. I couldn't see it but I knew he was smiling under his face mask. He whispered, "I love you, too. More than words can say." He used his right hand to remove the ring from his left hand. "Hold on to this for me. I don't want anything to happen to it or get lost. You can give it back to me when I get well." He handed me the ring.

Just then, one of the orderlies came over and assisted Brian away. I watched them go through a set of doors that closed behind them.

I went to see him late this morning. The nurses said he was sleeping and they were trying to reduce the fluid in his lungs. I told them I'd be back tomorrow to see him. To say, I'm seriously concerned would be a complete understatement. I'm not feeling good about this at all. I wish I could have seen him today. I told them to call me if there were any improvements regardless of the time.

The phone rang a little after seven this morning. It was the hospital. What they had to tell me has destroyed my life. My Brian was gone. He had died during the night. I let them know that someone would be coming for him later on. I went into my room, closed the door, got in bed and screamed and cried into my pillow.

Later in the day when I finally gathered some composure, I went to the funeral parlor and asked them to go get Brian, have him cremated and placed in an urn. I told them that he had no extended family, so I was the only one who could give instructions. The funeral director knew who I was since he was one of my clients and was aware of Brian's and my friendship. He had seen us together at many parties given by influential, powerful and wealthy people and was aware of my connection with them. There would be no problem. When this was done, I would come and pick up the urn. I called the hospital to let them know the funeral home would be there to get him.

Over the next several days I notified all Brian's clients as well as my own. I knew I needed to get away. I donated all of Brian's drawing equipment to one of the local schools. All his clothes were donated to the needy. I sold his car to one of my clients.

When I was notified by the funeral director, I went and picked up Brian's ashes and brought them home. I would pack them in a trunk along with several other items I would be taking with me when I went to the island. All I did was cry the whole day.

I hired a company to come and move my bed, several other furnishings I had bought from the landlord, along with some clothes and other items I had boxed up. They were to take them to the house on the island and put everything in the upstairs library and sitting room. I even did a quick drawing of the floorplan of the upstairs, so they would know the correct room. I gave them the key to the front door. They could return it when they had completed their mission. They indicated this could be completed in about two weeks. I would sleep on the bed in the second bedroom of the apartment. All my other things I would give to the needy when I finally left in the spring.

In the meantime, I did some paperwork of specific notes and information. Going to Macy's, I found the perfect wooden box to keep my paperwork, this book and the cloth pouch in which I would keep a few things. The box was meant to be a jewelry box but I would use it for this purpose.

I also hand-wrote my last will and testament. I would have it witnessed and kept at the firm of Brice and Walters.

Something I knew that would be very important was to make a quick visit to my banks in New York to let them know I was leaving town and the circumstances of having Brice and Walters taking charge. While at several, I obtained several hundred-dollar bills, several twenty-dollar bills, around fifty ten-dollar bills and almost one hundred one-dollar bills to use for different purposes down the road. I also got a large bag of quarters to use for general tips whenever needed. All this money went into the trunk I would be taking to the island and most of it would be kept in the secret room at the house when I got there. Letters were sent to other banks, not in New York, of my decisions.

April of 1919 finally arrived and it was time for me to leave. I paid my landlord through the rest of the year which made him very happy. Before getting to the island, I stopped in Boston. I put the trunk in storage at the station while I went to Brice and Walters. I wanted to put a few more things in the box there and also give them my last will and testament to put in my file. I also told them of possible future shipments that might arrive from Africa and to keep them in a safe location there. With this flu virus going around and it being so contagious, everyone's longevity was in question. It was also to let them know about my twin brother and that possibly one day he might be found and claim his inheritance should something happen to me. It was all mentioned in the will.

Two requests that I had were rather unusual. First I wanted them to send a messenger boy up to the island on a monthly basis, so I might correspond or have him bring money to pay for things in town. Second, I would like that messenger to also bring me at least twenty small envelopes that I could put messages in as well as about fifty plain sheets of paper, so I could write notes. A bottle of ink and a new pen would be good as well. They indicated this would be no problem and would begin the very next month. We decided on the second Monday of every month. I got several envelopes, paper, pen and ink before I left the office.

I also visited the bank suggested by Brice and Walters and opened an account. I indicated that the firm of Brice and Walters recommended them and that they would have full access to my account to pay necessary fees or charges. They would also be depositing any monies such as stock dividends. This would continue into the future regardless of how much time went by until such time

I closed the account or a legitimate heir came to make any changes. I did this in case somehow my twin brother was eventually found.

With everything completed in Boston, I got the trunk and got on the early train and headed north. Arriving at the station, the baggage attendant assisted me in getting my trunk off the train. One of the local men with a wagon saw me and came over asking if he could be of help. I was very appreciative since I could not easily move my trunk alone. Several others that were there made reference, regarding what happened with my fiancée and expressed how sorry they were. Little did they realize but the sorrow I now felt and showed this time was very genuine but not for some conniving woman.

The man helping me had no problem when I wanted to stop by the restaurant to see if Williams would be so kind as to resurrect their daily deliveries like they used to do for the workers when construction was going on at the house. Williams indicated it would not be a problem at all and was happy to do it. I also asked if he had a large pot I could use, so I could heat some ocean water and wash myself. If he could find one, he could send it along with the first food delivery the next day. He would keep a tally and I would reimburse him every week.

That completed, the man helped me take the trunk down to the boats. I went into my wallet and pulled out a one-dollar bill, handing it to him. "Thank you so very much for your help. I do appreciate it."

He bowed his head then looked at me. "Sir, you are so very welcome and thank you for your generosity." He smiled, holding up the bill.

After a few moments, the man from whom I used to always rent a boat was there. I nodded. "Jack. Good to see you again."

He responded, "Mister Cavenaugh, good to see you again as well. I am so sorry about what happened to you. You're a fine gentleman and you don't deserve to be treated so poorly."

I actually began to start crying with tears running down my face, feeling the loss of Brian. I gathered my wits and spoke with sadness in my voice, "Thank you so very much for your concern. I gratefully appreciate it." It took me a few moments to gather myself before I spoke again, "I don't need to rent a boat this time but I was wondering if you could take me over and drop me off?"

Jack immediately responded, "Not a problem, Sir. Glad to be of service."

Jack helped me load the trunk into the boat and we were off. When we arrived in the cove, Jack pulled the boat close to the beach and helped me get the trunk out, placing it on the sand. "Mister Cavenaugh, let me help you carry that up to the house." He pulled the anchor out of the boat and placed it in the sand.

"Thank you so very much. With your help, I will definitely get it to the house much quicker."

We each grabbed a handle and headed up the driveway.

Finally reaching the house, I unlocked and opened the door and we walked into the entryway. "This will be just fine, Jack. Again. Thank you so very much for helping me and your concern." I reached in my wallet, grabbed a ten-dollar bill and handed it to him.

Jack bowed his head. "Thank you very much, Mister Cavenaugh. You've always been so kind and generous. Again. I am so sorry for your circumstances." He looked around at the empty spaces with concern on his face. "Are you sure you are going to be all right?"

"Yes, Jack. Thank you for your concern but Williams will be delivering food to me every day, so if I need you for anything, I will let the one delivering the food to me know to tell you."

"Yes, Sir. That's good. Again, thank you." He bowed his head again, turned and headed down to the boat and back to the mainland.

It was late afternoon and I decided to organize things upstairs. Entering the front room, I was pleased to see everything arranged in an orderly fashion. It would take no time at all to make up the bed.

I'd not eaten all day but I wasn't hungry. I was depressed and very tired and decided to turn in early. Night was slowly closing in as I got in bed and pulled the covers up over me. I lay there in the darkness and whispered, "Brian. I love you and I miss you so badly. I cannot believe you are gone from me." I began to cry.

CHAPTER XV

The next morning I got up and had no idea what time it was. To be honest, I didn't care. I got dressed and went rummaging through the boxes in the room to get one of my pots, so I could make a cup of tea. I'm so glad I had labeled all the boxes, so I knew what was in them. I got out one of my big coffee mugs along with the canister of tea, one of sugar and one of my teaspoons. One thing I knew I definitely was going to need was one of the rolls of toilet paper. Since the plumbing in the house was incomplete, I was going to have to rough it outside with nature.

Heading down to the kitchen, I set everything on the counter next to the stove. I had my fingers crossed that there still might be a jug of water in the pantry leftover from happier times. Opening the door, I was very pleased to see two unopened containers over in the corner. I picked one up and brought it out, setting it on the counter.

Next, I went out to the pump room to make sure the valve on the gas tank was open so I could use the kitchen stove. I saw that it was shut. Probably a good thing to prevent any gas leaks. I opened the valve and went back to the kitchen.

It only took a few minutes to get the water boiling. I turned off the gas, threw in several teaspoons of loose tea and let it brew.

While waiting, I walked into the large great room and gazed out the windows to the ocean beyond. I whispered, "I miss you so much. You should be here with me. I'm so lost without you." Tears were streaming down my face and I began to cry.

Suddenly, I heard a knock at the front door. I could not imagine who it might be. But then I realized, "Of course, it's the guy from the restaurant. Damn. Is it that late already?" I wiped my eyes and headed to the door.

Opening it, there stood a young man with a big smile on his face, "Mister Cavenaugh. Good morning to you. How are you today? I have your food basket for today and a big soup pot."

I responded, "It's still morning? I thought it was much later."

He shook his head. "No, Sir. It should be going on noontime soon though."

I nodded. "I've completely lost track of time. Thank you so very much for bringing this to me. Please wait a moment." I placed the basket and pot on the floor, turned and hurried upstairs to get a quarter for the young man. Returning downstairs, I handed it to him. "Thank you so very much for taking your time to bring this to me. If at all possible, could you bring me a jug of drinking water tomorrow when you make your delivery? I would gratefully appreciate it."

He nodded and smiled, "I don't think that will be a problem. I'll tell Williams to include it."

"By the way. What is your name?"

"My name is Robert."

"Thank you so much, Robert. I appreciate it. I was wondering if you would wait just a few minutes as I will walk down with you. Did Jack bring you over here?"

Robert nodded. "Yes, Sir. He did."

"Wait and I'll be right back." I went upstairs, got out two ten-dollar bills and put them in a small envelope then returned to the front door. I looked at Robert. "Okay. Let's head down to the boat."

As we reached the beach, I saw Jack next to the boat waiting for Robert. He called out, "Good morning, Mister Cavenaugh. Are you settling in?"

"Yes, Jack. I'm trying to adjust." I walked over to him and stretched out my hand with the envelope in it. "I want you to have this. I will be giving you one every week for bringing Robert over with my food basket every day. I gratefully appreciate it."

Jack took the envelope. "Thank you so very much, Mister Cavenaugh. That is so gracious and kind of you." He bowed his head.

I turned to Robert. "I will see you tomorrow."

He nodded. "Tomorrow, Sir! And I'll bring your water, too." He turned and got in the boat.

I watched them push off and start back to the mainland. I waved a goodbye then headed back to the house.

I closed the door and took the basket and pot into the kitchen. I placed the pot on the counter. I was very pleased with what I saw inside the basket. I fixed my tea and set it on the counter. I then went upstairs, grabbed one of the chairs, bringing it to the kitchen. Next, was the small table. I was so glad I didn't trip while bringing it down the steps. This is where I would eat from now on.

After I finished eating, I made another mug of tea and went upstairs. Walking over to the bookcases, I felt for the latches to open the secret door. In no time, I had the door open and I went inside. It was the large painting of Brian and me that I wanted.

I lifted it up. It was very awkward due to its size as well as being quite heavy. I went out to one of the boxes and found a bath towel. I went back into the secret room and placed the folded towel under the frame of the painting. Now, it would be easier to move by sliding it on the floor. Slowly dragging it out into the room, I leaned it against the east wall of the room. I went and sat on the bed, staring at the painting. Seeing the smile on Brian's face filled me with emotions and I lay on the bed, screaming and crying into the pillow, "It's not fair! It's not fair! You should be here with me!"

After a while, I gathered myself together and went to the linen closet out in the hall, getting the wooden box with all my papers in it from the secret compartment in the bottom of the cabinet. Going back to the room, I sat on the bed and opened the box. I saw the cloth pouch where I was keeping the key to the safe deposit box at Brice and Walters and took it out. Pulling off the ring Brian had given me from my right hand and looking at it, turning it in my hands, I read the inscription inside. I began to cry, "You can't be gone. It's not fair. We had so many years together ahead of us. I love you so much." I put the ring in the pouch and the pouch back in the box. I was so depressed I went back to bed.

It's the second Monday of May. I'm expecting the messenger from Brice and Walters. If he took the morning train, he should be here soon.

I was correct. There was a knock on the door. Opening it, I saw a young man standing there with a medium-sized box in his hands.

He looked right at me. "You must be Mister Cavenaugh. The gentleman at the firm told me to give you this."

I took the box from him. "Thank you so very much. I have a message to go back to the firm. Let me get it for you." I quickly went upstairs and obtained the message I'd already written and placed it in an envelope. I also got two one-dollar bills for the young man. He had come all the way from Boston and deserved much more than a quarter or two. After heading back downstairs again, I handed him the envelope and the gratuity. "Thank you very much, again. I'll see you next month."

He looked at the two single dollar bills. "Wow! Thank you so very much, Sir! I'll see you in June." He turned and headed down the driveway.

I went upstairs with the box, placed it on the small desk and opened it. Just as I had requested. There were envelopes, plain paper, a jar of ink and a new ink pen. There was also a pencil. I was pleased.

With every passing day, I had time to think and ponder. I brought a chair down from the upstairs room and placed it in front of the large windows in the great room at the back of the house. I would sit and stare out the windows at the ocean beyond. Pain and anguish would fill me as I sat there, contemplating all of the 'might have been's. Tears would stream down my face. Memories of times I'd spent with Brian made me cry. Every day the pain and depression grew. I knew I could not take it much longer. I was going to have to leave.

It's now the second Monday in June of 1919. I'm now forty and extremely depressed and lonely. The young man from Brice and Walters is arriving shortly. I will be giving him an envelope to take back with him. The instructions in it should be quite clear. The key to the house will also be in it.

It is now Tuesday. Robert came by with the food from the restaurant. I gave him a written message in an envelope to give to Williams. It would be self-explanatory. I also gave him an envelope to give to Jack. I handed Robert a one-dollar bill which put a huge smile on his face. He thanked me profusely before heading down the drive.

The notes to Williams and Jack indicated that a good friend was coming on his yacht to pick me up along with all my important personal belongings. I wasn't sure if or when I would be returning to the island. I had to get away as I was very depressed with all that had happened. I would be locking up the house and no longer have need of their services. Of course, there was also enclosed a large gratuity to express my appreciation for their wonderful services.

Going upstairs, I sat on the bed and stared at the portrait. I was overwhelmed with emotion and cried uncontrollably. Sometime later, I calmed down and looked at the portrait again. "I love you so much. I miss you so much." I opened the secret room and dragged the painting back inside it, leaning it against the back wall. I left the room and closed the door. The 'click' sounds let me know it was shut. I sat on the bed.

I cannot take the pain any longer and shall not be writing any more in this book. I will place it back in the wooden box along with the other papers. Then, I shall place it in the secret compartment Brian built for me in the linen closet.

I began to recall what Madame Faruschka had told Brian about a closed door that she could not open and the thick fog she could not see beyond for me. It was all making sense to me. There is nothing for me to say anymore.

This house is filled with pain and sadness and grief. It's time to move on. "I love you so much Brian and I always will. And so, I close this book for the last time."

After a moment's pause, Ethan slowly closed the book and looked out at all of us sitting there, not saying a word. Finally, he spoke quietly, "Is there anything in the legend, indicating what happened to Andrew? Did a boat actually come and take him away?"

Luke spoke up, "The story goes that in the message he sent to the restaurant owner, Williams, Andrew had said it was time for him to get away and move on and stop delivering food. There was too much sorrow and pain in the house. Everyone believed it was because his fiancée left him. No one had a clue it was because of Brian's death. The thinking at the time was because work on the house had stopped due to the war, his architect, Brian, had gone on to do other work. That's why he wasn't around. Everyone believed that the boat coming to pick him up was taking him back to New York."

Alan commented, "Maybe there will be some information about where he went when we go to Brice and Walters tomorrow afternoon. After all, he sent them a message, too."

Tom spoke, "Alan's correct. We may find out more tomorrow. I'll put the book back in the box. We are definitely taking it with us tomorrow to Brice and Walters. If at all possible, I would like for all of us to meet here again tomorrow late morning. I want to hear any comments or questions that have come to anyone's mind. That way, I can bring them up tomorrow afternoon and see if we can find some answers. Right now, I recommend we all go get something to eat. Not to worry. I'm paying."

Sounds of approval came from everyone.

As I lay in bed that night, I could only imagine what tomorrow would bring. The information we might learn at Brice and Walters could be phenomenal. Somehow, I just knew that Ethan would have a major role in this. For him to look so much like the ghostly image as well as the drawing I did of Andrew was beyond coincidence.

A smile came to my face as I pictured Ethan in my mind. I whispered, "I cannot get over what a handsome man he is. He seems to have a really nice personality, too. Since he's in finance and stocks, I just might have to have him do some investing for me. That'll give me a good reason to stay in contact with him." I started snickering as ulterior motives flashed through my mind, "You idiot. There's not the slightest indication he's on my side of the tracks."

Little did I realize that when I fell asleep, I was going to have a significantly important dream.

I found myself on the island, walking up the driveway to the house. Slowly, I moved forward toward the front door and just as in my other dreams, I passed right through it without opening it. I knew I was there for an important reason.

While standing in the entry hall, I saw Andrew coming down the staircase. I wasn't sure why but he was completely naked and looked to be in a world of his own. I followed him as he walked into the great room of the house, through the French doors and to the outside terrace. He paused for a moment, looking to the east and out to sea. He then began walking to the edge of the bluff.

He stood there, peering out to sea. His whole appearance was that of a broken man.

I watched him take a deep breath and then let out a loud moaning scream. He then began sobbing uncontrollably. After a few moments, he called out, "Brian. I love you so much. You can't be gone. I miss you. It's not fair. It's not fair. It's not fair." He raised both of his hands up and buried his face in them, again weeping in agony.

"Brian, I understand now. Madame Faruschka couldn't open the door she saw in your reading because there was nothing on the other side for you. It was a sign that your life would be over. And so it was for me. She saw a thick fog for me that she couldn't see through. It's because there was nothing for me on the other side. Again, it was a sign. It was a sign my life, too, would be over." He continued his crying.

A few minutes went by before he calmed down and looked out to sea, "Brian. I'm coming. I'm coming to you. I love you. I love you. Brian, I love you." He took one step and slowly leaned forward beyond the point of no return. Over the edge, he went to the rocks below.

I screamed out, "NOOOOOO!" In so doing, I woke myself up. It was very disturbing. I sat up and shook my head. I was so affected, it brought tears to my eyes, "Everyone thinks he went away. They have no idea he killed himself. How sad. Such a tragedy."

Suddenly, I realized what I had done. I quickly got up, wrapped myself in a towel and went to the door of the hotel room and opened it. I looked out in the hallway and saw no one. "Good. I'm glad I didn't wake anyone up with my yell. Geez."

Heading back in the room, I thought about going back to sleep but the dream I'd had was very disturbing to me. After lying there for a few minutes, I decided to go down and see if the restaurant or bar was open. I needed to eat something. I commented, "That's not true. I really need a drink."

I got up, got dressed and walked out into the hallway. To my surprise, I saw Ethan coming out of his room. I spoke quietly, "Ethan. What are you doing up so early?"

Ethan turned and looked at me. "I might ask you the same thing." After a moment he responded, "Actually, I had a most disturbing dream."

I was shocked, "What!? You can't be serious."

"Yep! It was so distressing, I thought I'd go down and see if I could get something to eat." He bent his head down for a moment then looked back at me. "No, that's a lie. The dream was so disturbing to me, I need a drink."

I was very surprised hearing what he said, "Well, believe it or not, the same thing happened to me. That's where I was going. And to be honest, for the same reason. Have to tell you. The dream I just had is going to answer some long-awaited questions."

We headed to the elevator as Ethan continued, "It was truly unsettling. Yeah. Scary as shit."

I looked right at him. "Really? That bad?"

Ethan looked right at me with a tense expression. "Yep. It was like watching my own death."

I grabbed his arm. "What!? You can't be serious. That's distressing."

Ethan continued, "You've got that right. I'll explain more when we get downstairs."

As we walked into the restaurant, they were just beginning to open it for the day. Shortly, we were seated at a table. A few minutes later, a young man came by to take our order. We both ordered something light as neither one of us was really that hungry.

Ethan looked at the young man. "By any chance, is the bar open? I know it's early but I'd really love to have a drink."

A frown came to the young man's face, "I'm so sorry, Sir. The bartender's not here yet and it won't be open until he does. I'm sorry."

Ethan responded, "No harm in asking. In that case, I'll have coffee and keep it coming."

The young man looked over at me. "And you, Sir?"

I looked at him. "Since the bar's not open, I'll have coffee as well. And I absolutely agree about keeping it coming."

The young man bowed slightly as he left the table.

Shortly thereafter, the young man arrived with our coffee. "I'll bring out your food as soon as it's ready." He headed back to the kitchen area.

After taking a sip of coffee, I looked over at Ethan across the table from me. "Okay. I'm ready. Let's hear it. I hope it wasn't some horrible car crash or plane crash."

Ethan had been drinking his coffee and set the cup down. "Thank you for letting me take the floor first. I really can't get it out of my mind. And it's so disturbing. I found myself entering a house I'd never been in before. I must admit, it was very disconcerting to pass right through the front door without even opening it."

Hearing this was jarring to me, recalling how I always entered the house on the island the same way. I set my cup down and watched Ethan intently as he continued.

"Looking around, I realized I was in an entry hall with a wonderful staircase directly in front of me. I turned to my left, peering through a large archway and into a large room. The room was completely empty. No furniture. Nothing. It was the same for the room on the right. Suddenly, it came to me. It was the house I'd seen in the video on Roger's laptop. The report done by Tom and Alan about Cavenaugh Island."

I gasped and a shocked expression filled my face.

Ethan could not imagine what was wrong. "What's the matter? Are you all right?"

I composed myself, "I don't believe it. You were there? In the house? The house on the island? Andrew's house?"

Ethan nodded. "Exactly. And what's so strange about it is I wasn't surprised. It's like I was supposed to be there. Not long after, I saw a man coming down the staircase. Naked. No clue why. BUT! He looked exactly like me. I mean. EXACTLY like me."

Again, I was very shocked, "Oh, my God! And I know what happened next."

Ethan tilted his head. "Ah. How could you know?"

I looked directly at him. "Because I was there. In MY dream. I saw exactly the same thing. I also know what happened next and it's so very sad."

Ethan's eyes opened wide and surprise filled his face, "Really? Now, that's just so freaky and kind of scary. It definitely explains what happened to Andrew. He didn't just move away and hide."

"That's right. You and I know exactly what happened to him. We both witnessed what he did, sad and horrific as it was."

Just then, the young man brought our food order. "If you gentlemen need anything else, just let me know. Give me a wave. And not to worry, I'll be by periodically to fill up the coffee again."

As we ate, both Ethan and I continued to comment on the dreams. Both of us agreed at what a tragic ending Andrew had.

Ethan shook his head. "For a love to be so profound you would end your life is incredible to me. It makes me think of Romeo and Juliet. Sad. Just sad. I should be so fortunate as to find someone I could love so strongly, who would love me back the same way."

I agreed, "I know what you mean. I've had several encounters in my life but none of them were worth their salt. So many are users and takers. It's a shame." I looked at Ethan. "Something tells me that two major reasons a woman would be interested in you would be because of your handsome good looks and your bank account." I shook my head. "I've met and talked with several very good-looking and well-to-do men in my life and many of them indicated I was right on the mark."

Ethan gave a big grin, "Funny you should say that. But you have one thing wrong in what you said."

I was surprised, "Really?"

Ethan giggled, "Yeah. Really."

I looked right at him. "Okay. What part was wrong? Your looks or your bank account? 'Enquiring minds want to know.'"

Ethan bent his head down and continued giggling, "Neither."

I jerked my head. "Neither? Then, what?"

Ethan looked right at me. "You said reasons a woman would be interested."

I jerked my head again. "Well?"

Ethan looked very hard at me and spoke quietly, "It's because I'm not interested in a relationship with..... a woman."

Shock and surprise filled my face, "No. No way. There is no way you're..." I looked around to see who was nearby.

Ethan gave a big grin, "Yep! Give that man a cigar!"

I almost spilled my coffee. "Ethan! No one would ever know. I got no indication. My 'gaydar' never suspected. Damn!"

Ethan flexed his eyebrows a few times. "So, you find me good-looking?"

I had to pause for a moment. "Don't you own a damn mirror?"

Just then, the young man arrived with more coffee, filled our cups and left again.

Ethan chuckled, "I really appreciate that. I've been trying to find an opportune moment to talk with you. But there has never been a time when we were alone together. From the beginning, when I saw Tom's video online, heard you were an artist and a writer and I saw your face, I knew there was something about you. Something happened inside me. I knew I had to find you and meet you."

I was totally taken aback. "Do I dare tell you? The moment I saw you, something happened inside me as well. I cannot lie. From then on, you have been inside my head. But I didn't dare want to even consider mentioning it to you. I had no clue." I paused for a moment. "But you're such a handsome man. You could have anyone you wanted."

Ethan grinned, "That may be. But the problems I've faced are exactly the ones you mentioned. No one sees ME. The ME inside."

I nodded. "Interesting. I may not be the best-looking guy on the block but the ones I've run into only want to be taken care of. As I said, none of them were worth their salt."

Ethan continued, "Don't sell yourself short in the 'looks' department. And no pun was intended when I said 'short'. Personally, I find you very attractive and sexy as hell.

I thrust my right fist into the air. "YeeeHaw!"

Ethan gave a big smile, "Well. Now, that we've cleared the water and know that we're both in the same pond, why don't we both take a swim together and see how it goes."

We both reached across the table and smacked our hands together in a high-five.

CHAPTER XVI

After our morning coffee, Ethan and I decided to go sit in the lobby and talk as we waited for Luke to come down before heading to the TV station. Our conversation happened to be about our days in college. Luke came down to the lobby just as the van was arriving to take us to the station.

Entering Tom's office, Luke called out to him, "Wait till you hear what these guys told me in the van coming over here."

Tom gave a salute with his right hand. "Good morning, gentlemen. Hope you all slept well."

Ethan and I looked at one another and just shook our heads.

Tom was curious, "Okay. What the hell is going on?"

Luke looked at Tom. "Just wait till you hear."

Ethan responded, "What Luke is alluding to is something that did disturb our sleep."

I commented, "Yes. Ethan and I both had a very disturbing dream last night. And they prove that Andrew did NOT just leave the house, go off possibly to New York in a yacht and disappear." I turned to Ethan. "Please. You go right ahead."

Ethan described his dream in detail. When he finished, I confirmed everything he said, "Yep. I had that exact same one. Exactly the same."

Tom was surprised, "Wow. You have to be kidding me. Wow. That could have very incredible and severe implications with what we find out today at Brice and Walters. Has anyone come up with any more questions about what we already know? If so, I want to make note of them."

We all shook our heads in the negative and responded, "No."

Just then, the door to Tom's office opened with two guys delivering cups of coffee and a bag of sausage biscuits. They placed them on the nearby table.

Tom spoke out, "Thanks, guys for doing that for me." He turned to us. "Wasn't sure if you'd eaten anything yet, so I had these brought in for you."

Everyone expressed their appreciation with positive comments.

It was around one o'clock when we got in the van and headed to Brice and Walters. On the way, Tom indicated he wanted to hear everything Brice and Walters had to say and show us before we said anything unless we felt it was important. We all agreed that would be a good idea. Tom told me to carry the wooden box with all its contents, so we would have physical proof of the need for our visit.

The van driver dropped us off and Tom told him he would notify him by cell phone when we were ready to leave. Then, we all went inside and the receptionist led us to a conference room. I placed the wooden box on the table where I was going to sit as we sat down. Alan began getting his camera ready.

I looked around the well-appointed room. "From what I can tell, this doesn't seem to be one of those fly-by-night firms."

Tom added, "Don't forget. They've been around over a hundred years."

Shortly thereafter, the door opened and in walked three individuals. We all stood to greet them.

The oldest gentleman, who looked to be about sixty years old, was first with a smile on his face, "Good afternoon, gentlemen. I'm

Matthew Brice." He turned to the young lady. "This is Stella Walters and this gentleman is Jeffrey Walters." They appeared to be in their early thirties.

Everyone shook hands with introductions.

Tom expressed his appreciation, "I definitely want to thank you all for allowing us to film this. Parts of what may be said or provided today could go in a future report."

Stella spoke up, "Hey. Any good publicity for the firm is always a good thing. We promise. We'll watch what we say."

I spoke up, "I realize this is way off the subject at hand but I just know Jeffrey has to have a really interesting story with his last name being Walters." I looked directly at Jeffrey. "If you wouldn't mind, I'm a writer and I just might like to talk with you sometime. It's possible I might get a short story out of it or maybe even a novel."

Jeffrey was of African-American heritage. He spoke up, "I wouldn't mind at all doing that with you as you are quite right. It all goes back to the early nineteen sixties and the fight to allow blacks and whites to marry." He paused for a moment before making a clarification, "No. Stella and I are not married. She's a distant cousin."

I acknowledged him, "Okay. Now, I know it's going to be a great story. Thanks, guy. I do appreciate it."

A few moments later, a man walked in, carrying a metal box, looking very much like a bank safe deposit box with two cloth pouches on top of it, placed it on the table then started leaving the room. Matthew thanked him as he left.

Matthew then instructed, "Everyone, please have a seat and we can get started. I must say from the information Tom gave me over the phone, this should be a very interesting conversation. I have never dealt with a situation where information regarding a client involved his ghost."

This had everyone snickering as everyone took their seats except for Alan and me. He would be moving around the room, videotaping the whole thing.

I stood at my place and opened the wooden box and got out the signed paper that Andrew had drawn up to prove our legitimacy. "Mister Brice. I wasn't sure if you needed to see this before you could give us information regarding Andrew Cavenaugh." I held the paper up in the air. "It's a document Andrew drew up and placed in this box to prove we aren't just some off-the-wall folks." I passed it down the table to Matthew then took my seat. "I will have to tell you how we actually have this box and these documents. As crazy as it may sound, Andrew came to me in a dream and showed me where he had hidden them in the house on the island. The next day I went and found the box just where he had said it would be."

Matthew nodded. "Very interesting and I do appreciate it. Please call me Matthew. Mister Brice is so formal." He looked at the paper for a few moments then looked at everyone.

He continued, "We will place a copy of this in our files as proof should any questions come up in the future." He passed it back to me. "Please, have my secretary make a copy of that later on."

I responded, "I certainly will." I placed it back in the box.

Matthew continued, "After seeing Tom's report on the TV, there was no doubt in my mind, regarding the authenticity and legitimacy of why you are here. I've seen many of Tom's reports and all were legitimate, open and above board. I knew he would never be perpetrating a hoax. He's an excellent reporter."

There were sounds of approval in the room. Alan happened to be near Tom and patted him on the back.

Matthew continued, "I think the best place to begin would be when Andrew Cavenaugh first came to us. Well, I should say this firm since none of us were alive back then."

His story began from the time Andrew hired the firm, to oversee bank accounts and stocks, all the way up until they received his final communication in June of 1919, indicating he was going away. "It was everyone's impression at the time that he needed to get away to some place and get himself together. They all expected him to finally get back in touch with the firm when this happened but he never did. All the firm could do was continue with his previous instructions of overseeing his affairs."

"Yes, his communication indicated he was going away to New York. He also indicated that he wanted someone to go to the house on the island and dispose of all the things in it. They were to be given to local people, donated to the needy or sold with the money being donated to the needy. It would leave the house completely empty. From what I understand, there wasn't that much. Just a bunch of boxes filled with clothes and household stuff and a few pieces of furniture. Oh. There was an icebox, too. He wanted someone from the firm to go to the house around every six months to check on things and make sure there were no major problems. He had sent the key to the house in his last communication to the firm. Since the house was built like a damn fortress, there were never any major issues."

"He also indicated that there could possibly be deliveries to the firm from Africa by secret security services. Actually, there were deliveries of two very heavy wooden boxes and two cloth pouches."

He looked at the pouches on top of the safe deposit box. "Believe it or not, to my knowledge, no one has ever opened the boxes or the pouches. We were directed to just keep them in a safe place. Since the boxes are so heavy, I didn't have them brought here to the conference room. Several years after the last delivery, a message was sent to us, stating that due to political and revolutionary events, there would be no more deliveries. I wanted you to be aware of that information. That correspondence is in the files."

Ethan raised his hand and spoke, "From what was said in Andrew's journal, the wooden boxes contain gold and the pouches diamonds. Their true value can be determined down the road."

Matthew smiled at Ethan, "Thank you, Ethan. I will show you where the boxes are located in the company vault after the meeting is over. If you would like to check the contents of the pouches, please feel free to do so." Then, he continued where he had left off, "Andrew also indicated that he wanted the firm to oversee everything until such time a possible heir might make a claim. From information he had given us, we knew he had a twin brother, so there was a possibility he or one of his heirs would show up one day. This never happened." He looked back over at Ethan. "Well. Probably not until now."

Everyone smiled with sounds of agreement.

Ethan spoke with an apologetic expression on his face, "Ah. This really is a serious situation and all the cards need to be on the table. Now. Damn. Where do I begin?"

Matthew looked at Ethan. "What can be the problem? You look exactly like the apparition. Personally, I have no doubt you are Andrew's relation."

Ethan bent his head down, shaking it. "Yes. But there could be another."

Everyone was shocked and yelled out. "WHAT!?"

Ethan continued, "Let me explain. Let's say, Albert, my distant relative, truly was Andrew's twin brother. Yes. He was an adopted child. Adopted by the Groves as they medically could not have children. Albert grew up, married and had two sons. I am the last of the relations of one of the sons. But!" He paused for a few moments. "But there is one other, a cousin, who could be the remaining relation of the other son. He, too, could be an heir."

Matthew spoke out, "Really!? This is very interesting. Since you know about this other person, where is he?"

"If he's still alive, he would be in his late sixties or early seventies. It's kind of a very weird and strange story."

Alan called out, "Hey! We're all ears."

Ethan began, "I was very young when it happened but the story was told to me by my parents. My parents heard it from his. His name was Michael. Michael Groves. He was an artist and lived in Atlanta. I have never seen any of his paintings but I was told he was quite good. In April of nineteen eighty-two, he went on vacation to paint. He had been saving up for a long time to go to this very exclusive and not cheap hotel in the mountains of North Carolina. The name of the hotel is the Sandora."

Matthew spoke up, "Wow! My wife and I have been there! It is an incredible and amazing hotel. When you walk in, you almost could think you have walked into Versailles. There are wonderful gardens and a beautiful lake. An artist could go there and paint landscapes forever. It makes perfect sense. There's even an art gallery next to the hotel filled with amazing paintings. Piano music is playing there the whole time the gallery is open. And, yes. It is NOT cheap to stay there." He stopped and looked at everyone. "Oh. Sorry for interrupting. Please, Ethan. Continue."

Ethan nodded. "Well, the story goes that one morning he went running out the front door of the hotel, yelling out, 'If I can, I'm saving yesterday!' and he disappeared. After he didn't show up, the police were called in to see if they could find him. They were told what he had yelled out but it didn't make any sense to them. Everyone looked but no one could ever find him. He literally just vanished. The hotel and grounds were searched but not even a body showed up. Believe it or not, I've thought about going down there and looking into it. It was so strange. So, it's possible there could be one more heir to Andrew's legacy if he's still alive.

I raised my hand. "I hate to say it but that sounds weird as hell. Was he a druggie? I mean, 'If I can, I'm saving yesterday!'. What exactly does that mean? Sounds like he was on some damn drug trip."

There were snickers from everyone.

Ethan shook his head again. "Actually, that was investigated. His parents said he wasn't into drugs, so what can I say? The police had no idea what it meant, either."

I spoke up, "Well, maybe one of these days you really should go down there and see if you can find anything out. Especially, with him being a relative. If you don't mind, I'd kinda like to go with you. I possibly could get a short story or novel out of it. Yeah."

Matthew looked at everyone and spoke, "I think we need to get back to the subject at hand. We can address the issue of a cousin another time.

Since we were returning to the subject at hand, I just had to know about the paintings. I raised my hand. "Matthew. Sorry for interrupting again but I had one question. I'm an artist as well as a writer and was just curious. I understand there was a portrait done and I would love to see it. When everything was removed from the house, where did it go? If there was one, maybe I could go to the person who bought it and get a photo of it in case I do write a novel about all this. I'm sure Tom would like to have a photo as well for his report." I didn't want to say anything more regarding the other paintings right now.

Matthew nodded his head. "Yes. I know. I saw your portrait drawing and the painting of the house in Tom's report. If you don't mind me saying so, you're quite an exceptional artist. Wouldn't mind having you do a nice landscape or seascape for us to purchase for the office here." Then, a questioning expression came to his face, "To my recollection, there is no indication that any painting or anything of real value was removed from the house."

I immediately responded to prevent any more questioning on it, "Thank you, Matthew. And I do appreciate the kind words. Actually, the art gallery I deal with in Atlanta has several of my works. I'll have them send some pictures of them in an email to you. That way you might see if any of those would be suitable." What Matthew said made me realize that no one most likely had ever found or discovered the secret room behind the bookcase.

From the look on the faces of those who had heard the whole story, it was obvious they were thinking the same thing. Hopefully, the secret room really was still a secret.

Matthew then looked at the metal box on the table. "This box has not been opened for at least a hundred years. Andrew is the only one who had the key. And since he took it with him, no one has ever opened it."

I opened the wooden box and pulled out the cloth pouch. Opening the pouch, I reached in and pulled out the key. Holding it up, I commented, "I'm pretty sure this is the one that will do it."

Everyone gathered around the box.

I immediately looked at Ethan. "Since Ethan looks so much like Andrew, I think he's the one who should do the honors of opening the box and going through the contents." I handed Ethan the key.

Ethan spoke, "Before we open the box, let me just check one of the pouches." He picked them up, placed one on the table then opened the other and carefully poured the contents onto the table. "Rough diamonds. Wow."

Everyone was quite surprised with sounds of approval.

Ethan placed the stones back into the cloth pouch and set it on the table. Then, he took the key, inserted it in the safe deposit box and turned it. The telltale 'click' let us know it had worked.

More cheers of approval along with clapping filled the room. Alan got in the best position to film the event.

Ethan slowly opened the box and looked inside. "There's a small box in here and I think we all know what's in it."

Jeffrey questioned, "Ah. Not all of us."

Alan commented, "That's right. They have no idea what was in the book." He focused his camera in on the small box in Ethan's hand. "And when you open it, DO NOT touch its contents."

Luke jumped into the conversation, "An old gypsy lady told Andrew to save his wisdom teeth when they were pulled out. He had no idea why but did exactly what she instructed. The box contains his wisdom teeth."

Jeffrey snickered, "Andrew may have had no idea why he needed to save them but they sure as hell could contain proof with DNA that Ethan is truly a blood relative."

Ethan removed the lid from the box and smiled as he peered inside it, "You've got it." He turned the open box in everyone's direction, so they may see the contents.

Alan focused in on the box to show the two teeth inside it. He also repeated his previous comment, "Don't anyone touch the teeth! It could damage or contaminate the DNA!"

Stella spoke up, "Alan's correct. We don't need to contaminate items of possible proof of Ethan's heritage."

Matthew added, "When we finish here, we can run down to the police station and have them draw some of Ethan's blood. We can give them one of the teeth to use and see if they can do a match as quickly as possible. It might take some time to confirm the fact." He shook his head. "Personally. The DNA information will only prove what is quite obvious. Ethan is definitely a blood relative."

Ethan put the lid on the small box and placed it on the table.

Next, he reached in and grabbed an envelope. Opening it, he pulled out a couple of old sepia photographs along with a written note. He started going through the pictures first. He'd read the note later. A smile came to his face. He flipped the first picture over and read what was written on the back, "Here's a picture of Andrew." He held it up for all of us to see. He then held it up next to his smiling face to show the comparison.

Everyone clapped their hands and cheered at the likeness. Alan zoomed in to get a closeup of the two together. The likeness was truly uncanny.

He placed the first picture on the table then flipped the next one over to read what was written on the back of that one, "Here's a picture of Brian." He started laughing very loudly. He turned and looked directly at me. "Oh, my God! You look like Brian!! I mean, seriously! You really do look just like Brian!" He held the picture up for all to see.

Luke called out, "This is freaky as shit! Wow!"

Again, everyone was extremely shocked and surprised at the resemblance, clapping and verbally expressing their approval as Alan zoomed in on me and then the picture.

Tom also expressed his surprise, "Holy shit! This truly is incredible. What are the chances? Ethan looking exactly like Andrew and you looking exactly like Brian. This is unbelievably bizarre. This is the first time anyone has known what Brian looked like. Wow." He paused for a moment and his face was filled with shock, "I just thought of something that is remarkable. Brian was Andrew's architect." He then looked directly at me. "And you not only look like Brian but you also have a background in architecture. Holy shit! What are the chances?" He turned and looked at Ethan. "Andrew was in finance and stocks just as Ethan is." He raised his hand in the air and called out, "Okay! Now, I get it! You reminded Andrew so much of Brian. That's got to be the connection when he said 'our house' to you. Because they were going to be living together and it was going to be their house."

I looked at Tom. "I think you're absolutely correct. Seeing me must have brought back all his memories of Brian."

Ethan looked at the next picture. "Here's a photograph of Andrew and Brian together. It's obvious, these were all done by a professional photographer. Everyone back then didn't have cameras to take pictures like they do today with their cell phones." He handed the picture around.

Ethan looked down at the last picture and began to roar with laughter. He shook his head and then looked over at me, continuing to laugh as he spoke, "Those of us who know the whole story in Andrew's book will totally understand this last photograph. For those of you who know the legend of Andrew having a fiancée, this picture will have you totally on the clue bus." He looked at Matthew, Stella and Jeffrey. "We'll explain in detail in a minute." He paused for a moment and looked at me. "Here's what you would look like in a dress!" He held the picture up for all to see of Brian all dressed in his 'fiancée' outfit but without the veil, revealing his smiling face with full facial hair and a wig.

The picture had everyone just roaring with laughter, cheering and whistling.

Luke called out, "It's one of the outfits Brian wore to fake out the townspeople but he also wore a heavy veil, so no one could see his face."

Stella questioned, "Okay. For those of us not on the clue bus, would someone please enlighten us?"

I responded, "It's all in the book." I reached in the box and pulled out Andrew's book. "It was a ruse they had concocted to make everyone think Andrew had a fiancée. When in fact, Andrew and Brian are the ones who had a major relationship going on."

Jeffrey was floored and shocked, "Holy cow! You ARE shitting me! You have to be kidding! Are you saying Andrew was gay? And Brian was his partner? No way! Seriously?"

Ethan yelled out, pointing at Jeffrey, "BINGO!! Give that man a cigar!"

Jeffrey bent his head down, shaking it and looking down at the floor. "What are the chances? What are the chances?"

Matthew shook his head and spoke with surprise in his voice, "There was never any indication of that in any of the information that's been passed down to us over the years. Oh. Wow. That really is a zinger."

Ethan picked up the note that accompanied the pictures and read it allowed, "These pictures were taken by a very good photographer who happens to be one of my clients. We told him that the picture of Brian all dressed up in women's clothes was one of his Halloween outfits. He actually laughed during the whole time he was taking that picture. I hope all who may see that picture in the future will realize the great love Brian has for me to concoct such a skeem. Since you are reading this note, it is obvious you have found the wooden box hidden in the special compartment in the linen closet of the house, containing the book as well as the key to this safe deposit box. If you have read the book, you know the whole story and not just the false one we propagated."

Jeffrey spoke up, "Tom, I sure hope in your TV special on all this you tell the story of what's in the book mentioned in the note."

Tom responded, "Yep. We actually will have Ethan reading the whole story in the book for all to hear. He's already read half of it on camera."

Next, Ethan reached in the box and pulled out a cloth pouch. He opened it and carefully dumped its contents into his left hand. He spoke softly, "Oh, my God. It's their rings." Immediately, he became extremely emotional with tears streaming down his face.

I quickly went over and wrapped my right arm around Ethan yet looking at Matthew, Stella and Jeffrey. "Andrew had the rings made. On New Year's Eve in nineteen fourteen, they both pledged their love for one another at the stroke of midnight and placed the rings on each other's hands. The writing in Andrew's book explains how he had Brian's ring because Brian gave it to him in the hospital. But there was never any more information as to where they were or what happened to them. Well. Now, we know."

Matthew looked at Ethan. "Since these items are so personal, I believe you should keep them. It's only fitting. Once the DNA proves your relationship to Andrew, there will be no problem with you taking them."

Ethan quickly composed himself, placing the rings back in the pouch, "I'm so sorry folks. But it just hit me like a ton of bricks. And Matthew. Thank you. I would gratefully appreciate it if you would keep them here in this box for safekeeping. That way, I will always know where they are. Now, I'll explain a little more."

Ethan paused for a moment then continued again, "When Brian died of the influenza in October of nineteen eighteen, Andrew was so distraught over losing him, he told everyone he was going away. Everyone at the time assumed it was because of the story of the legend. The story of his fiancée not loving him. But to the contrary, he was distraught over Brian dying. It took some time but he got his affairs in order and moved to the house on the island in early April of nineteen nineteen. Being alone on the island, it was these emotions that finally overwhelmed him, causing him to walk out to the edge of the bluff overlooking the ocean and jump off, committing suicide. Virtually everything is in Andrew's book, leading up to the point just before him taking his own life."

I interjected, "The reason we know he went off the cliff is because Ethan and I both had a significant dream last night where we watched the event occur."

Jeffrey shook his head. "Oh. Wow. This is so over-the-top and so sad. What a profound love they must have shared and those fucking religious assholes who condemn us, saying it's a sin and an abomination." Jeffrey immediately stopped and looked at everyone in the room. He bent his head down. "Wow. I'm so sorry. I kind of got wound up there. Sorry about that. Yeah." He looked back at everyone.

Ethan looked at Jeffrey. "Jeffrey. You said 'us'."

Matthew immediately jumped in and looked at everyone. "Yes. Jeffrey is gay. We here at the firm don't give a damn. He's a terrific and wonderful employee and we all love him. I hope this is not a problem."

Instantly, Ethan, Luke, Tom, Alan and I started clapping, cheering and yelling out, expressing our approval of Matthew's comment. Quickly, Stella and Jeffrey joined in. A big smile filled Matthew's face.

Luke chimed in, "It's so nice to see there are those who have a legitimate understanding and knowledge of the issue and are accepting. Thank you, Matthew."

We all clapped and cheered again.

The rest of the afternoon was spent giving Matthew, Stella and Jeffrey the more detailed story described in Andrew's book. They were quite surprised at the information they discovered. The rest of the contents of the safe deposit box was also checked out. It was mainly stock certificates, other legal papers and information about several banks where Andrew had accounts. There also were the papers indicating ownership of the island.

When all was done, Matthew turned to Ethan. "We will be glad to continue to oversee everything until you are ready to take it all over yourself since you are in finance and stocks. It hasn't been proven yet, but I have a great belief you will come out on top."

Ethan nodded. "Thank you, Matthew. An excellent idea. You all have been taking care of business for at least a hundred years. I see no reason to make any major changes now. And if information does come back that I AM a legitimate heir, I have a feeling I will still require your firm's assistance, expertise and services with everything."

I spoke up, "Matthew, your firm has more than proven itself. I can tell you right now. I will be calling you to set up an appointment to help guide me with any future legal issues I may have. I hope it doesn't matter that I live in Atlanta."

Jeffrey immediately interjected, "I'm sure Matthew will agree that distance is not a problem. And I'm sure we will be glad to be of assistance to you in legal issues."

Luke raised his hand. "That goes for me, too."

Tom made a grunting sound, "That goes for me and I'm sure Alan as well. I definitely could use some guidance on making sure either one of us is protected should something happen to the other." He looked over at Alan with a strange expression.

Alan saw it, snickered and shook his head, "Oh, hell. Yeah. Why not."

Tom smiled as he turned to Ethan and me, "Wasn't sure if you had picked up on it but Alan and I have been partners for several years now. We try to keep it low profile." He looked at

Matthew, Stella and Jeffrey. "So, Jeffrey, you are not the only one here that's gay."

Ethan shook his head. "Wow! I never had a clue. Well. Kudos, guys."

I smiled, "Actually, I've known for a while now. It came up in a conversation I had with Luke. I know he wasn't trying to break any confidences. I'm sure he thought you both wouldn't mind that I knew. I think it really is fantastic. You seem to work extremely well together. And seriously, no one would ever know unless you told them."

Alan gave a big grin, "And that's not all. Right after it became legal in June two thousand fifteen, Tom and I tied the knot. Yeah. All the folks at work know about it and are cool with it but we try not to flaunt it around. As Jeffrey said, there are still those who have a real problem with it."

Ethan spoke up, "Wow! More kudos! And congratulations to you both."

"Wow! That's something I didn't know." I clapped my hands and called out, "YeeeHaw!! I'll second that!"

Everyone in the room was in a congratulatory mood with smiles and hand-shaking of approval..

Ethan looked at me and asked, "Should I? You don't mind, do you?"

Everyone's face showed a questioning expression.

I looked at Ethan with a big smile on my face, "Go for it."

Ethan looked at everyone. "To be honest with you all, so there are no hidden secrets, I'd like you to know that we are gay as well. I think Luke knew already."

Luke pointed at me. "Yeah. I knew about him." Then, he looked at Ethan. "But I had no clue about you. Wow! I think that is so damn cool!"

The room was filled with joyous laughter and sounds of approval.

Jeffrey spoke with a big smile on his face, "Wow. This is so incredible. Wow! Wow! Wow!"

Tom spoke up, "I really do feel for Luke, though. There's no way he'll ever find a partner up there in nowhere land." He looked over at Luke. "And you're such a great guy."

I responded, "I feel the same way. During one of our conversations, it came right out as to where he was coming from. He's so happy for us and yet, he is getting left out. That's so sad. As you said, Tom. He's such a great guy."

Alan nodded. "Yes, he is. But he loves it up there. What can I say?"

Luke commented, "Maybe one day someone will come along. One never knows."

I added, "He's correct. As my mother has always told me, 'You never know what's around the next corner.'"

A huge smile filled Jeffrey's face, "Damn! I love it! I'm so happy for all you guys! That is so cool."

Even though it was going into early evening, Matthew thought it most important to run down to the police department and get the blood work started. Afterward, we all went to dinner at the restaurant Tom liked to frequent. After dinner, Matthew, Stella and Jeffrey headed home. Tom asked if we could meet again at his office the next morning around ten o'clock. He also took the wooden box and its contents for safekeeping.

It was going on ten o'clock at night when the van driver dropped Luke, Ethan and me at the hotel.

I spoke before we got on the elevator, "I don't know about you guys but I could use a drink. I'm heading to the bar."

Luke just smiled, "To be honest, I'm exhausted. What a day. I'm heading up to my room. See you guys tomorrow morning at breakfast."

Ethan turned to me. "Would you like some company at the bar?"

A big grin filled my face, "Sounds good to me."

We waved at Luke as he got on the elevator and the doors closed. Ethan and I headed to the hotel bar. After getting our drinks, we went and sat at a table.

I tilted my head. "Okay? I'd like to compare notes here. I mean, from what we heard today and what we know was written in Andrew's book. It's obvious since there was no mention of it in the conversations today, the paintings must still be in the secret room. If you're lucky, maybe they will have some value. I mean, they are over a hundred years old, so they are antiques."

Ethan agreed, "Not to sound like a money-grubbing asshole, but I'm sure you're right. And not just his paintings but his 'rainy day stash' as well. If no one has discovered that room, all that stuff should still be in it."

I looked at Ethan. "And when the DNA proves you truly are a blood relative, you're going to have a chunk of change to claim as an inheritance. I just hope to hell you don't get socked with a huge inheritance tax."

Ethan responded, "You've got that right. I think with Matthew and his gang helping out, I'm sure that will be a no-brainer for them to work out. Now, not to brag." He bent his head down as he snickered, "But with my current wealth, this inheritance could just be icing on the cake, I'm sure." He flexed his eyebrows several times. "The value of the house and the island can be figured out quickly. But I have no idea what the value of the gold and diamonds will be. That will have to be determined when we see how much there is. And let's not forget the ones at Brice and Walters."

I gave a sigh, "Okay. Can we be honest here? You say you're interested in me. Ethan! You're an incredibly handsome man. You obviously have money and you're most likely going to have a lot more. You could have anyone you desired. Why? Why would you be interested in me? I have nothing to give you and would never be able to pay my fair share. That would not be fair to you. I have always believed that people should pay their fair share in a relationship."

Ethan reached across the table with his left hand and placed it under my chin, so I was looking right at him. Then, he pulled his hand back and looked directly at me. "All through my adult life, I've wondered if there was someone out there who I could love and would love me. Never have I had feelings about a person like the feelings I have developed for you. They began and continued to grow from the moment I first set eyes on you. Call it Fate. Call it Destiny. I knew deep inside me you were the one. I knew I would love you like no other and I knew you would love me like no other. All the money in the world can't buy you love. Especially, a love like that. So, don't tell me you have nothing to give me. You have love. And I know you do."

I was totally taken aback. "Ethan. I feel the same way about you. But I wouldn't want you to feel like you were taking care of me or being cheated."

Ethan continued, "Let me explain something to you since money seems to be a problem for you. Yes. I do have money and many would consider me well-to-do. But! If it were not for you and you going to the island to paint, none of this would ever be happening. Do you understand that? Because of you, it is quite likely my wealth is going to be significantly increased. Well, maybe not significantly." He paused and gave me a big grin, "That would never have happened if you had not gone to the island to paint. So. Whatever inheritance should come my way would be as if you were handing it to me on a silver platter." He began to giggle, "Let me correct that. Not a silver platter but a golden one. Do you understand what I'm trying to tell you?"

I was surprised, "Ah. Well. I never really thought about it that way."

Ethan continued, "Well. It's true. This inheritance has been sitting around for a hundred years and no one has ever claimed it or realized it even existed for that fact. You're the one who opened the door. You're the one that found Andrew's book. And honestly, I don't believe it was by coincidence. I believe Andrew's ghost saw you and thought of Brian. You saw the pictures. You're the spitting image of Brian. Andrew's ghost wanted you to get this ball rolling."

I smiled and looked right at Ethan, "I feel so much better now. I understand. I just didn't want you to feel cheated or taken advantage of. And maybe you're right. Maybe Andrew did see me and I reminded him of Brian. Actually, I'd like to think that was true. I just feel so sad that they both had their whole lives in front of them and it was taken away so soon."

Ethan nodded. "You're right. You and I have our whole lives in front of us. Let's continue where they left off. We can share the love and happiness they never got to. And we can do it in their memory. For them. Also, think about this. If you had not gone to the island

and the report had never been on the TV and internet, I would never have seen it and we would never have known each other existed. I believe that it was not the Fates that stepped in for this to happen but it was somehow Andrew and maybe even Brian. Not only for the island to have an owner again but for us to meet and live the life Andrew and Brian never got to have."

I raised my glass in the air. "To Andrew and Brian."

Ethan raised his glass. "To Andrew and Brian."

We clinked our glasses together as we called out, "Hear! Hear!"

CHAPTER XVII

The van came to pick us up the next morning around nine-thirty. Luke, Ethan and I had just finished breakfast in the hotel restaurant. We arrived at the TV station just before ten and were directed to Tom's office.

Tom had been sitting at his desk but stood with a big smile on his face, "Good morning, gentlemen. I hope you all slept well. I got some very interesting news this morning. The station wants Alan and me to do a major special on this whole event. They thought it was so controversial, unusual and bizarre, it would draw a huge audience. Remember." He raised his right hand up, pointing with his index finger. "It's all about ratings."

This had us all laughing.

I raised my hand. "Tom. Ethan and I were going to head up to the island tomorrow. Ethan wants to see it firsthand. I was hoping you and Alan would be there when we open the secret room. Today is Saturday and it's the weekend. I didn't know what the schedule is for you and Alan."

Tom snickered, "When you're in the news business, there is no schedule. You go where and when it is happening."

This made everyone laugh again.

I continued, "From all that we've heard so far, no one has known of it and the contents should still be in it. Is it possible you both could come with us? I'm sure its contents could be of great importance to your special report." I looked over at Ethan. "Ethan! I'm so sorry!

It's your house! You're the one who should be doing the inviting, not me!"

Ethan had a big smile on his face, "Well, it's like what Andrew said to Brian. 'It's our house.' I now say that to you. It's our house."

There was a moment of silence before Luke spoke up, "Oh, my God! This is incredible. Really? Does this mean what I think it does? Personally, I think it's terrific. It just adds more to the whole story."

Tom called out, "Hot Damn! REALLY? Luke's right. This does add more to the story. WOW! And YES! Alan and I would love to go up there with you all. We can take the first train up and head out to the island by early afternoon." He paused for a moment. "And I believe you need to hold onto the box and Andrew's book. Something tells me with you being a writer, you will probably get a novel out of this, especially with all the information that's been revealed and is in the book."

Luke laughed, "And for me, it will be great to get back to my normal routine. I've been missing the restaurant and bar."

We all cheered.

Tom added, "Okay. With all that settled, we'll be in the van tomorrow morning to get you all and go to the train station. Remember, it's the early train and it will still be dark outside. I'll call the lodging house and make sure we have rooms for at least one night. Maybe two."

The van arrived in the very early morning and dropped us all off at the train station. We all helped carry Alan's camera equipment along with everyone's luggage.

Arriving at the town's station, we all got off the train. It was late morning. Luke spoke out, raising his arms in the air, "Home at last!"

Everyone expressed their joy of being there.

Luke continued, "Okay, guys. I need to get to the restaurant. You all go do what you have to on the island. When you get back, I'll see what I can whip us up for dinner."

We all said our momentary goodbyes to Luke and went to the lodging house. The landlady was very glad to see us and showed us all to our rooms.

After she left, Alan commented, "Guess you and Ethan are trying to keep a low profile by getting separate rooms. I totally get it. Don't need any staring by the locals. At least, not yet."

Ethan commented, "Alan, you are so correct. We may be in the twenty-first century but there are still problems with some folks and we don't need to ruffle any feathers right now. Especially, here in small town USA."

Tom responded, "Yep. It's one reason Alan and I get separate rooms." He paused a moment then continued, "Okay, guys. We do need to get this show on the road. Now, let's get Alan's stuff and go get a boat. I'm sure Abel will let us use the same one we used the last time."

Tom was absolutely correct and we headed over to the island. After anchoring the boat, we grabbed Alan's equipment and started walking up the drive to the house.

Ethan kept turning his head around trying to gather everything in. Finally, standing in front of the house, he looked up at the front façade. "This is a magnificent house and it's bigger than I thought it was. If this was finished, it would be a grand home."

I didn't dare say anything about my idea as a bed and breakfast. He might want it as a vacation house.

Entering, we carried everything up to the room where the secret room was behind the bookcase. Alan called out, "Tom and I will get everything organized here. Go show Ethan the rest of the house."

Since we were upstairs, we took a quick walk-through. Then, we went downstairs and walked through it. I even took him out to the pump room.

I pointed at the LP gas tanks. "I know Andrew was eventually going to have a cable run under the water from the mainland, so there would be electricity in the house. He was going to have that done when all the construction was completed. He just never got to it. Of course, the existing gas tanks would have to be replaced as I'm sure they are way too old to even consider using today. When that's done, a nice water pump can be installed as well to get water out of the cistern." I pointed at the floor. "It's under here."

Ethan had said nothing but was mentally scrutinizing everything as we walked around. As the tour of the house ended, he spoke, "Could we go see the great room again? I want to see that view that looks out over the ocean."

Finally, we were standing in the middle of the great room and Ethan turned slowly around to see the whole thing more closely than we did before. Then, he walked over to the windows and looked out to sea. "What an amazing view. And what an incredible space this is. Interesting." He reached up with his left hand and stroked his beard. "Interesting. But I think we should head upstairs and check out the secret room."

Shortly, we were up in the room and Alan turned to Ethan and me. "Okay. Which one of you geniuses knows how to open it?"

I turned to Ethan. "You're a lot taller than me. Look in the last bookcase on the right. On the left-hand side of that case and against the wall, you should feel some sort of something to pull or push to open the latches on the door. There should be two of them."

Ethan put his head into the upper shelves on several levels to look. He didn't see anything. Then, he reached up onto the next to the top shelf and felt around. After a second, he called out, "Think I've got one of them." After a moment we heard a 'click'. "That's one. Now, for the other one. It's probably down lower." He knelt down on the floor and looked into the lower shelves. "Eureka!" There was another 'click' sound. "That should do it."

He stood up, grabbed two of the shelves and slowly pulled. As he did, the bookcase started to move and open slowly to the right, revealing a three-foot wide opening in the wall directly behind the bookcase.

Tom and I clapped and cheered as Alan kept filming. Alan did join in with the cheering, "If you need a flashlight, there's one in my case over there." Alan pointed to one of his cases. "But before you go in, I'd like to film what it looks like in there for posterity."

Alan slowly entered the room and continued to film. The bright light on his camera fully illuminated the room.

We all listened to Alan calling out from the room, "Unbelievable! Unbelievable! This is unbelievable! I can't wait for all this stuff to come out, so we can actually see it." Shortly, he emerged from the room. He turned his camera off. "You're NOT going to believe what's in there." The expression on his face was one of shock, surprise and wonder.

Tom looked at Alan. "Really? It's that incredible? Really?"

Alan looked right at Tom. "Yes. Really. Because of how everything is arranged and leaning against the walls, I could only make out a few but what I saw is unbelievable."

Ethan spoke, "Well since we know it's there, I think the first painting that should come out is the portrait of Andrew and Brian. I'll go get it."

Alan called out, "It's in the back against the back wall. If you walk in there slowly, there should be enough light for you to see it. It's pretty big. I think you're going to need help with it."

Ethan slowly entered the room. "Yes. I see it. Alan, you're right. It's a very large painting. I'll absolutely need some help." He grabbed hold of it with both hands. "Wow. It's not only big but it's a bit heavy."

I called out, "Wait! I'll come help." I went into the room and grabbed one side of the large gold leaf frame. We carefully carried it out and leaned it up against the east wall of the library and sitting room. We all stood back and looked at it.

Ethan shook his head. "Now, that's something. Wow!"

A questioning look came to my face, "I know this is going to sound really strange but there's something about the painting. The style. It's like I've seen that style before. Just can't put my finger on it."

Alan called out, "You and Ethan go stand next to the painting. It's remarkable how you look exactly like Andrew and Brian." He snickered, "I already know the artist as well as others in the room. Wait till you see. That's one reason I was so surprised before." He looked at me. "You being an artist should know who the painter is. He was no slouch when it came to portraits."

I was curious because there was something familiar about the way the painting was done. "I have a feeling I know but that just couldn't be possible. No way. I'm checking to see who's the artist. It's such an amazing painting." I got down close to the floor and examined the signature. I yelled out, "Oh, my God! Oh, my God!! It is! I knew it! I was right! It is who I thought it was! I knew I recognize the style but couldn't imagine it actually being true! You're not going to believe this!" I stood up and looked at everyone. "THIS is a Sargent! John Singer Sargent did this portrait! This painting is worth a fortune!" I looked at everyone. "Sorry to sound so dollar sign oriented but it's true. A portrait by John Singer Sargent is not just some run-of-the-mill painting."

Alan turned on his camera again and zoomed in on the signature. "As I said, wait till you see who did the other ones." He began to chuckle.

Tom, Ethan and I went into the secret room and one by one slowly started bringing out the paintings, leaning them up against the walls. All of us shouted out our disbeliefs regarding the artists. There were twenty of them. Mostly landscapes and a few still life ones.

As we did, I could see them more clearly in the light of day and the styles of several were quite clear. I bent down to examine them to reassure that I was correct. "Holy Shit!! Unbelievable! There's a few Monets and these over here look like Renoirs." I walked over to two of the others. "These are two early works of Picasso. And those over there look like Matisse." I pointed at one. "That has to be a Van Gogh and those two look like Gauguin." I looked right at Ethan. "Ethan! Holy Shit! There are enough paintings here to open your own damn museum! My mind never imagined there would be paintings by such artists as these. The value of these paintings will DEFINITELY increase your wealth."

This had everyone laughing.

Alan nodded. "He's so right. You have several million dollars worth of paintings here. Probably serveral HUNDRED million dollars worth. SEVERAL! I'll bet museums will be begging you for them."

Ethan looked at me. "Regarding my comments about whatever might be in the secret room, THIS is definitely an unexpected major find." He then looked hard at the portrait. "Whatever happens, the Sargent painting is eventually going in the great room in the middle of the inside wall. It belongs there. I know that's what Andrew and Brian would've wanted."

I was so glad to hear that as I totally agreed. Hearing that made me very happy.

Tom joked, "Well, with any inheritance taxes you might have to pay on what you're going to get from Andrew's estate, donate one or two of these and you might be off the hook. Yeah. Now, let's see what else is in there."

Tom went in and yelled out, "There are two very heavy wooden boxes here with rope handles. They are just like the ones we saw in the vault room at Brice and Walters. I can hardly lift one up. Ethan. Maybe you and I can drag them out. We'll bring them out one at a time."

Ethan entered and soon they both came out with one of the boxes. From the way they were carrying it, its weight was obviously significant. They placed it near the middle of the room then went for the other one. Bringing it out, they placed it next to the first one.

I looked at the boxes. "From what was written in Andrew's book, they most likely hold some gold just like the ones at the law firm."

Ethan clapped his hands. "Well, let's see." He pulled on the latch and pulled the lid back on the hinges. There inside the box were small ingots of gold, filling the box. "You are absolutely correct." He closed the lid.

Alan started laughing, "And there is a total of four of them. Two here and two at Brice and Walters. Wow."

I headed into the room and lifted a small wooden box off one of the shelves and brought it out. "I have a feeling I know what's in here, too." I handed the box to Ethan. "I got to open the first wooden box. Now, it's your turn."

Alan kept filming.

Ethan took the box and placed it on top of the wooden boxes on the floor. He slowly lifted the lid. Inside were two cloth pouches. "These are identical to the two in the vault at Brice and Walters. And we know what's in them." He took one out, opened it and slowly dumped the contents out onto the nearby floor. Out poured several large rough stones. He spoke quietly, "Yep. Just like what we saw at Brice and Walters, uncut diamonds." He dumped the second pouch out onto the floor. Several more of the same landed next to the ones already there. "Wow." He put them all back in the pouches and back into the box.

I called out. "There's a large cloth bag on the shelf in there. Let me go get it." I went in and retrieved the bag and handed it to Ethan. "When I picked it up, I could hear what sounded like a bunch of coins shifting around."

Ethan took the bag and opened it. He pulled out several piles of monetary bills, stacking them on the floor. Then, he pulled out another bag containing a large amount of coins. He looked in the bag. "It's a bunch of quarters." He set the bag down next to all the money.

Tom called out, "This truly is remarkable. Twenty-one paintings by very famous artists, four boxes of gold ingots, four bags of uncut diamonds and a bag of antique money that could fetch a hefty price with coin collectors. Ladies and gentlemen. I would like to introduce you to Mister Ethan Groves. One of the richest men in the world!"

This had us all bending over with laughter, clapping our hands and patting Ethan on the back.

Finally calming down, I went into the room and grabbed the urn sitting on the shelf and brought it out. I held it up. "It's Brian's ashes. So sad."

Ethan got a sad expression on his face, "Since no one knew Andrew went off the cliff outside, maybe it's possible some of his remains are down somewhere in the rocks below. If we can have someone go search and find them, we can reunite him and Brian together with their remains."

Alan agreed, "Ethan, that's a wonderful idea. I know some forensic guys in Boston who could do it. They would know what to look for."

Ethan smiled, "Thanks, Alan. That would be fantastic. We could put them in a memorial. Have one built out near the pavilion. I can also have a container made, so Andrew's bones and Brian's ashes can be in the same container. They loved each other in life and should be together in death."

Tom looked around. "So. That's everything? How about we put it all back, close it up again and head back to the mainland for something to eat?"

Ethan raised his right arm in the air. "I'll second that. And I sure as hell could use a drink."

This made us all clap and cheer as we picked things up and started placing them back in the secret room. Everything back in their places, Ethan slowly closed the bookcase door until we heard the 'click's. We gathered Alan's stuff and headed to the boat.

As we walked down the drive, I turned to look back at the house again. That's when I saw two figures, standing on the front steps of the entry portico. I yelled out, "Oh, my God!"

Everyone stopped and turned around to look. Alan quickly opened his camera case, grabbed his camera and turned it on. He aimed it at the front entrance to the house. "I'm getting it. Not to worry."

Ethan spoke quietly, "It's Andrew and Brian. Both of them. Together. This is the first time I have seen Brian."

We all watched as the figures smiled and waved at us. Then, they did something that put huge smiles on all our faces. They both stretched out their arms giving a 'thumbs-up'. We all reacted and returned the gesture while laughing joyfully. After nodding, they turned and went back into the house, walking right through the closed front door.

Alan quickly turned the camera to film Ethan and me standing there. "I'm doing this for one reason. It shows that you two are right here and it would have been impossible for those figures to be you propagating a hoax."

I was becoming emotional, "That's the first time I have seen them together. And did you see their smiles? I can't help it but I am totally bowled over by seeing that."

Ethan responded, "I have the same feelings. Wow. Come here." He grabbed me and held me tight.

Alan checked his camera and let out a big sigh, "YES! And I got it all on video! YES!"

I shook my head. "Now, I really do need a drink."

Tom called out, "I'll second that!"

Tom's comment broke the tension as we all continued heading to the boat.

CHAPTER XVIII

Getting back to the mainland, we went by the lodging house to drop things off and then headed to the restaurant and bar.

Luke saw us all walk in and gave us a wave. He came over and led us to a table. "I hope everything went well out on the island."

Tom answered, "For me and Alan, it went very well. We got some great footage for the special. For Ethan, I would say it went EXCEEDINGLY well."

We all started chuckling at his comment.

Luke crossed his arms. "Okay. What's the joke? I'd like to be included on the clue bus."

I turned to Luke. "What was discovered in the secret room should make Ethan an incredibly wealthy man. More so than he is right now."

Luke's face was filled with surprise, "Really? Well, that's terrific! Good for him. You can tell me more later. Okay. Now, I know you all must be hungry, so let me take your order and we'll get it cooking."

After Luke took our order and before walking away, I commented, "Turn in the order and come join us."

Luke turned with a smile, "Thanks. I'll be there in a few."

Shortly thereafter, Luke came to the table just as drinks were being brought. "Cook says things should be coming out in a little while. Now, I can't wait to hear what happened today over there."

As we drank and ate, everyone told of the events of the day. Alan closed with the sighting of Andrew and Brian that he caught on video.

Luke turned to Ethan. "So. Are you going to do anything about the house?"

Ethan tilted his head and his face squinted. "This may sound off-the-wall but I actually have a great idea. All the construction needs to be completed. I want to get a cable over to the island as soon as possible and have an electrician check out all the wiring there. If any of it needs updating, I want that done. Then, some really nice light fixtures should be installed. I'm leaving that up to you." He turned and looked right at me. "You have an architectural background and also an artistic flair that I don't have."

Ethan continued, "The same goes for the plumbing. Anything that needs it will be replaced. I'm really glad Andrew decided to have three bathrooms built upstairs other than the one for the master bedroom. Then, there's the one downstairs near the kitchen, the one for the servant's quarters and the other one in the south end of the house. Of course, they will have to be updated significantly along with the kitchen. I'll see about getting a connection to the town water system and run a supply pipe under the ocean from the mainland to the island and to the cistern at the house. There would be other connections installed for any future needs."

"Outside and adjacent to the back terrace, a nice swimming pool would be great. Then, out hear the pavilion but somewhat out of the way would be a nice place to build the memorial for Andrew and Brian where their remains can be placed."

Tom nodded. "Wow. You really have been thinking about this. So, when are you moving in?"

Ethan responded, "Well." He paused for a moment and looked at everyone at the table. "It took seeing the whole house to make me think outside the box. Instead of a private dwelling, I was thinking more along the lines of a bed and breakfast."

Luke and I immediately roared with laughter and did a high-five.

Tom turned to us. "Okay. What's so funny?"

Luke pointed over at me. "That's exactly what he said after he'd taken a major tour of the house. He said it would make a terrific bed and breakfast."

Ethan broke out laughing, "Seriously? Well. I'm so glad we see eye to eye about that. I'll drink to that." He raised his glass. "To a bed and breakfast!"

Everyone raised their glasses and clinked them together. "Bed and breakfast!" Then, everyone cheered.

Ethan turned and looked at the painting I had done still on the easel Luke had set up. Then, he looked at me. "That's the painting you did that made Andrew write the words on the wall. Correct?"

I responded, "Yep."

Ethan continued, "What does everyone think about this idea? To keep the words Andrew painted on the wall from being damaged, cover them with a clear plastic piece attached to the wall. Due to its height on the wall, frame and hang your painting right above it, so people can see what the words are referring to. Interestingly enough, it would be at the perfect height for viewing. And off to the right of the painting, mat and frame your portrait drawing of Andrew and hang it there. That way everyone can see what Andrew looks like. Small plaques can be attached to the wall to describe everything."

Tom and I began clapping and cheering, pointing at Alan who bent his head down snickering.

I looked at Ethan. “Believe it or not, Alan made the same suggestion when we were here to make the video for Tom’s first TV report. We all think it’s a great idea.”

Ethan was happy, “I’m so glad we all see eye to eye on all this.” He then turned to Luke. “Luke, I know you are a part-owner of this place along with Tom and your buddy, Bob. But maybe we could steal you away periodically to oversee the restaurant and bar when the bed and breakfast opens. You’d still have this place but ours would be a little side job and I promise I would pay you well.” He gave a ‘thumbs-up’.

Tom slapped Luke on the back. “I know you can do it. You have a flair for this shit. You know what you’re doing and you can find someone to help you and hire folks to do specific jobs. Now, I don’t have a crystal ball but I have a sneaking suspicion this bed and breakfast is going to be very very popular. So, that being the case, I know they’re going to need significant help there. What I think you should consider is this. You hire some folks to help you out both here and there. I’ll still be paying you the same for overseeing work here and Ethan can pay you for working virtually full-time there. How does that sound?”

Luke’s face was filled with surprise, “OH, MY GOD! REALLY!!?”

Tom continued, “Hey! You deserve a life. And a decent one at that. I’m sure Ethan will agree with me that we don’t want you to feel overworked or like you’re being used. You’re one of us. You’re an equal. You deserve to be treated as one.”

I called out, “YeeeHaw!!”

Ethan turned to Luke. “I’d love to get this ball rolling as quickly as possible. You know the folks here in town and in the area. I need good people to help in finishing the work on the house and the other projects." He turned to Alan. "Can you contact your forensic guys to go find Andrew? And I need to hire a boat to collect a few things and take them to New York." He paused for a moment. "BUT! We can prepare but we really can't get the ball rolling until I find out the DNA results."

Tom shook his head and snickered, "Let me say this. The chances of you NOT being a blood relative of Andrew's are like one zillion to one. This is a done deal."

Everyone raised their glasses and clinked them together. "Hear! Hear!"

The next day, we all went to see Tom and Alan off at the train station.

Tom turned to Luke. "We'll let you know when we plan to have the special. It's going to take some time. Possibly a month. So, we're talking about late July at the earliest."

I commented, "There could probably be the results of the DNA test by then. I'm sure the folks at Brice and Walters will let you know. I know they'll be calling Ethan as well."

Shortly, the southbound train arrived and we said goodbye to Alan and Tom. Luke drove us down to the boats. Ethan and I wanted to head back out to the island to look around some more.

Abel rented us a small motorboat. We told him we'd return it later on that afternoon. It wasn't long before we were pulling into the cove and to the beach.

Ethan and I spent the rest of the day walking through the house and discussing the possible uses for all of the downstairs rooms. Obviously, virtually all the upstairs rooms that were not bathrooms or closets would be bedrooms for guests except for the library and sitting room.

Ethan commented, "I called one of my clients last night who owns a boat. Well, it's really a yacht. What can I say? I asked him if he would mind coming up this way in the near future. It would be a way to get the paintings from the secret room back to New York."

I gave a 'thumbs-up'. "That's a great idea."

We walked into the great room and stood in front of the large windows, looking out to sea.

Ethan stared out the window then spoke quietly, "I know I'm having great expectations for this place but there is still the issue of Michael. That has never been resolved. When his parents died, he never showed up. They were both killed in a car accident around nineteen eighty-nine. Everyone basically believes he is dead. But if he does show up, we will have some legal issues to straighten out. I have no problem sharing with him as he is legally an heir."

I looked right at Ethan. "You will cross that bridge when you get there. I agree that it is most likely he is no longer alive. You really should go down to North Carolina and check things out. You never know what you might find out." Then, I shook my head with a somewhat disgusted expression. "It's already the twenty-fifth of June and I've only done one painting. I thought I'd at least get four done before heading back to Atlanta. I told folks at work I'd be back by the first of July. Since it takes me two days to drive it, that leaves me just three days left to be here. The folks at the art gallery are going to be really disappointed."

Ethan turned to look at me. "Wow. I know we've talked about how we feel about one another but we've never really discussed the ramifications of it. It's true. You have a life in Atlanta. I have a life in New York. I definitely would like to find a way to fix that."

I looked right at him. "You're correct. We've not sorted that out yet. Not to sound forward or bold, but I do believe it would be easier for me to change my location than it would be for you. And with my architectural background, it would be no problem for me to be up here and make sure the completion of the projects needed would be done in a satisfactory manner. It would take a little time but I think I could get everything in Atlanta taken care of in less than a month."

Ethan suggested, "What do you think about this? You head back to Atlanta tomorrow. Take care of everything there. How much furniture do you have?"

I bent my head down. "I rent a furnished apartment. Always wanted to buy a house but I don't make enough money to take out a large enough loan to get one. So, to answer your question, the few things that I do have are of little consequence and could be donated to charity. Except for my piano. I can have that put in storage until it's time to have it shipped up here. We could put it in the house here. I'll have the strings replaced with plated ones. It will prevent rusting due to the salty atmosphere here. The rest of the things I have that are of importance will fit in my car. If I came back up here, I could not only oversee the completion of the things on the island but maybe help out Luke as well till he finds someone significant to help him."

Ethan's face was filled with joy, "Damn! I had no idea you played the piano. Geez."

"I'll bet there are lots of things we don't know about each other. We'll just have to find that out as we go along." I looked at him and grinned. "But I swear, I'm not an axe murderer."

Ethan gave a strange look and then began to laugh. I joined in.

Ethan nodded. "Seems you've got it all figured out right down to the finish line. I really like that in a person. What can I say?"

He walked over to me and looked down into my face. "If you only knew the feelings I have for you. I already know I will love you forever."

I looked up into Ethan's face. "I can't believe a man such as you could ever love someone like me. The love I have for you just grows every day. I promise you, I will do my best to make you happy for the rest of our days."

We hugged each other tightly and passionately kissed for the very first time.

The next day, I asked Luke if he would take care of the things I had there. Ethan and I had told him the plan the previous night at dinner. He would be driving Ethan to the train station right after I left. I would let both of them know when I was returning.

Interestingly enough, it didn't take me as long as I thought to get things taken care of to leave Atlanta. All my friends had seen the original report online and when I told them about Ethan, they were overjoyed for me. I told them all to be on the lookout as Tom's special report could be out by the end of July and most likely would immediately be posted online. Many of them indicated they would love to come for a visit sometime after the bed and breakfast was completed and opened.

It was the middle of July when I finally returned and it made me so happy when I saw Luke and Ethan, standing in front of the lodging house. Ethan had arrived from New York on the afternoon train, not long before I arrived. Luke drove them both over to the lodging house to wait for me to get there. Little did I realize that Ethan had changed his plan right after I drove off, heading back to Atlanta. I would discover that very soon.

Luke told me to follow him in his car. Ethan had called early the day before and rented a storage unit for all my things to be kept temporarily. Since my car was totally full, Ethan rode with Luke. It didn't take long to get everything out of my car and into the unit. Then, it was back to the lodging house.

The landlady was glad to see me and we put my things up in the room. Next, it was to the restaurant and bar to have something to eat and drink. It would be the celebration of a new beginning for me and Ethan. But we were not alone.

After seating us at a table, Luke went into the back, returning shortly with another young man by his side. He looked to be a few years younger and shorter than Luke and sporting a very nice mustache and goatee. Luke had a big smile on his face, "I'd like you both to meet Mark. He's going to be helping me a lot around here."

Immediately, I knew something was up. "Ah. Something tells me there's more to this. Why don't you both sit down here and tell us all about it."

Everyone had big smiles on their faces as Mark sat down at the table.

Luke stayed standing. "Okay, folks. I know you must be hungry and I'm sure you'd like a cocktail, so let me get your food order and get it going while Mark catches you up a little on why he's here."

Luke took our order and headed to the back and also began making our drinks.

Mark smiled as we all shook hands and made introductions. Shortly, he began to tell his story, "It's really kind of crazy how and why I'm here. It all started with the video that was online about the house on the island. It sounded interesting, so I thought I'd watch it. In the report, there was a segment interviewing Luke and what he did up here. To be honest, an overwhelming feeling filled me when I saw him. Even after seeing the video, I couldn't get him out of my head."

"Thoughts of him were driving me crazy. Just over two weeks later, I knew I couldn't take it anymore. There had to be something to this and I needed to find out if it was real. It took some doing but I finally got in contact with Tom at the TV station. It was one of the last days of last month. I was dead honest and upfront with him. Needless to say, he was rather surprised but told me more about Luke since they had known each other since high school. Tom was really pleased when he found out my background was in restaurant management. He knew Luke could definitely use my help. He told me to get my things in order then head up here. He told me to call him when I was ready to head this way, so he could let Luke know I was coming. I was surprised but Tom actually sounded ecstatically happy."

"It didn't take me that long to get everything done where I was and got here the end of the first week in July. I was really happy that Luke was right there to meet me at the train. The minute I stepped off and saw him the emotions that swelled up in me were beyond words. He told me Tom had called him to let him know I was coming."

Ethan commented, "Well, I guess things have turned out just fine since you're working here."

I smiled, "I hope things work out. Luke's a great guy and he deserves to have someone special. I believe if you treat him right, you will not be sorry."

Just then, Luke arrived back at the table with a tray full of drinks, handing one to each of us. He took the last one, set the tray on an adjacent table and sat down, joining us. "So, did Mark get to explain a little of why he's here? Strangely, Mark had called Tom the day after you both had left to go get your affairs in order. Tom told him to get up here ASAP. Yeah. He has a background in restaurant management. And from what I've witnessed so far, he's damn good at it."

Ethan was ecstatic and looked at Mark, "Did Luke mention to you about the help we will need on the island?"

Luke interrupted, "I didn't want to say anything. I thought it would be more important to hear it from you guys."

Mark questioned, "More work?"

Ethan continued, "Yes. When all the construction is completed out on the island, it's going to be made into a bed and breakfast. There will be an area for dining and a bar for the guests. We've mentioned that to Luke. We were hoping he would find someone with some expertise to help him here as well as on the island. It seems he has found the perfect person who'll be able to help him in this endeavor."

Luke patted Mark on the back. "With what you know about the restaurant business, we would be in like Flint. And they want us to hire more folks to help us out. What do you think?"

I had to chuckle inside at Luke's reference to the old comedy movie, 'In Like Flint', that came out back in the mid-1960s. I had actually seen the movie starring James Coburn.

Mark clenched his fist and thrust it in the air. "WaaaHoo!" A big smile filled his face, "I know this may sound strange and crazy but I truly believe that Destiny and the Fates led me here. If I'd not seen that video online and Luke's handsome face, I wouldn't be sitting here right now."

A memory crossed my mind, recalling the restaurant I frequented in Atlanta. "Now, all we have to do is find someone who can play the piano once in a while. It would be great at meals and maybe some evening dancing. I play but not that well. It would be great if we could find someone who could play tunes off the top of his head. There was this great piano player at the Prince George, a restaurant I used to go to in Atlanta. His name was Patrick. He could play any tune at the drop of a hat. It totally amazed me. Yeah. If we could find someone like that." I looked over at Mark. "Being in the restaurant business, maybe you know of someone."

Mark bent his head down and started to laugh. "Funny you should ask. It's one reason I went into the restaurant and bar industry. I could provide my own entertainment for my guests."

Ethan's face was filled with surprise, "You're kidding! Seriously? You play the piano, too?"

Mark just gave a huge grin.

I looked at Mark and was very much surprised, "Well. What can I say? Providence is shining on us more and more. With your thinking and abilities, it's obvious you're going to fit right in with this crowd. Yes, the Fates have been kind in more ways than one."

A huge smile filled Ethan's face, "I swear. You are absolutely correct." He paused for a moment, bent his head down and started snickering, "I know this is going to sound so strange and off-the-wall but believe it or not, I have a feeling that it wasn't Fate and Destiny. It was Andrew and Brian who have somehow had a hand in Mark getting here. So much has actually happened due to their influence. I have a sense they want this to be as much a fantastic endeavor and success as we do." He looked at Mark. "I know you know a little about Andrew since you saw Tom's video but Luke is going to have to fill you in on so much that has happened since that video. I believe Andrew and Brian are with us all the way."

We all raised our glasses in the air, clinking them together and calling out, "Hear! Hear!"

CHAPTER XIX

While I was in Atlanta getting my affairs in order, Ethan had changed his mind, regarding the paintings and other valuables in the secret room at the house. Instead of taking the train down to New York, he went to Bangor and rented a truck, packed it with all the paintings and valuables and took them himself. He had the time and he wouldn't have to depend on his friend with the yacht. Luke helped him get the paintings from the house and to the mainland in a boat. He also helped in loading them into the truck and packing them so they would not get damaged. It was the same for the two wooden boxes of gold ingots. They brought those over from the house one at a time.

On the way down, he stopped at Brice and Walters and dropped off the two boxes, the diamonds and the antique bills and quarters. They could possibly be of value to coin collectors. The value of the gold and diamonds would be worked out down the road.

When he arrived in New York, he took the paintings to the Metropolitan Museum of Art for safekeeping, some cleaning as well as to get an idea as to their possible value. All that completed, he returned the truck to the rental company at their facility in New York. While there, he did some catching up on his business at his finance and stock company. When he knew I was returning, he took the train back north. Luke would pick him up at the station on the afternoon when I was to return and we would all meet at the lodging house.

Returning to Maine, we began to start dealing with necessary things that needed to be done to get the island project moving.

Doing his investigating, Ethan found an excellent contractor who began working on the projects on the island. This contractor would be using quite a number of the townspeople to help out. He knew this made the folks in town very happy.

He got with the electric company to work out a plan to extend an undersea cable from the mainland to the island, so electricity would be available there. This work started immediately. The electric meter would be in a secure box on the mainland, not far from where the cable entered the ocean. That way the meter reader wouldn't have to come out to the island to do his job.

Freshwater was another necessary utility. Eventually, a heavy-duty four-inch aluminum pipeline was connected to the local water system and run along the ocean floor to the island. The large cistern in the main house and any others that would be built would have automatic floats, so the cisterns would stay filled at all times. This eliminated the need to have water delivered to the island.

Alan was very helpful in getting his forensic friends to come up and search in the rocks below the bluff for any of Andrew's remains. Luckily, many bones as well as the skull were discovered and collected. We were all glad that the ocean waves crashing on the rocks and currents hadn't washed them far and wide. These and Brian's ashes would be put together in a special container and placed in the memorial structure when it was completed. Ethan even decided to put Andrew's signet ring that Brian gave him in the container holding the ashes and bones. He believed that no one should ever wear that ring. It was part of Brian and Andrew.

Tom was absolutely correct. At the end of July, notices began to show up on television regarding his special. Tom notified us when it was going to be aired and wanted all of us to come down to his and Alan's place in Boston to watch it.

On Sunday, August the 5th, Luke, Mark, Ethan and I took the early train down to Boston. Tom had rented two hotel rooms for us. Each one had two double beds. Luke and Mark would have one room. Ethan and I would have the other. After getting all of our things to our rooms, we all headed over to Tom and Alan's place.

It was good to see Tom and Alan again and make them aware of the plans ahead. Drinks were served all around as well as some finger food. Tom planned to serve dinner at seven o'clock before the TV special which was to begin at ten.

As we sat eating, Ethan made a gruff sound to catch everyone's attention. Then, he spoke, "I wanted everyone to know I have some interesting and important news. I got a call today from Matthew at Brice and Walters. The DNA test results came back." He paused for a moment, bent his head down and spoke with a sad tone, "I'm not related to Andrew and I have to stop everything and return everything to the house."

Everyone looked at Ethan with shock on their faces as we gasped and cried out, "WHAT!!??

I almost choked as I cried out, "THAT'S IMPOSSIBLE! I don't believe it! They had to have made a mistake!"

After a moment, Ethan and Tom began to start laughing, getting louder and louder.

Ethan slapped his right leg with his right hand and roared with laughter, "I'm kidding! I'M KIDDING! I'm kidding!"

Luke called out, "You damn BITCH! You FUCKING BITCH! You got us AGAIN!

Realizing we'd all been had again by Ethan, we all could not stop laughing.

While laughing I said, "Not to worry. I'll get him later. Not to worry." I gave a sly grin and flexed my eyebrows.

This made everyone laugh even louder, thinking what I might do.

Tom shook his head. "I heard Ethan knew the DNA was a match. Matthew called me from Brice and Walters to let me know that Ethan was the very first one they called to let know the results. But I wanted to see how Ethan was going to tell you all about it. And I see he did it just as he did with Madame Faruschka. Yep. He got you all.... again."

Dinner was finishing up around nine when Tom spoke up, "Okay, guys. Everyone get to the bathroom if necessary before the show begins. Then, let's all get to the living room and get comfortable. Drinks are on the way."

Finally, we all gathered in front of the TV to watch the show. Tom looked at us all with a big smile on his face, "I believe you all will be very pleased with how it turned out. One thing I've not told you is that this is not going to be broadcast just locally. When the national affiliate saw the incredible interest made by the public with the online video of the original report we did and that there was going to be an hour-long special devoted to the story, they wanted to incorporate it simultaneously with the local broadcasts. That's why it's being shown here in Eastern Time at ten o'clock, so the affiliates across the country would have the showing in the evening after most had eaten their dinners. Also, because of its content. So, guys, this story is going to be seen nationwide. I was super pleased as that is a major feather in Alan's cap as well as mine." Alan had refreshed everyone's cocktails just as the program was beginning.

Tom's smiling face filled the TV screen, "Good evening, ladies and gentlemen. Some of you may have seen my original report on this story back in June but I'm sure many of you are not aware of it unless you saw it online. Much has come to light since that report."

"Actually, this is a tragic love story. Yes, I do want to warn you right now. If you're a person that is not comfortable regarding relationships other than mainstream, you may not want to watch this program. Why? Because this is a story about a love that was considered illegal and unheard of at the time. No, I'm not talking about the love that was illegal between blacks and whites due to racism like the kind Jeffrey's grandparents faced and finally overcame in the nineteen sixties. You will meet Jeffrey later in this story. No, I am talking about the love between........ two men."

After pausing for a few moments, he continued, "That's right. Two men. Andrew Cavenaugh and Brian Durnam. Two men living at the beginning of the nineteen hundreds and the stigma attached to their love at that time period that unfortunately, continues even today.

Tom looked directly at his audience and his full face filled the screen. "Yes, I could sit here and express my opinions about this issue but I don't want to detract from the incredible story this is and what was done to preserve an amazing love between two individuals."

He paused again for a moment and then continued, "Now, my first question to you may possibly make you laugh. I totally understand if it does. When I first heard of it, it definitely raised my eyebrows. But as I investigated the story and saw what I saw, it completely changed my entire perception and thinking on the matter. Yep! Knowledge is power. So. Here is the question. Do you believe in ghosts?"

Tom smiled, "Okay. I can hear the snickering. But trust me, you may think differently after this story is told. And remember this. All that you hear and see tonight is true. No tricky camera work was done. I know because I was with my incredible cameraman, Alan, the entire time every video was taken."

Tom started off with an interview with Luke, telling the original legend of the island. Then, there was one with me at the house. He continued his interviews with Ethan, Matthew, Stella and Jeffrey. Alan's camera work was exceptional, showing interior and exterior videos of the house, the pavilion and scenic views around the island. This tour was accompanied by excerpts being read from Andrew's book by Ethan, telling Andrew's story. Alan's camera work and lighting were excellent, showing all the items from the secret room. Superb explanations accompanied them all. The sepia photo from the security box of Brian in the dress only emphasized the ignorance and intolerance that existed at the time, forcing them to create such a ruse.

The telling of Andrew's story ended with Alan's camera work, walking through the French doors of the great room, across the terrace and lawn to the edge of the bluff, all the while hearing Ethan repeating the words from his dream that Andrew spoke. This was the path Andrew took, crying out then ending his life on the rocks below. The camera slowly lowered, showing the crashing surf on the rocks at the bottom of the cliff then faded away.

Tom also explained the bizarre coincidence that Ethan looked like Andrew and I looked like Brian. The comparison was quite clear when the old photographs were shown and then focused in on Ethan and me. It was the same with the showing of the portrait painting done by John Sargent.

As Tom continued his discussion, regarding the possibility of Andrew's ghost haunting the house, that's when Alan's video clip slowly focused in on the image of a man on the top of the front portico. After holding for several moments on that scene, the TV screen was filled with Tom's smiling face again, "Here are some recent images of not one ghost but two. These are the images of Andrew and Brian." As Tom was speaking, the images were being shown of Andrew and Brian, standing on the front steps of the front portico, smiling and waving. The camera work continued even as they turned and walked into the house through the unopened door. Then, to prove there was no faking, the camera immediately swung around focusing on Ethan and me.

Tom continued, "You have now heard the story of Andrew Cavenaugh and the legend of the island. The images you saw in the last scene were not some hired actors. They were actually the ghosts of Andrew Cavenaugh and Brian Durnam. And how do I know this? Because I saw it with my own eyes. That's correct. I was there when that video was taken and saw the images of the men myself. Whether you believe it or not is up to you. But I know what I saw as Alan captured it on video."

"I will also tell you this. The house is being completed and turned into a bed and breakfast. Andrew's bones were found in the rocks below the cliff by forensic specialists. They, along with Brian's ashes, will be placed in a memorial to be constructed on the island. So, if any of you out there are ghost hunters, you might want to consider making some reservations when the house opens. And who knows? You might even catch a glimpse of Andrew Cavenaugh yourself."

"So. Ladies and gentlemen. I hope you have enjoyed the story and the legend of Cavenaugh Island. I'm not sure but it's possible I may do an update down the road after the bed and breakfast opens which is scheduled for next spring. Thank you for tuning in and may you all have a wonderful evening." Tom shook his head and snickered, "And as the great Paul Harvey used to say at the end of all his radio shows, 'And now you know.... the rest of the story. Good day.'" He gave a big smile and looked directly at his audience. "Ladies and gentlemen. Good evening." The screen faded to dark.

We all clapped our hands, cheered and started jumping up and down, hugging one another.

I called out, "Tom! That was an incredible program! Well done! And the same goes for you, Alan. Excellent camera work. And that look over the edge of the cliff scared the shit out of me. Yeah. It should be very interesting to hear the reactions to your show."

Mark started to chuckle, "Yeah. I can hear all those damn fucking evangelical fundamentalists, bitching and moaning about how sinful the show was. That is if any of them actually watched it."

Alan grinned, "You know they did. And why? Because they just had to see the whole thing, so they'd really have something to bitch about and maybe protest march at the TV stations for showing it."

Tom added, "You know, I was so tempted to go on a rant regarding my opinions of stupid, ignorant, morons who refuse to accept the legitimate and unbiased facts on the subject. But the story was about Andrew and Brian, not my personal opinions. As for those protesting TV stations, that would actually be great. It would bring more notice to the broadcast and maybe others would watch it again when it's posted online."

Luke called out, "Hey! Ignorance is a choice. You can't fix stupid!"

What was left of the evening was spent in conversation, catching up on progress at the island as well as more information on Mark's background. Ethan and I mentioned we would be traveling back and forth from New York to oversee the projects on the island and the completion of the house.

Mark spoke up, "Just to let you know, I'm computer savvy and would love to set up a website for the bed and breakfast. Of course, Ethan would give his approval and any suggestions."

Ethan gave a 'thumbs-up'. "Mark, that's a terrific idea. Thanks for the offer. And know you will NOT do it for free."

Everyone cheered.

August, September and October showed much being done and completed on the island. One of the first things on the agenda was to put up a secure fence about four feet from the edge and along the bluff. This would prevent folks from getting too close to the edge.

The terrace area outside the great room was extended, so it would be at least sixteen feet wide and the same length as the great room. Ethan even talked about enclosing it like a glass solarium. This could be done sometime in the future after all major necessary work was completed.

Installing the swimming pool adjacent to the terrace was somewhat of a chore. Jackhammers had to be used due to the amount of rock. Everyone joked that with this much support, it was doubtful the pool would ever crack. Ethan also mentioned the possibility of glass enclosing it as well.

Putting in heating and air conditioning systems took some creative thinking, so as not to destroy the aesthetics of the interior of the house and not have ugly units showing on the outside of the building. The large area on the flat roof offered a huge help in accomplishing this. Units would be placed on the roof above where there were interior structural wall members in the house. This would give the support needed, so the roof would not sag from the weight.

Ethan was also investigating the possible installation of solar panels on the flat roof of the house and any other structures built on the island. This, of course, would help in the electric usage on the island.

Ethan did something that I thought was totally incredible. He had Abel go find two boats with seating capacity for twenty passengers each. Abel knew exactly the kind that would be reliable and durable. Ethan paid cash for them but got a receipt since they would be tax deductible.

When they were delivered, Ethan told Abel to use them and charge customers a minimal fee to transport them to and from the island as well as trips out and around the island. Abel was to keep the fees. If there were any special events where both boats were needed, he was to hire someone to pilot the other boat during that time period. Abel would be paid for any trips he made to and from the island as would any additional pilot.

Also, a pier was constructed, jutting out into the cove, making it easier for boats to load and unload passengers. The pier would have a walkway right to the paved drive, heading up to the house. This would make it easier for anyone, so they wouldn't have to walk in the sand on the beach. Any visiting yachts would have its people disembark at the pier then go anchor farther out in the cove, so the pier would never be obstructed.

Ethan and I wanted the great room finished first. By mid-October, all the construction and decorating had been finished in that room. I had the piano shipped up and delivered. There was a man in the nearby town who worked on pianos. I had him change out all the strings to plated ones to resist rusting from the salty atmosphere. He also tuned it. We told him to come back every six months to keep it in tune. Striking a few chords on the piano, I was totally amazed at the acoustics of the room.

Ethan contacted the museum in New York, asking them to ship the portrait painting. When it arrived, it was hung in the middle of the west wall of the great room just where Andrew and Brian wanted it placed. It looked terrific there.

Ethan and I became closer and closer. I could not believe I had found such love from and with another.

One night in early November, we both went to bed, hoping for a good night's sleep. I had no idea I was going to have such an incredible dream.

I was walking right next to Ethan and we were walking in the direction of the house on the island. Up the steps to the portico and to the front door. Just as before, both of us just passed right through the front door without even opening it. We were standing in the entryway.

It wasn't long before we saw the figures of Andrew and Brian coming down the staircase. They got to the bottom and stopped, standing together. Both had big smiles on their faces.

Andrew walked forward and came within about five feet of Ethan and me. "You have both done exceedingly well. What you've done with the house is remarkable. It exceeds all of my and Brian's expectations. We love where you've hung the portrait. It's exactly where we were going to put it. And the grand piano right down from it is terrific. We also love what you did over there." Andrew turned and pointed at the painting I did of the house, hanging above the words he had painted on the wall with his portrait next to it.

I spoke up, not even knowing if I would be heard, "Andrew. In the beginning, I only saw you. Alone. How is it that Brian has been able to join you?"

Andrew smiled and Brian began to chuckle, "It's because of what you did. In the beginning, when I first saw you, I immediately had memories of Brian and me together. Before that, I had no memories. I was a lost soul, wandering without reason. Seeing you, reminded me of Brian and the time we had shared together. It gave me the impetus to try and make things happen."

Ethan spoke, "But Andrew, all that time you wasted without having memories and being with Brian. That's so sad."

At that, Brian walked forward and stood next to Andrew. "Time is something that has no effect on us. A hundred years for you is insignificant for us. When there is infinity and eternity, there is no time." Brian looked at me. "Because of you and Ethan, Andrew and I are now together for all eternity. We will both be forever thankful for allowing it to happen."

Andrew returned next to Brian and spoke, "I did want to explain about how you both knew of how I ended my life. It had happened long before but I believed you both needed to know the truth, so I re-enacted it all over again for your benefit."

I spoke, "Andrew, it was extremely helpful in understanding where you had gone."

Ethan had a question, "Now, that you are together, what's going to happen?"

Andrew started laughing, "Actually, we both wanted to stay here. But under the circumstances, it looks like we're not really wanted."

Ethan and I both called out together, "Oh! No! No!"

I shook my head. "It's your home. This is where you both belong."

Ethan snickered, "As strange as it sounds, I totally agree."

Brian turned to Andrew. "We could be quiet and stay in hiding. That way, we could stay here."

Again, Ethan and I both called out together, "Oh! No! No!"

Andrew and Brian looked at both of us very curiously.

Brian continued, "I don't understand."

Ethan started chuckling, "We want you to stay! We would love it if you would be visible once in a while to guests and visitors. Those who will come here would love that. They are the kind of people who believe in entities like yourselves. And those who don't will be coming here trying to believe. And so you both will have your own space, I will set up one of the bedrooms for you both. It will be your bedroom. Your space. We will keep the door to the room closed and locked."

Andrew and Brian both began to chuckle. Andrew spoke up, "There is no need to keep the door closed and locked. Visitors might like to see the room you have set aside for us. It might even give everyone the realization that when they pass over, it's not so bad here."

This made us all feel filled with happiness.

Ethan responded, "Sounds good. That's the way it will be. But should you change your mind, you know you can tell us by coming to us in this way."

I added, "Ethan is correct. Please, feel at home. And I don't mean to sound crass but with you both periodically being visible and accessible only enhances the popularity of this place. So, please. Don't hesitate. We'd love it."

Andrew and Brian began to laugh and Brian commented, "Unbelievable. Thank you. We will try to be discreet. We don't want the house to get a bad reputation."

I smiled, "Andrew. Brian. I'm so glad I was instrumental in you both being together again. In reading Andrew's book, it was so evident the great love you both had for one another. Seeing you now, only makes me realize your love still continues. It makes me so happy to see you together."

A big grin filled Ethan's face, "I totally agree. It's just that it's such a shame your earthly love was so short-lived."

Brian spoke with a smile on his face, "I have a great feeling that both of you will continue where Andrew and I left off. Share the love you have for one another. Be grateful it has happened for you. So many go through life and never know love at all. You two are the lucky ones. Don't squander it."

Ethan chuckled, "I remember a comment that was made in Andrew's book about our kind of love being accepted. Well, it's not completely accepted now but it is by most and believe it or not, if you didn't know, marriage between two men or two women was legalized in June of twenty fifteen. Yes. Seriously."

Brian called out, "Wow. That is terrific."

I shook my head. "I wish. I wish Ethan and I could pull you both close to us and hug you. Because of you both, Ethan and I found one another."

Andrew looked at Brian and they both smiled as they turned and looked at us. Andrew giggled, "Well. Nothing says we can't try it. Who knows? Maybe we CAN hug one another."

All of us began to laugh as we walked towards one another and began a huge hug-fest. As we did, we all were laughing out loud at the experience. It was as if all of our bodies were joined and melded together as one.

Ethan called out, "It's working! It's working! I can feel it!

I called out, "Yes! I can too!"

Andrew and Brian both called out, "Yes! We can feel it, too! It's wonderful!"

Finally, after a few moments, we all backed off and kept looking at one another with huge smiles on our faces. Shortly, Andrew and Brian turned, walked towards the staircase and started up. They'd gone up five steps when they both turned and looked at Ethan and me. Andrew spoke, "We will be watching. Keep your love burning. Be an example for others." He paused for a moment then spoke again. "I'm so glad our efforts worked out on influencing Mark to come here. We both knew he was just what Luke was looking for, not only for his expertise in business but the love he would give Luke. Luke is a fine young man and deserves to have love. We both know he will give great love to Mark as well. All of you take care and stay happy." They both smiled then slowly faded away.

Ethan and I turned and hugged each other.

CHAPTER XX

I quickly sat up in bed. At the same time, so did Ethan. We looked at each other and realized we had both had the same dream. We turned and hugged each other tightly.

I whispered, "Ethan. I love you so much. I love you forever."

Ethan whispered, "Thank you for being in my life. I will love you forever, too."

I continued, "I'm so glad they're together. I'm so glad we got to hug them."

Ethan giggled, "I must admit. That was a strange experience. I'm so happy they're together, too."

I pulled back and looked into Ethan's eyes. "That was so incredible. For some reason, I believe it never would've been able to happen except in a dream. In dreams, we are not actually in our physical bodies. We are ethereal like ghosts. I'm so glad it got to happen. And I'm so happy for Andrew and Brian being able to be together forever. After that, I must say, I'm not going to be able to get back to sleep again."

Ethan nodded. "I know what you mean. Let's go have a cup of coffee. I can't wait to tell Luke and Mark what we just heard."

All through November and December, we looked for furnishings to place in the house. We definitely wanted some very special furniture to go into the bedroom we were setting up for Andrew and Brian. Ethan also wanted me to go to several of the art galleries in New York and pick out paintings to go throughout the first story. He wanted several of my paintings to be added when I had the time to do some. I jokingly told Ethan that with all the wall space in the house, we could turn it into a museum. Ethan thought that was very funny.

Mark had done an incredible job setting up the website for the place. He was getting hits already from folks wanting to book reservations when it was finally ready and open. The people in town were gearing up for potential visitors and customers due to the publicity that had occurred from Tom's special.

Both Mark and Luke were amazed yet so very glad that Andrew and Brian were influential in their coming together. They both agreed that knowing that made their love that much stronger. It was meant to be.

The grand opening of Cavenaugh House was set for the end of April even though everything had been completed by the middle of March. Ethan and I wanted to make absolutely sure everything was set up and ready to go. Everything was tested several times to make sure there were no glitches. We were all totally astounded at the reservations for the island as well as many facilities in town. Tom and Alan were going to do a report on the grand opening as an update to the story.

A week before, Ethan indicated he had to run into New York to check on a few things at the office there. He left on the early morning train and came back the next day on the one in the evening.

Luke and Mark had ordered special outfits for everyone who would be working at Cavenaugh House. Ethan and I were extremely pleased with the outfits as they were very smart yet comfortable. No. Ethan and I weren't going to be wearing them.

The opening day finally arrived. The weather was cooperating beautifully. Everyone was dressed to the nines. It had been forever since I'd worn a tux. Tom and Alan had arrived the day before. So had Bob, Tom and Luke's other business partner. He said he wasn't going to miss this come hell or high water. All the major ceremony was going to take place on the front portico and the paved area in front of it with everyone starting to gather around noon. All attendees would be standing on the driveway area adjacent to the front steps.

A party with dancing would occur afterward in the great room. A bar and several portable tables had been set up at the south end of the great room. They would be used to hold all the edibles and drinks that were going to be served after the opening ceremony. Since the weather was so nice, tables and chairs were set up out on the terrace adjacent to the great room. Mark indicated he would love to play the piano for the event.

Many guests had arrived the night before. The house was full of those who were spending a week or more. The lodging house and all rentals in town had been sold out to those who were staying for a night or more.

Many of Ethan's clients arrived on their boats, anchoring them in the cove. Virtually all of the townsfolk arrived by late morning into early afternoon. It was a good showing.

Alan, along with several other news outlets, had cameras set up and ready to go to record the happenings of the day. Tom was there to assist him if needed.

It was just after two o'clock when the mayor walked up to the podium and tapped on the microphone, trying to draw everyone's attention. "Ladies and gentlemen! May I have your attention, please!? This event is about to begin! For those of you who don't know, my name is Jimmy Jones and I'm the mayor of our fair town across the water and west of here."

Claps and cheers rose from the crowd.

The mayor continued, "If someone had told me a year ago I'd be standing here today at the opening of Cavenaugh House, I'd probably have shaken my head and laughed. But here I am. This morning when I woke up and knew I was coming here, I had to pinch myself to make sure it was for real. Something tells me this is going to bring some prosperity and publicity to this area. That will be a good thing."

"But now, I'd like to introduce you to someone who has enabled this project that began over a hundred years ago to finally come to fruition. Yes, the original concept was for this to be a private home. But, HEY! That was a hundred years ago. Times change."

Everyone laughed and clapped their hands.

He continued, "I'd like to introduce Mister Ethan Groves. It was his ancestral uncle who began the building of this great house."

Everyone clapped and cheered as Ethan walked up to the podium.

Ethan looked out over the crowd and smiled, "Good afternoon, ladies and gentlemen. I thank you all for attending today. Today is the end of a tragic love story and the beginning of a new and happy one. I'm sure most of you have seen the special on television, regarding the story of Andrew and Brian. Such a sad, sad ending for two wonderful individuals. Cavenaugh House may have a tragic past but we intend for its future to be filled with fun and happiness."

"I would like to thank our friends, Tom and Alan from the Boston TV affiliate for doing that incredible special." Ethan pointed toward Tom and Alan who both smiled and bowed several times.

Tom called out, "And we are doing an update very soon to include this grand opening of Cavenaugh House."

Hearing that, the whole crowd cheered and clapped their hands.

Ethan continued, "I must point out also that none of this would ever be happening if not for someone who is now near and dear to me. If he had not come here to paint almost a year ago, this would not be happening. Because he saw the ghost of Andrew Cavenaugh, a ball began to roll that has brought us to this day. And believe it or not, it is one reason Andrew Cavenaugh and Brian Durnam have been reunited together even in death. How do I know this? They came to us in a dream to explain how it happened. Many may be skeptical of things such as this and that's okay. But for me, I know the truth."

"So, welcome all of you to Cavenaugh House. But before the festivities begin, there is something very special about to happen here. It has to do with Luke and Mark who were originally overseeing the restaurant and bar in town. But now, they are going to be of significant assistance here on the island. They are terrific individuals and will be glad to be of assistance should you need any. I will also tell you that it was Andrew and Brian who are the ones that led us all together. So. Ladies and gentlemen. I introduce you to Luke and to Mark. And remember. Something very special is about to happen."

Luke and Mark both walked out in front of the podium dressed in their new crisp outfits and onto the clear area between the podium and the crowd. They both bowed numerous times as everyone clapped and cheered.

Luke then took Mark's hand and turned to face him as Ethan took the microphone off the podium and walked over to Mark and Luke, standing between them and the podium. Luke went into his vest pocket, pulled out a small box, opened it and pulled out a ring. Smiling, he knelt down in front of Mark and looked up into Mark's face. Ethan held the microphone so everyone could hear.

Luke began to speak, "Mark. I do know it was Andrew and Brian who brought us together. Because of where they are, they had a greater vision and were influential in us meeting. And honestly, every day I share with you is amazing and is something I never thought I'd experience in my lifetime. I love you and I will love you forever. With this ring, I'm asking if you will marry me?"

A huge smile filled Mark's face, "Luke. You are correct. I truly believe that it was Andrew and Brian who brought us together and I am so grateful for it. I love you and I will love you forever. And to answer your question. Yes. Yes, I will marry you."

Luke eased the ring on Mark's finger, stood, hugged Mark and they passionately kissed. At that, the crowd roared with clapping and raucous cheers.

Then, Luke took the microphone from Ethan as Ethan turned and looked at me. Ethan raised his right hand and with the first finger wiggled it in the 'come here' signal. This had the crowd chuckling.

I had no idea what was happening but walked down to where Ethan, Luke and Mark were standing. Mark took several steps back as Luke held the microphone.

Ethan knelt down, smiled and looked up at me. He opened his right hand and I saw what was there. Two rings. They were the rings that were in the safe deposit box at Brice and Walters. The two rings that belonged to Andrew and Brian. I now understood. The supposed quick trip to New York was a ruse. He actually went to Boston to get the rings. I immediately knew what was going to happen and my entire body was filled with joy.

Ethan took the smaller of the two rings out of his right hand. Still holding the larger ring there, he used it to take my left hand. He eased the ring onto my ring finger and smiled, "Words will never explain how much I love you. And as Luke and Mark have already said it, I already know it was Andrew and Brian who have had a significant influence in all that has happened and is happening and I thank them for it. I love you. I will always love you. Will you marry me?" He stood up in front of me.

I took the ring from his right hand and took hold of his left with mine. "Ethan. I'm so lucky to be standing here with you. I love you and I will always love you." I slid the ring on his ring finger. "Yes. I will marry you."

We hugged and kissed passionately.

Again, the crowd roared their approval. After a few minutes, the attitude of the crowd changed. There were loud gasps and everyone began pointing to the roof of the front portico. Everyone turned to see what was there. The crowd went silent.

Standing next to the front balustrade on the roof of the portico, looking down at the crowd below, were the images of Andrew and Brian. Both had big smiles on their faces and they were waving their arms in the air. Then, they began clapping their hands and bowing several times. It was as if they were giving their approval of what was happening. After several moments, they stopped clapping and they both stretched out their right arms, giving a 'thumbs-up'.

Seeing this, the entire crowd started roaring with laughter and cheering as everyone raised their arms in the air, returning the 'thumbs-up' gesture.

Andrew and Brian had huge smiles on their faces as the crowd continued their clapping and cheering. Finally, they bowed one last time, turned and walked through the French doors into the house without opening them.

Once again, the crowd exploded with cheers and clapping. Expressions of approval and surprise erupted as well.

When the ruckus finally calmed down, Luke spoke into the microphone, "Ladies and gentlemen. You have been extremely privileged to witness a very special event here today. If you don't know it, those were the ghosts of Andrew and Brian. It is obvious to me, they came as witnesses and to express their approval of the events taking place here. I'm so glad that my friends, Tom and Alan, who came to video this event, have captured all of this. I'm sure it will be incorporated into Tom's next update on his story, regarding this island and Cavenaugh House. Now, at the conclusion of this ceremony, we hope everyone will join us. Refreshments and drinks are being served in the great room of the house. Thank you so very much for attending today." He handed the microphone to Ethan.

Ethan spoke, "Luke! Thank you so very much. You put it so very eloquently. He is absolutely correct. Now. Come join us in the festivities."

The crowd cheered and clapped again.

And so, life at Cavenaugh House had begun. Ethan and I were so pleased with how Luke and Mark were handling everything, we actually put them in charge. Tom, Alan and Bob were so pleased, they had Luke and Mark hire more individuals to run the restaurant and bar in town. They would continue to be in charge of overseeing that operation as well.

Eventually, several cottages would be built on the island to not only be used by future guests but one would also be where Luke and Mark could live. Ethan and I would be staying in the master bedroom suite in the house. Ethan gave up his New York City apartment. He wanted to continue working as a financier and stockbroker which made his company very pleased, so he had an office building built on the island, not only for the island business but for his finance and stock business as well. The architecture was in keeping with the other structures there. Eventually, many of his clients told him how much they enjoyed coming to the island rather than some busy city office. Ethan's bosses were very pleased.

Finally, the glass solarium over the terrace of the great room and the swimming pool was built. A heating and air conditioning unit was installed and located in an unobtrusive place on the ground outside the solarium. This made using the swimming pool a year-round thing.

Interestingly enough, the ghosts of Andrew and Brian would periodically show up, making the guests extremely happy and thrilled that they got to see what they had come for. Yep. They became known as 'Andrew and Brian, the Friendly Ghosts'. Not to completely outshine Casper.

Tom and Alan's updated report was superb. It brought significant recognition to both of them for their reporting and video abilities. I should also mention that it also significantly increased the interest in the subject matter as well as the number of people wanting to come to the island.

Ethan and I finally took a trip down to North Carolina and we stayed at the Sandora. That visit was a true eye-opener with what we discovered there. The painting, hanging above the fireplace in the lobby done by John Singer Sargent, was the icing on the cake. Ethan and I looked at it and then at each other, shaking our heads, chuckling and doing a high-five together. We realized that love had won again. It also made it perfectly clear that Ethan had no worries about another heir to Andrew's estate and definitely inspired me to start writing another novel.

Eventually, Ethan did end up donating all the paintings that were in the secret room to the Metropolitan Museum of Art in New York. He believed that keeping such works of art away from the world would be a travesty. All the paintings would be listed as 'on loan' to the museum. But one by one, each year they would be given to the museum. Because of their value, this would significantly help with Ethan's taxes and how much he would or wouldn't owe the IRS. This made him very happy for many years. The portrait painting of Andrew and Brian would remain at Cavenaugh House right in the place where they had planned to put it.

As for me, I finally got to do paintings on those three other canvases I'd planned to do the year before. They were hung in a few of the rooms of the house. I even completed one for Matthew Brice for their offices in Boston. He was very pleased with it.

In mid-June 2019, not long after the opening of Cavenaugh House, Luke, Mark, Ethan and I had a private double wedding in Boston. Several close clients of Ethan's, several of my friends from

Atlanta, of course, Tom and Alan, Bob, Tom and Luke's business partner, Matthew, Stella and Jeffrey came as well.

Jeffrey's comment at the wedding hit the nail on the head, "In the nineteen sixties, my grandparents had to march in protest to allow them to marry. In June of nineteen sixty-nine, there was the Stonewall event, organizing the gay community as one and fighting for equal rights. Then, in twenty fifteen, it finally became legal for me and you guys to get married. The wheels of progress ARE moving. Even if it is very slowly. Congratulations to all four of you."

As I sit here writing, I look back on all the events that happened and they make me ponder. "What if I had never taken that trip here to paint? What if I hadn't gone out here to the island but just stayed on the mainland and painted the lighthouse? What if I hadn't looked like Brian, awakening the memories in Andrew's ghost?" All I can do is shake my head and wonder.

Then, I think of every day I share with Ethan. How blessed I am to know I am loved by such a man, "I know my life is and will forever be filled with love and joy. I could not be happier. Every time I look down and see the ring on my left hand, it makes me smile. I hear Andrew, telling us to continue where they left off. Live the life they never got to. I also hear Dolly Parton singing in my head, 'And I will always love you.'" I nod my head and smile, "Ethan, I will always love you."

The End

POST SCRIPT

Okay. I'm sure you noticed that I pulled a Daphne du Maurier again, just like I did in another one of my novels. I won't tell you which one as you may not have read it yet and I don't want to spoil the surprise. She did it in her novel, Rebecca. If you haven't read the book or seen the movie with Laurence Olivier and Joan Fontaine, let me explain.

The first time I watched the movie, I love it. Not long afterward, I was telling someone about the movie when I suddenly realized I couldn't remember the name of Joan Fontaine's character. I pondered for a while and still couldn't remember her name.

Sometime afterward, I watched the movie again. This time I was determined to remember the character's name. As the movie came to a close, it finally dawned on me. She was called: my darling, my dear, Mrs. DeWinter, ma'am. I had to laugh. She never has a name. I found it so funny that the character of Rebecca is constantly called by her name even though she is dead. I thought it was incredibly creative to do such a thing.

So, here in this story, the character telling the story has no given name. I hope Daphne doesn't hate me for stealing her idea for a second time.

Printed in the United States
by Baker & Taylor Publisher Services